So this *is* Cyr

This was as good as it got. Th
in appearance didn't come a
was an impressive-looking man. What she hadn't been
expecting was the charisma, the air of authority that
appeared entirely natural. Obviously Cyrus Bannerman
was ready to take over his father's mantle, when many
a son with a tycoon for a father finished up with a
personality disorder. Not the case here, unless that
palpable presence turned out to be a facade.

He was tall, maybe six-three, with a great physique. The
loose-limbed long-legged stride was so graceful it was
nearly mesmerizing. He had thick, jet-black hair, strong
distinctive features, his eyes even at a distance the bluest
she had ever seen. She knew instinctively she had better
impress this guy with her professional demeanor. No
contract had yet been signed.

"Ms. Tennant?"

Though every instinct shrieked a warning, she offered
him her hand. It was taken in a firm cool grip. Jessica let
out her breath slowly, disconcerted by the thrill of skin
on skin. "How nice of you to meet me."

"No problem. I had business in Darwin." The startling
blue eyes continued to study her. She had already
grasped the fact that despite the smoothness of manner,
he hadn't taken to her. Was it wariness in his eyes? A
trace of suspicion? *More's the pity!* she thought. Anyone
would think she had coerced his father into hiring her.
Not that it mattered. She didn't altogether like him. She
did, however, like the *look* of him. A teeny distinction.

Dear Reader,

It is with much pleasure I introduce to you the first in my four-book series MEN OF THE OUTBACK. The setting moves from my usual stamping ground, my own state of Queensland, to the Northern Territory.

The Northern Territory is arguably the most colorful and exciting part of the continent. Even today it is frontier country. The Territory comprises what we call the Top End and the Red Centre. The Top End has as its capital Darwin, the gateway to Australia and a hop, step and a jump from Southeast Asia. The chief town of the Red Centre is Alice Springs, which lies in the middle of the fantastically colored MacDonnell Ranges, the setting for one of the stories. The Top End lies well above the Tropic of Capricorn. The Red Centre is the desert, the home of our most revered monuments, Uluru and Kata Tjuta. Thus we have in a vast area two extreme climatic and geographical divisions. World Heritage–listed Kakadu National Park, crocodiles and water buffalo to the Top, the Dead Heart to the Centre (though not dead at all, only lying dormant until the rains transform it into the greatest garden on earth).

The pervading theme of the series is family. It can be a difficult and provocative subject because many highly dysfunctional families are out there—fighting, loving, hating, struggling, exploiting, betraying. Family offers endless opportunities for its members to hurt and be hurt, to love and support or bitterly condemn. What sort of family we grew up in reverberates for the rest of our lives. Were we blessed with a rock-solid foundation or left with memories that plague us? One thing is certain—at the end of the day, *blood* binds.

I invite you, dear reader, to explore the lives of my families. Not all of it is invention. Such people as I write about *do* inhabit families. What sort of family is yours? Now and *then*.

Margaret Way

THE CATTLEMAN
Margaret Way

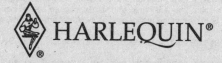

TORONTO • NEW YORK • LONDON
AMSTERDAM • PARIS • SYDNEY • HAMBURG
STOCKHOLM • ATHENS • TOKYO • MILAN • MADRID
PRAGUE • WARSAW • BUDAPEST • AUCKLAND

ISBN 0-373-71328-2

THE CATTLEMAN

www.eHarlequin.com

Printed in U.S.A.

PROLOGUE

Mokhani Station
Northern Territory, Australia
1947

ALL THE WHILE THEY WERE riding, Moira felt a stab of anxiety as sharp as a knife beneath her breastbone. She tried to tell herself not to be afraid, but it did no good. A sense of foreboding weighed on her so oppressively, she slumped in the saddle, her hands trembling on the reins. If her companion noticed, Moira saw no sign. It was another hot, humid, thundery day on the verge of the Wet, or the Gunummeleng, as the station Aborigines called it. There were only two seasons in the Territory, she'd learned. The Wet and the Dry. The Wet, the time of the monsoon, extended from late November to March, the Dry lasted from April through October. It was mid-November now. She had arrived on Mokhani in early February of that year to teach the Bannerman twins, a boy and a girl aged seven. Nearly ten months of sharing her life with extraordinary people; the ten most life-changing months of her life. Ultimately, they had turned her from just out of adolescence into a *woman.* Her great fear was she had chosen a tragic path.

Nearing eighteen and not long out of her excellent

convent school, she'd craved *adventure*. Mokhani had offered it. After years of hard study and obeying strict rules, she'd been ready for a liberating experience. It was understood that at some time she had to continue her tertiary education, but if her parents hadn't exactly encouraged her to take a gap year, they'd put up no great objection when they'd seen how much she'd wanted it. As a much-loved only child, "the wonderful surprise" of her parents' middle years, their only wish was for her to be happy. The family solicitor, a good friend of her father's, had come up with the answer. His legal firm handled many Outback clients' affairs. It just so happened, the Bannerman family, pastoral pioneers with huge cattle interests in the Northern Territory and Queensland's Gulf country, wanted a governess for their children, someone of good family and proven academic ability, a *young* woman preferably, to better relate to the children.

She qualified on all counts. Her father was a well-respected family doctor. Her mother, an ex-nurse, helped out several days at his surgery. Moira had been a straight-A student, winning a scholarship to university. The Bannermans, for their part, were rich, powerful, influential. The present owner and heir to the Bannerman fortune was Steven Bannerman—ex-Squadron Leader Steven Bannerman, seconded to the Royal Air Force during the war, survivor of the Battle for Britain, who'd returned home a war hero. His wife, Cecily, was a niece of the South Australian governor. In short, the Bannermans were the sort of people to whom her parents felt no qualms about sending her.

The great irony was, they might have been signing her death warrant.

Moira lifted one hand, pressing it hard against her heart

to stop it from bursting through her rib cage. If her companion addressed a stray comment to her, she heard nothing of it. There were too many demons clamouring inside her head. She knew she wasn't very far away from a breakdown. In a sense, it was another version of the Aboriginal *kurdaitcha* man, the tribal sorcerer, pointing the bone. Yet nothing had been said to her. Her throbbing fears were virtually without proof, but like all victims, she had the inbuilt awareness there was threat ahead.

It was deliriously hot. That alone caused profound dislocation. Temperature nearing a hundred and rising. A thunderstorm was rolling in across the table-topped escarpment that from a distance always appeared a deep amethyst. The storm revealed itself as magnificent. Majestic in cloud volume, black and silver with jagged streaks of livid green and purple that intensified the colors of the vast empty landscape and made the great cushions of spinifex glow molten gold. Even *she* knew it was risky taking this long ride. If it poured rain, the track could become slippery and dangerous and they would have to walk the horses. But it wouldn't be the first time a thunderstorm had blown over, for all the fabulous pyrotechnics.

Nearly everyone on the station, even the Aborigines, the custodians of this ancient land, were feeling the peculiar tension the extremes of weather created. Heat and humidity. The humidity alone left one gutted. The monsoon couldn't come soon enough even if it brought in a cyclone. Not that she had ever lived through the destructive cyclones of the far north. Still she understood what the Territorians meant when they talked about going "troppo," a state of mental disturbance blamed on extreme weather conditions.

Was that it? For one blessed moment, she felt a lightening of her fears. Was she going troppo? Were her fears imaginary rather than real? No one meant her any harm. It was all in her mind. Her companion appeared almost serene, hardly the demeanour of an avenger. The heat did dreadful things to people, especially those not born and bred to the rigours of the inland.

We're white people living in the black man's land.

Steven Bannerman had said that to her when she'd first arrived, looking down at her with a strange intensity, his handsome mouth curved in a rare smile. Steven Bannerman was not an easygoing man. Many attributed that to his traumatic experiences during the war. Steven Bannerman was the symbol of power and authority on the station, as daunting in some moods as a blazing fire.

Steven!

She'd been destined to fall in love with him. Her heart leaped at the sound of his name. It resonated in her head and through the caverns of her heart. If she never saw him again, his image would remain etched on her mind, his touch imprinted on her skin. It was truly extraordinary the bearing *one* person could have on another's entire life.

She had felt it such an honor to work for a war hero. She had handled the high-spirited, mischievous little imps of twins who had seen off not one but two governesses remarkably well. Everyone said so. Particularly Mrs. Bannerman, Cecily, a benign goddess who, at the beginning, had sung her praises. Not that she had ever been invited to call the Missus, as the Aboriginal house girls called Mrs. Bannerman, by her Christian name. Steven, too, was only Steven when they were alone. At all other times, he was Mr. Bannerman.

A prince in his own kingdom; everything in the world to her. He had been since the first moment she'd looked up into his beautiful, far-seeing blue eyes—though it hadn't been revealed to her then. But each week, each month that passed, they'd grown closer and closer, learning so much about each other. Nothing had happened until a short time ago when their feelings for each other had broken out in madness.

Fate had delivered her like a sacrificial lamb right into his arms.

She had gone from innocence to womanhood all in one sublime destructive day. She was certain in her heart neither had deliberately chosen it. It had just happened, like an act of God; a flood, a drought, an earthquake, a deadly bolt of lightning from the sky. Acts of God were merciless.

The voice inside her head started up again. She let it talk. It was the next best thing to a conscience.

You know what you have to do, Moira. You have to get out of here. Leave before tragedy overtakes you. Worse, overtakes Steven. A scandal that would be talked about all over the Outback, affecting everyone, even the children.

She couldn't bear that. She had to make her decision. She had to put a thousand miles between herself and Steven. Steven had made his decision years ago before God and man. He had a wife and children. He would never leave them. Not that she'd dreamed for a single moment he would. His role had been drummed into him from childhood. He was the master of Mokhani Station. Outback royalty. She was nothing more serious than a passing affair.

Only, that wasn't true. Both of them knew it wasn't true. She had lain awake far into the night searching the corridors of her soul. There was a strong two-way connection between them, an instant bonding. Steven had told her she was his other half. His reward for what he had suffered during the war. They shared a dangerous kinship of body and spirit that opened the doors to heaven, but also to hell. Steven was passionately in love with her, as she was with him. Hadn't he told her he didn't know what love for a woman was until she'd come into his life? The admission hadn't been merely an attempt to break down her defenses; it had been wrenched from deep down inside him, causing him agony. A war hero, yet he had stood before her with tears in his eyes. Tears she understood. She too was on a seesaw.

Love and guilt. Their love was so good, so pure, yet she knew it could be equated with shameful, illicit sex. Women of other cultures had been murdered for less. When it came to dire punishment, the women were always the victims. Men were allowed to go on exactly as before. Except for the Aborigines, who meted out punishments equally.

Whether he loved her or not, Steven's marriage couldn't be counted for nothing. It was his *life*. He had married Cecily in a whirlwind ceremony before he'd gone off to war. He'd told Cecily he had wanted to wait. They'd been living through such tumultuous times and he could very easily lose his life. But Cecily had become hysterical at the thought of not becoming his wife there and then. She'd wanted his children, and what was more, she had conceived on their brief honeymoon. Cecily was a cousin of his lifelong friend, Hugh Balfour. Hugh had introduced them, and then been best man at their wedding. The tragedy was that after the horror and brutality of war, Steven had come home a different man. So had Hugh, once so full of promise, now well on the way to self-destruction. "A full-blown alcoholic" Cecily scathingly labeled him. "Hugh can't cut it as a civilian!" Cecily Bannerman, Moira had quickly learned, was extremely judgmental, like many who had lived only a life of ease and privilege.

But the tragedy hung over both families. She saw it clearly the first time Hugh had visited Mokhani after her arrival. Hugh idolized Steven. Steven in turn always welcomed his old friend, defending him even when Hugh's own family had written him off. Hugh had been so charming to her, offering friendship, asking her all sorts of questions about herself and her family. He'd made every attempt to get to know her, he had even painted her. Many times. Until, strangely, Steven had put a stop to it. She couldn't think about that now.

Moira plucked a long strand of her hair from her cheek. It glittered with drops of sweat. She had been so happy at first. Lost in the uniqueness of this exciting new world. This was real frontier country where nature in all its savage splendour dominated everything. A city girl, born and raised, she had grown to love this strange and violent place. It revealed itself to her every day, this paradise of the wilds. The space and the freedom! The absolute sense of grandeur. She loved the incredible landscape, saturated in Aboriginal myth and legend. The blood-red of the soil, the cobalt-blue of the sky. She looked up at it briefly. It started to spin above her.

They were heading up the escarpment, the track littered with rubble and orange rocks the size of a man's fist. The promontory overlooked the most beautiful lagoon on the station, lily-edged Falling Waters. No crocodiles were thought to swim this far inland, though they had done so in the past. Nowadays it was argued that from numerous rock slides the neck of the canyon had become too narrow. Besides, it was a known drinking place for the great rainbow snake, owner of all water holes in the vast arid inland.

She could hear the falling of water now. It grew louder,

sighing, hissing, splashing. From the track, the lagoon appeared like giant shards of glittering mirror lost in the thick grove of trees. White-trunked paperbarks and graceful red river gums adorned the water hole, the sun turning their gray-green leaves metallic.

She remembered the first time Steven had brought her to this magical place. The two of them *alone*. Her heart contracted at the memory, one she would cherish until the day she died: how with a tortured oath he had pulled her body close…how her lips had opened spontaneously under his…how his hand on her naked breast had made an indelible brand. She would remember the way he'd picked her up and laid her on the warm golden sand. She had given herself to him willingly, overtaken by a great tide of passion, her blood sizzling, as he played her virgin body, his hands so knowing, so masterly, in turn demanding and tender. One could surrender the world for such lovemaking. Hadn't she? She had abandoned the tenets of her faith, honor, loyalty, cold reason. So many codes of conduct on the one hand. On the other?

Steven.

A world lost for love.

THEIR ARRIVAL ON THE PLATEAU, heralded by a miniature landslide of eroded earth and rocks, caused a huge congregation of waterfowl to rise from the glittering waters with a thunder of wings. They dismounted. Moira removed her wide-brimmed hat, shaking out her thick blond plait. Her body was soaked in sweat, not only from the heat and exertion. Dark forces were at play and she knew it. She had gone way beyond anxiety, moving toward acceptance. She followed her companion nearer the edge, acutely aware they were keeping their distance from one another as if a contagion were upon her.

The view from the top was sublime. There was nothing, *nothing,* like the vast burning landscape. The *sacred* land. It stretched away into infinity and beyond. She could see the length of the rocky, winding corridor of the gorge, the terraced walls glowing a rich, deep red with bands of black, rose-pink and ochre-yellow. The creek bed was little more than a chain of muddy water holes in the Dry, but the permanent lagoon, an extraordinary lime-green was very deep at the centre. There was an Aboriginal legend attached to it; the Aboriginals had a legend for everything. A beautiful young woman, called Narli, promised to a tribal elder, had drowned herself in the lagoon following the killing of her lover for having broken the tribal taboo. Narli's spirit was said to haunt Falling Waters, luring young men to their deaths. There was danger in being young, beautiful and seductive, Moira reminded herself. Beauty inspired obsession. Obsession inspired violence.

Half fainting, she drew breath into her parched lungs. Her tongue was dry. It tasted of dust, making it difficult for her to swallow. She wondered what lay ahead, in part, knowing she had already surrendered. The air still quivered with fierce vibrations. Not by nature timid, she'd allowed herself to be brought low by shame and guilt. She had a sudden image of Steven and her deliriously locked together, his mouth over her, cutting off her ecstatic cries. In her defense it could be said she was incapable of withstanding him.

The waterfall tumbled a hundred feet or more to the pool below, sending up a sparkling mist of spray, as intoxicating as champagne. In the rains, she'd been told, the flow that today ran like a bolt of silver silk down the blackened granite turned into a spectacle of raw power, with a roar that could be heard from a great distance. At those times, the breadth of the falls widened dramatically as it thundered down the cliff face, tiered like an ancient ziggurat to drop countless tons of water into the lake. So augmented, the lagoon broke its banks, engulfing the floodplains with enormous sheets of water—which become huge swamps that were soon crocodile rich. People and cattle had to be moved to higher ground. Afterward, the earth responded with phenomenal abundance—lush green growth and an incredible profusion of wildflowers, native fruits and vegetables. She'd been so eager to witness that sight. Now she felt she never would.

There was no redeeming breeze. Nothing swayed. No petals of the wild hibiscus scattered. All was quiet save for the tumbling waters and the heavy *thud, thud, thud* of her heart. Even the birds that fed on the paperbarks and the flowering melaleuca trees—the honeyeaters, the gorgeous lorikeets and parrots—normally so restless, were strangely silent. Moira dared to look across at her companion, who could at that very moment be settling her fate. Despite all outward appearances of calm, violence simmered just below the surface. Violence generated by perhaps the most dangerous and deadly of sins.

Jealousy.

GOD HELP ME! MOIRA WAS BEYOND all thought of trying to escape. Escape to where? This land was hostile to those on the run. She hadn't seen her parents in many months. The tears started to trickle down her cheeks as their dear, familiar faces swam into her mind. She loved them. Why had she never told them just how much? She should have stayed at home with them where she was safe. Instead, she had betrayed them. Betrayed herself. Betrayed Cecily, who had been kind to her in her fashion. She had inspired a devouring love that overwhelmed all else. In exchange, she had inherited consuming hate. She could feel that hate everywhere, even to the tips of her shaking fingers.

Moira lifted her unprotected face to the burning sun as if there were good reason to blind herself to what was coming. If she survived this, she would have to live with her sins for the rest of her life. It she didn't...*if she didn't...*

Hadn't Sister Bartholomew, in what seemed another lifetime, said to her whenever she landed herself in trouble, "Moira, you have no one to blame but yourself!"

Slowly her companion turned away from the lip of the precipice, jaw set, grimacing into the sun. The distance between them dramatically narrowed. "I've been waiting for this, Moira," came the chilling words.

What could she answer? Words died on her lips. There was no chance. None at all.

Moira's knees buckled under her. She was tired. So tired. The matter had to be decided. She was guilty. She deserved what was coming to her. She sank to the ground, for one extraordinary second so disoriented she thought there was someone else besides her and her companion on the escarpment. If only she could turn around...

CHAPTER ONE

The Present

RETURNING FROM LUNCH—no fun at all, she *loathed* hurting people—Jessica found a note from Brett De Vere, her uncle, summoning her to a meeting in his office. It was probably about the Siegal place, she thought, carefully hanging up her new Gucci handbag. It had cost an arm and a leg. She felt a tiny spasm of guilt, but she had decided she *must* have it.

And why not? She was single. She had a great job, a challenging, exciting life. Swiftly she took a hairbrush from the bottom drawer of her desk and ran it briskly through her long blond hair, which was naturally curly but straightened at the moment. The action freed her a little from thoughts of the upsetting lunch with Sean, who really was a thoroughly nice guy, as wholesome as rolled oats. Most girls would be over the moon having a guy like Sean love them. The sad fact was he hadn't found a way to her heart.

Jessica stowed her hairbrush away, then turned to stare out the huge picture window directly behind her desk. It offered a tranquil view of the quiet leafy street. It was the *bluest* day. A day to hold in the memory. She loved the location of their offices, the avenue of mature jacaranda trees that in November, six months away, broke out in blossom. At that time, the whole city of Brisbane became tinted with an exquisite lavender-blue no sooner spent than the great shade trees, the poincianas, turned the air rosy. She loved life in the subtropics. Not too hot. Perfect!

In the distance, the broad, deep river that wound through the city's heart glittered in the afternoon sunlight. Nature stirred her, gave her strength. Comforted, she tried to work out what she was going to say to Brett. Her uncle, trained as an architect from whence, becoming bored, had branched out into interior design, had given her the commission. She was desperate to show him she measured up, but despite her best efforts, things weren't going very well. She'd lavished a lot of time and effort on her designs for the Siegals' resplendent new river-front home. But the Siegals were proving to be rather difficult clients. At least the wife, Chic, a fixture at charity functions, was. Couldn't be her real name, Jessica suspected, though she stood by Mrs. Siegal's decision to make one up. She must have considered Chic had impact. After all, she was only five-two standing fully erect.

But it was hell trying to deal with her. The fact that her husband was a multimillionaire might have had something to do with her endless waffling. De Vere's Design Studio had a few millionaires on the books, but most of its clients staved off mini-heart attacks by having a firm budget in mind. Her uncle Brett was in his late forties and had reached the point in his career when he could handpick his clients. Such a shame, then, he'd let Chic Siegal through the door.

About ready to join her uncle, Jessica checked herself over in the long narrow wall mirror. The lime-green suit and the fuchsia-pink-and-lime camisole beneath it had cost a month's pay, but Brett was a stickler for looking good, considering it was part of the job. He, himself, was polished perfection. In her entire life, Jessica had never seen her uncle slide into sloppiness. She winked at her reflection then walked down the corridor to his office, waggling her fingers at Becky, a senior designer, and stopping at her door. Becky's desk was awash with swatches of gorgeous new fabrics she was tossing around with abandon. Turquoise, aquamarine, malachite. Jessica smiled. *Malachite* sounded much better than *olive*. As a schoolgirl hired for the holidays, Jessica had adored being in Becky's office. She still did. The space was a veritable Aladdin's cave.

Becky beamed back. "Love your suit, kid! Watcha pay for that?"

"Not telling."

"We're friends, aren't we?" Becky, fifty for a few years now, in her youth powerfully pretty and still hanging in there, peered over the top of the glasses she had finally made the decision to wear.

"Sure. I just can't get my tongue around the price tag."

"Well, you look like a million dollars." Becky gave her a thumbs-up.

"Thanks, Beck."

Jessica resumed walking, smiling left and right at staff, eight in all, clever, creative people very loyal to the firm. She had joined De Vere's Design Studio soon after completing her fine-arts degree with honors. As a result of her degree, she'd been offered a position at the Queensland art gallery, with good prospects for advancement, but she'd turned it down. A decision about which her eminent lawyer father, a pillar of society, a man who thought he had a perfect right to speak his mind at all times, had been most unhappy. "Working for your uncle is a very *frivolous* decision, Jessica. Your mother and I had high hopes for

you, but our hopes don't seem to mean anything to you."
Her father generally spoke with all the authority of the
pope.

The fact that her stunningly handsome and gifted uncle
was gay might have had something to do with it. Brett's
sexual orientation made quite a few people in the family
a tad uncomfortable, but she had dealt with the issue by
moving out of the family home into a nice two-bedroom
apartment in a trendy inner-city neighbourhood. She was
able to do so thanks to the nest egg that Nan, her beloved
maternal grandmother—Brett's mother, Alex—had left
her. Jessica had been very close to Alex. In fact, her full
name was Jessica Alexandra Tennant. Christening her
Jessica had not been her mother's decision. She had
wanted the name *Alexandra,* after her own mother, for her
newborn, but such was her deference to her husband that
she had given in to *Jessica* after her baby's strong-minded,
paternal grandmother, a large imposing woman who wore
so many layers of clothing that one never knew exactly
what sort of body lay beneath. It was she who had descended on the young couple like a galleon in full sail, for
frequent, unscheduled visits. Jessica's mother had once
confided to her daughter that the early days of her marriage
had been like living in a police state.

Jessica had been devastated when her beloved nan, with
never a complaint, had died of cancer when Jessica was
eighteen. She knew Brett greatly missed his mother. Nan
had offered that rare thing—unconditional love. Jessica's
formidable maternal grandfather, much like her own
father, had great difficulty accepting Uncle Brett's homo-
sexuality, seeing it as a blot on the family escutcheon and
a major hurdle in life. The hurdle part Jessica was forced
to concede had come into play; she had seen it in action.

But she loved and admired her uncle, and she got on famously with his partner of twenty years, both in business and in life, Tim Langford. Tim was a sweet man, exceptionally creative, with a prodigious, largely self-taught knowledge of antiques. Tim handled the antiques-and-decorative-objects side of the business.

Brett was working at his desk, smooth blond head bent over an architectural drawing, but when she tapped at his door, he looked up with his faintly twisted, rather heartbreaking smile. Very few people saw the full picture of Brett De Vere. "Hi! How did the lunch go?"

She took the seat opposite him. "Perfectly awful! Thanks for asking. At least it didn't amount to a *scene.* Sean's a really nice person, but I couldn't let him go on thinking sooner or later we were bound for the altar. That wouldn't have been fair to him. Besides, I like my independence."

"How could you fall in love with someone like that, anyway?" Brett, who had never hit it off with Sean, asked. "He could never make you happy. He's so damned *ordinary.*"

"Maybe, but it took me a while to see it."

"At least you have," Brett said dryly.

"Next time I'll go for a Rhodes scholar," she joked. "I'm not ready to settle down yet. I'm enjoying my life just the way it is."

"Until the right guy comes along," Brett murmured, sitting back and making a steeple of his long, elegant fingers. "Then you'll change your mind. Have you managed to get that truly silly woman who never shuts up on side?"

"Ever so slowly," she sighed. "The trouble with having too much money is it opens up too many options. Mrs. Siegal spends her time trolling through design magazines to the point she simply can't decide whether she wants classical, traditional grandeur, lots of drama, ultramodern or a hybrid of the lot."

"Give her pure theatre," Brett advised. "The only trouble with that is De Vere's puts its name to it. Maybe *I* should make an attempt to help her decide?"

Jessica looked at him. Her uncle was an elegant, austerely handsome man with fine features and an air of detachment. Extremely intelligent, he was inclined to be sharp-tongued, even caustic at times. His eyes were green. Like hers. His hair ash blond, again like hers. They shared the family face. Alex's face. Alex's coloring.

"Well?" he prompted breaking into her brief reverie.

"Why not? She fancies herself in love with you." Indeed Brett's air of unattainability drove some women wild.

"A lot of good that will do her," he said with biting self-mockery.

"What I don't get is they know you're not interested, yet they fall in love with you all the same."

"A bitter pill no woman worth her salt can swallow," he returned. "It's the Liz Taylor–Montgomery Clift syndrome. Women always want the man they can't have."

"Is that what it is?" Jessica swiveled a quarter turn in her black leather chair. "Be that as it may, at this point I need help."

"Surely not the talented young woman short-listed for Best Contemporary Residential Project!" Brett raised a brow.

"It would be quite a coup to win it."

"A coup, yes, but not beyond you. You're *good,* Jass," he said, giving his professional, uncompromised opinion. "I haven't handed over a client who hasn't been delighted with your services. In fact, I could say with some confidence that my mantle, when I go to the angels, will fall on you. You're developing a following with your watercolor renderings of our clients' favourite rooms. They *love* them. Single-handedly you're reviving the old genre. Oh, and remember it was *my* idea."

"Don't I always give you credit?"

"Of course you do."

It was Brett who had encouraged Jessica to turn her hobby of painting interiors in watercolors, an art project carried on from her student days, into a lucrative sideline. For the past year, she'd worked very successfully on half a dozen commissions, along with the major commission of designing the stage sets for the Bijou Theatre's *A Midsummer Night's Dream*. Maybe one day she would follow her uncle into designing stage and movie sets.

"Is that what you wanted to speak to me about, the Siegals?" she asked.

"That was the second thing. First—" Brett ruffled through his papers again, this time finding a long fax "—what do you know about Broderick Bannerman?"

"Bannerman…Bannerman…rings a bell." Jessica sorted through her memory bank. "Hang on. Don't tell me." She held up a hand. "He's the cattle baron, right? Flagship station, one of a chain, by name of something starting with an *M…M…M…*Mokhani, that's it. Bannerman always figures in the *Bulletin*'s Rich List."

"The very one." Brett looked at her with approval. He leaned forward to hand over the fax, murmuring something complimentary about her powers of recall. "And he remembers *you!* He saw that interview on TV with the ubiquitous Bruce Hilton when he so easily could have missed it. That was just after you'd been short-listed for your award. Apparently he was so impressed he wants you to handle the interior design for his new temple in the wilds—'temple' is how some magazine described it. Lord knows what's wrong with the original homestead. I'm sure I read somewhere it was magnificent, or at the very worst, eminently livable."

Jessica, busy concentrating on the contents of the fax, lifted her head in amazement. "I don't get this. With all the established interior designers in the country, let alone *you,* purely on the basis of the proverbial fifteen minutes of fame on a talk show, he's singled out little ol' *me* with scant history in the business and only twenty-four?"

"It would appear so," Brett replied blandly. "Obviously he's a man who can sum up someone on the spot. Remember, you're a sophisticated twenty-four with natural gifts."

"How could he want *me* when he could have *you?*" Jessica asked in some wonderment.

"How sweet you are, Jass." Brett smiled. "In addition, you're respectful. Look, just believe in yourself. Take risks. I've taught you everything you know. Between you and me and the paper bin, I'm the best in the business. If I tell you you're ready, you're ready. I'm thrilled he wants De Vere's. I'm thrilled he wants *you.* For one thing, I love you, for another, there's no way I'm heading off for the Northern Territory. The great Outback isn't my scene, splendid though it is. Parts of it are downright eerie. Tim and I were quite spooked on our trip to the Red Centre. Wandering around the Olgas was a thoroughly unnerving experience. I could have sworn we were being watched by guardian spirits none too happy we were invading their territory. It was an extraordinary feeling and I'm told it's not that unusual."

"Well, it *is* sacred ground," Jessica commented, having heard numerous tales about the Outback's mystical ability to raise the hairs on the back of one's neck. "'There are more things in heaven and earth, Horatio, than are dreamt of in your philosophy,'" she quoted. "Getting back to the cattle baron, or should I say, king? Did you know Nicole Kidman is a descendant of Sir Sydney Kidman, the original Cattle King?"

"Few of us have your mastery of trivia, Jass. No, I didn't. Neither of them short of a bob."

"Unlike us, Nicole has a wonderfully supportive family," Jessica said. "Do you really think I'm ready for a project of this size?" she asked very seriously. The word had got around she was good, but she never thought an immensely rich Territorian would seek her services. Not for years and years.

Brett interlocked his hands behind his head, stretching his long, lean torso. "Are you doubting yourself?"

"I'm doing my best not to, but as I recall, Mr. Bannerman has a reputation for being ruthless. Who knows? Some of my designs mightn't suit him. He could turn nasty. I read an article about him a year or two ago. A lot of people interviewed weren't very fond of him, though most wisely insisted on having their names withheld. Word was, he did terrible things to them in business. His cattle stations represent only a fraction of Bannerman holdings. He's into everything."

"Don't let that worry you. As long as he's not into drugs. Then we'd have a problem." Brett straightened, shoving a file across the table. "On the plus side, he makes large donations to charity. Might help with his tax, but apparently he *wants* to, so he can't be all bad. He owns Lowanna Resort Island on the Great Barrier Reef. Highrise apartment blocks on the Gold Coast and the tourist strip in North Queensland, mining and exploration developments, foreign investments. He's loaded."

"Excessively rich clients are a pain in the neck," Jessica said from very recent experience. "We must consider he might be even more impossible to work with than Chic Siegal."

"Surely you're not going to turn the commission down." Brett shifted position, apparently trying, ineffectually, to make himself comfortable in his antique captain's chair.

"I have no intention of turning it down. I want lots and lots of commissions. Still, before I sign up, there's the small matter of crocodiles. They insist on getting their long snouts into the news." In a recent event on a remote beach in far North Queensland, one had waddled up from the water, crossed the sand and entered a camper's tent, dragging him out. All that had saved the hapless man was the incredibly brave action of a fellow camper, a grandmother in her sixties, who without hesitation had jumped on the crocodile's back, then another camper had shot it.

Brett grimaced. "It *was* a remote beach. One must treat crocodiles with respect like the Territorians do. We talk about their crocs. They talk about our traffic accidents. I don't imagine Bannerman has given crocs an open invitation to waddle around the station, anyway. Just think what could happen."

"You don't have to look so ghoulish. Speaking of which there was a big mystery on Mokhani many years ago." Jessica frowned, dredging her memory for more information. "Surely it's been the subject of articles over the years?"

"'The Mokhani Mystery,' as it came to be called," Brett said, having read a few of the articles.

"Didn't a governess disappear?"

"So she did," Brett said briskly, apparently not really

wanting to talk about the old story. "It made front-page news at the time. But for years now everything about it's been quiet, though I'm surprised someone hasn't written a book about it. Horrible business, but not *recent*. It must be all of fifty years ago. Which reminds me my big five-oh is coming. Aging is not fun."

"Don't take it to heart. You've never looked better." Jessica was sincere. "Anyway, you can always do what Becky does. Birthday every three years like the elections."

"Women can get away with these things. What's the old saying? 'If a woman tells you her age, she'll tell you anything.' I look after myself and I don't smoke. At least not for years now. Couldn't do without my wine cellar, but wine in moderation is good for you. I'll be very angry if the medical profession suddenly disputes it. But back to Bannerman. You can be sure he's put up plenty of signs warning visitors about nomadic crocodiles."

"You think a crocodile may have taken the governess?" Jessica asked with some horror.

"How can one not *hate* them?" Brett shuddered. "Poor little soul. I can just see her picnicking without a care in the world beside a lagoon and up pops a prehistoric monster. There have been a few cases of that in North Queensland in recent times."

"More likely in one particular case the husband pushed her into the lagoon," Jessica offered darkly, having come to that conclusion along with a lot of other people, including the investigating police officer, who just couldn't prove it. "I can't believe you're sending me up there."

"Sweetie, you're at no risk." Brett took her seriously when she was only teasing. "I'll be very surprised if you even lay *eyes* on a crocodile. I understand the station is a good way inland."

"I hope so, but I'm sure I've read it's within striking distance of Kakadu National Park, World Heritage area, reputed to be fabulous and home of the crocodile."

"I'm quite sure you'll be safe. The very last thing in the world I want is to have my favourite niece vanish into the wilderness. I love you dearly."

"I love you, too," Jessica answered. She resumed reading the fax. "He'd like me to be in Darwin by Monday, the twenty-second where I'll be picked up at Darwin airport and taken to the station. The twenty-second! That's two weeks away." Her green eyes widened.

"I know. Doesn't leave you much time." Brett gazed past her linen-clad shoulder, a smile transforming the severity of his handsome features. "Not *more* junk, Tim?" he drawled. "You're hooked on it."

Jessica swiveled around, a big, welcoming smile on her face. "Hi, Timmy. How did it go in Sydney?" Her eyes settled with considerable curiousity on a large canvas he was carrying beneath his arm. "What have you got there?"

"My dears, you'll *never* believe!" Tim, thick black hair, deep dark eyes, extraordinarily youthful-looking and dressed casually in T-shirt and jeans, staggered through the open doorway.

"We don't *need* any more paintings, Tim dear," Brett warned.

"You're going to love this one," Tim promised, his voice reflecting his excitement. "I had one hell of a battle to get it. Some crazy old bat I swear was in costume was after it. No manners whatsoever. We nearly had a fistfight right there on the floor of Christie's."

"If you've bought some bloody *flower* painting, I'll kill you," Brett said. Tim had excellent taste but he did overly favor flower paintings.

"Voilà!" Tim rested the painting against the wall of built-in cabinets, gesturing as if at a masterpiece.

There was total silence.

Then a stunned. "My God!" blurted out from Brett.

"Where in the world did you get this?" Jessica was equally transfixed.

"I told you. Christie's auction." Tim whipped a satisfied grin over both their stunned faces.

"That's one of the most haunting paintings I've ever seen," Brett murmured, standing up the better to examine it. "The girl could be Jass."

"Now you know why I wanted it." Tim suddenly slumped into a chair as though his legs were giving out. "It made my hair stand on end."

"So everyone has a double, after all," Brett muttered. "What can you tell us about this? What's the provenance?"

"I took a chance on this one," Tim admitted, addressing his partner, the dominant of the two. Both men were devoted to each other, though Brett had strayed a few times over the years, causing much suffering. Tim brimmed over with charm and good humor, far more comfortable in his own skin than the at-war-with-himself Brett.

"No one knows anything about the artist. It's signed in a fashion in the lower right-hand corner—H.B. It came in on consignment with a batch of paintings by established artists. There was comment about its beauty, but the serious collectors only buy *names*. The old girl I'm talking. about was after it, I can tell you that. She even offered me far more than I paid for it."

"It's beautifully painted," Jessica observed, making her own close inspection. "Perhaps the artist was in love with her. It has a decidedly erotic quality, don't you think? I wonder who she was?"

"No date on it?" Brett asked.

"Nothing. From how she's dressed I'd say late fourties, early fifties." Jessica, who had studied fashion through the ages, remarked. "She's very young. Seventeen, eighteen?"

"It's a particularly fine example of color and light," Brett said. He had excellent critical judgment. For some inexplicable reason he wasn't comfortable with the sudden appearance of this remarkable painting. The work struck him as decidedly odd.

"Notice the background," Jessica was saying. "It's fairly loose. No clear outlines, but I'd say it's definitely the great outdoors. Not a suburban garden. The long, curly blond hair is marvelous. So are the green eyes staring right at you. It's quite powerful, actually. Sort of mesmeric. Don't you feel that?" She looked back at the two men.

Brett nodded, turning to Tim. "How much did this set us back?"

"Twenty thousand," Tim said, looking like he was about to get up and run.

"Wh-a-t?" Brett snapped. "An *unknown* artist?"

"But plenty of panache! That old girl knew him. Or of him," Tim said defensively. "I'm sure of it. Besides I couldn't let it go anywhere else. It belongs here." His dark eyes appealed to Jessica. "*She,* the girl in the portrait, wanted me to buy it. She *moved* me to do it. You understand that, Jass. You're so sensitive. For all we know, she could be a relation."

"Don't be ridiculous. We know all the relations, more's the pity," Brett said acidly, giving his partner a sharp look.

"Well, we all agree Jessica is extraordinarily like her."

"Proving as I said, we all have a doppelgänger, nothing else. Next time you go off to these auctions I'm coming with you."

"I'd love that." Tim grinned.

"Actually, we could put it up in a prominent place in the showroom." Brett was starting to come round. "It'll certainly generate discussion."

"I thought that, too," Tim was suddenly all smiles. "Besides, what's twenty thousand? You've got plenty."

"That's because I spend little time at auctions," Brett said dryly, returning to his desk. "By the way, I can't come to terms with this chair. It looks good, but it's not kind to my tailbone. Find me something else, will you, Tim?"

"Sure. I'd remind you that I did say it wouldn't be all that comfortable, except you don't like being reminded."

"Thank you for that." Brett lowered his long, lean length into the mahogany chair. "Now, you've shown us your big surprise. Hopeless to top that, nevertheless we'll try. We've got a surprise for you."

"Do tell." Tim slipped Jessica something he'd taken out of his pocket.

"What is it?"

"Just a little prezzie." Tim smiled at her.

"If you'd be so good." Brett raised a supercilious eyebrow, then continued. "Broderick Bannerman, the cattle baron. Hails from the Northern Territory—"

"How absolutely thrilling!" Tim broke in enthusiastically. "I know the name."

"It gets better. He's offered De Vere's a huge commission. Specifically he wants Jass to handle the entire interior design for his new Outback temple."

Tim's expression turned to one of amazement. He stared from one to the other. "You're making this up, aren't you?"

"No, Tim, we're not," Brett replied, somewhat testily this time. "Hand him the fax, would you, Jass. Bannerman saw her interview with Bruce Hilton and was so impressed he shot off that little lot."

Tim scanned the fax quickly, then looked up. "Good grief, I'm blown away. So is she going? It's a *big* job."

"One never knows what one is capable of until one tries," said Brett. "Of course she's going. There's plenty we can do to help and advise. It's a huge commission. There's bound to be good coverage and flow-ons for us."

Tim's brow furrowed. "Are you comfortable about sending Jessica by herself? She's our baby. Now I think about it, wasn't there some murder up there? Passed into Outback folklore? Remember, we found the Outback one scary place."

"Hell, Tim, don't say that to anyone else," Brett begged. "What would people think?"

"Who cares what people think?" Tim said. "On the other hand people might agree if they'd been there. Those Olgas, they were fantastic, if kinda forbidding."

"Look—" Brett tried to be patient "—forget the Olgas, okay? Incidentally, they've been renamed Kata Tjuta. A governess disappeared. A tragedy certainly, but no murder. An accident befell her some fifty years ago, but alas there was no body. Bannerman is perfectly respectable. He's one of the richest, most influential men in the country. He's not a drug lord. I'm certain Jass will be safe. I'd never let her go if I thought otherwise. She's young for such a big commission, but that shouldn't be a deterrent. She's genuinely gifted and she'll have plenty of backup. If for some reason Bannerman turns out to be straight out of a Stephen King novel, she can come home."

"You want to do this, Jessica?" Tim still looked unsettled.

"Hey, of course I do." She shook his arm. "I'll be able

to brag about it for the rest of my days. Don't worry, Timmy. It should be quite an adventure." She started to unwrap his little present. "Ooh, earrings. Aren't they lovely?" She leaned over and kissed him. "Victorian."

He nodded. "I knew you'd like them. I picked them up at Maggie Reeves. She has some really nice stuff."

"You spoil her," Brett said, sitting forward to look.

"*You* should talk!" Tim shot back.

"I'm her uncle."

"And I'm her honorary uncle."

"Stop, you two. These are lovely, Timmy. Thank you." Jessica was delighted with the gift—drop earrings, peridots set in gold. She had a jewelery box filled with the little gifts Tim had given her since she was a child. Bracelets, gold chains, pretty pendants, a crystal-encrusted sea horse that she still loved and wore as a pin. "They'll go beautifully with that vintage dress of mine. The green chiffon." Sometimes she felt very sad that neither her uncle nor Tim would have children. They were loving, caring people. They had been wonderful to her.

"My pleasure, love." Tim smiled, picking up Bannerman's fax again. "They reckon there's a dark side to this Bannerman?"

"Tim, dear, there's a dark side to us all," Brett responded. "Not even *you* are nice all the time. If you're concerned, maybe you can fly up with Jass."

"Both of us? I would go, but I'm sure they don't want me."

"Not to mention how having a babysitter would make *me* look," Jessica protested. "What else do we know about this man?"

"Well—" Brett drew another piece of paper, hitherto unseen, from the pile on his desk "—he has a son, Cyrus.

His mother was the heiress, Deborah Masters. Masters Electronics."

"You said *was?* She's dead?" Jessica inserted one of the earrings in her right earlobe, remembering Tim had gone along with her for support when she'd had her ears pierced a few years back and had been a little fearful of needles.

"A riding accident," Brett informed them. "That was in the early 1990s. Bannerman remarried. A woman with a child of her own. A daughter, Robyn. Neither wife was particularly lucky. The second suffered from some rare syndrome—I don't know exactly what. She died two years ago."

"How very bizarre," muttered Tim, trying to grapple with all this. "It's right up there with the Olgas."

"Don't be silly, Tim." Sternly, Brett held his partner's gaze. "Tragedies happen."

"Indeed they do. But Bannerman could be looking for a new wife. He could fall in love with Jessica on sight."

Jessica laughed, but Brett blustered testily, "God almighty, Tim! I think you're losing it. Bannerman has to be nearing sixty."

"That's not a good answer." Tim resolutely dug in. "He could live for years and years. Aging men often turn to young women. Especially *rich* old men."

"He's hardly an *old* man," Brett said caustically. "You're nearly fifty."

"Forty-eight, thank you. Same as you. Keep it up and you'll really hurt my feelings."

"Stop it, you two," Jessica intervened again. "I'm not in the running for Wife Number Three." She took Tim's hand in hers. "Broderick Bannerman is old enough to be my father. Grandfather, if he were exceptionally precocious."

"For all we know, temptation could be overwhelming in the Outback," Tim said. "There's a real shortage of women. Besides, men never get falling in love with the young and beautiful out of their system," he warned. "I know I sound overanxious, but there's something a little odd here, Jass. You know how intuitive I am. No matter how gifted you are, you're young and inexperienced. I know you've won that nomination and you deserve to carry off the prize, but why not Brett, for instance? He's a colossus in the industry. Well, *he* thinks so."

"I *know* so." Brett was pleased to see Jessica elbow Tim hard. "For God's sake, Tim, what are you on about?" Brett was irritated that some of Tim's concern was starting to rub off on him.

"I'm not sure." Tim shook his head. "I live by my intuitions."

"And your intuitions tell you Bannerman has an ulterior motive in choosing Jessica?"

"Amazing, but true. I should join a training class for psychics. Seriously, I just had to get it off my chest. I don't actually *know* why."

"Then why are you trying to put us off?"

"I'm not," Tim protested. "I'm only trying to say Bannerman mightn't be quite the man he seems. Sounds to me like he's been struck by lightning."

"Lightning!" Brett said irritably. "How you give yourself over to the sensational!"

"Sensational?" Tim protested. "Men have been making complete asses of themselves over young women since forever. Besides, what man ever thinks he's too old?"

"Look, Timmy, I've dreamed about doing something like this." Jessica sought to calm Tim down. "You know you tend to worry about me too much."

"True." Tim's face broke out in his easy smile again. "I wouldn't mind if you were working within shouting distance, or even Sydney. But the Northern Territory! Hell, you might as well be rocketing off to Mars."

"Tim, dear, stop talking," Brett advised. "It's all fevered nonsense, anyway. Jass wants the job. I want her to have it. It'll be a considerable step up the ladder. If the slightest thing happens to cause her concern, she's to drop everything and come home."

"Hear that, sweetheart? You get on the phone right away. I'll be there like a shot. I wonder what the son's like?" Tim asked speculatively, then answered his own question. "Probably a dead ringer for his godawful father."

"Okay, enough's enough!" Brett lunged to his feet. "Where are we going to hang this painting?"

"Maybe above the console in the entrance," Jessica suggested, giving the painting a tender, welcoming look for its own sake and not because the subject bore an uncanny resemblance to her. "She'll be right at home there."

CHAPTER TWO

FROM THE TOP OF THE ESCARPMENT, Cy had a near aerial view of the valley floor, semidesert in the Dry except for the ubiquitous spinifex and the amazing array of drought-resistant shrubs, grasses and succulents that provided fodder for Mokhani's great herd, one of the biggest in the nation and thus the world. Today, four of his men were working flat out to round up of some forty marauding brumbies that were fast eating out the vegetation they desperately needed for the cattle until the blessing of rain. The wild horses had to be moved on. Not only that, two of the station mares were running with the mob, seduced by the leader, a powerful white stallion the men had christened Snowy. Snowy was too nice a name for a rogue, Cy figured. More like Lucifer before the fall. The stallion was so clever, it had long evaded capture, though Cy doubted the wild horse could ever be broken. He'd been close up to Snowy when they'd both been boxed into the canyon, so he knew he was dealing with a potential killer. There were few station pursuits as dangerous as trying to cut off a wild horse from its precious freedom. Ted Leeuwin, the station overseer, had lived to tell the tale of his encounter with Snowy. Just as Ted had been attempting to rope the stallion, it had closed in, terrifying Ted's gelding before biting Ted on the shoulder. Not once but several times.

Vicious hard bites that forced Ted, as tough as old boots, to give up.

Cy was aware of his own excitement as whoops like war cries resounded across the valley. He knew the thrill of the chase. The men were right on target to herd the wild horses into the gorge. Two of the station hands were on motorbikes; jumping rocks and gullies with abandon, another two were on horseback. He'd put one of the station helicopters in the air to flush the brumbies out and guide the men.

He'd have to leave them to it. His father, known as B.B. wanted him to fly to Darwin to pick up the interior designer, Ms. Jessica Tennant if you please, he was hellbent on hiring. As usual, they'd argued about it. Any suggestion that amounted to a differing opinion caused his father rage. B.B. wasn't a man to listen. Not to his only son, anyway. Often after such arguments, his father hadn't spoken to him for long periods, by way of punishment. But punishment for what? There could be a hundred things, and Cy had narrowed it down to two: for daring to cross a living legend and for being alive when his mother wasn't. He understood his father loved him at some subterranean level, but the very last thing B.B. would do was show it. Needless to say, they weren't close, but they were *blood*. That counted.

As far as this latest development went, his father had taken them all by surprise. What would a young woman of twenty-four be expected to know about furnishing from scratch what was virtually a palace? For that matter, what was wrong with the old homestead even if Livvy, his great-aunt, claimed it was haunted? He was sick to death of it all. The old story distressed him. He'd grown up with it, had been taunted about it in his schooldays. Poor tragic

Moira, the governess, had most probably been taken by a croc or she had fallen, her body wedged into some rocky crevice in a deeply wooded canyon, never to be found. God knows it happened. People going missing wasn't exactly a rare occurrence in the Outback. So why had journalists over the years continued to rake up the old story, when all the family wanted was to bury it? No one had ever been able to unearth any proof as to what had happened to her that fatal day.

His mind returned to Jessica Tennant. She might work for a top design studio, but surely there were many people more experienced and more qualified in that firm to do the job? He couldn't figure it out. B.B., who only dealt with the top people, never underlings, a man renowned for always making smart moves, had done something totally un-smart. He had hired a mere beginner to take charge of a huge project.

"She's coming here, Cyrus. I'm still making the decisions around here. As for you, Robyn—" B.B. had turned to his stepdaughter "—I don't want to hear one unpleasant word pass your lips when she's here. Is that understood?"

In that case, Robyn had better take a crash course on manners, Cyrus thought. For a moment he almost felt sorry for Ms. Tennant. She would be living in the same house as a very dysfunctional family. Perhaps not for long, though. Cy could still hope Ms. Tennant might decide the project was beyond her. There was no way, however, to avoid meeting her. He'd agreed to pick her up because he had business in Darwin, anyway. Otherwise, he'd have said he was far too busy, which not even B.B. could dispute. These days he ran Mokhani while regularly overseeing the other stations in the Bannerman chain. Unlike everyone else directly under B.B.'s control, he didn't toe the line unless there was substantial reason to. He had to accept his father was different. Never relaxed, never friendly, as though in doing so he would diminish his aura. The older he got, the more controlling B.B. became. Cy couldn't remember a time when he and his father had been in accord. Not even in childhood. The precious days when his mother, Deborah, had been alive. A few years back, after a particularly bad clash, he had stormed off, thinking his absence would solve the problem of their angst-laden relationship. In the process, he'd realized he could be throwing away his chance of inheritance. But what the hell! He had to be his own man, not the yes-man his father wanted. The sad fact was that B.B. liked grinding people into the ground. He had treated Robyn's mother, Sharon, like the village idiot. His own mother, who had won the love and admiration of everyone around her, had apparently been highly successful at standing up to her autocratic husband—a man given to unpredictable bouts of black moods—but a riding accident had claimed her when Cy was ten and away at boarding school. A *riding* accident, when she'd been a wonderful horsewoman. Cy was constantly struck by the great ironies of life.

On that last bid for freedom he'd been gone only a couple of months when his father had come after him. It'd been a huge backing down for B.B., who'd come as close to begging as that man ever could. After he'd had a chance to cool down, B.B. had seen the wisdom of not letting him go. For one thing, for B.B. to deny his own son would go down very badly in the Outback. Even he, Outback legend though he was, was afraid of that. And for another, B.B. knew that Cy was not only the rightful heir to the Bannerman empire, but he was *needed*. Cy's skills had been tested and proven. Many thought him the man of the future, serious, influential people who for years had muttered about B.B. and his ruthless practices. Things could be done right without throwing honesty and justice aside.

The conniving Robyn, though she was an excellent businesswoman and owned a very successful art gallery and a couple of boutiques in Darwin, couldn't hope to replace him. Though she'd try. Robyn *wasn't* a Bannerman, though she bore the name and fully took advantage of its clout. Robyn had a *real* father around someplace, but no one had heard of him for years. She was a year younger than Cy. She and Sharon had come to Mokhani two years after his own mother's death. Sharon had been sweet and kind. Robyn was anything but, though she trod very carefully around B.B. It was no big secret to insiders that Robyn's greatest ambition was to somehow usurp Cy and inherit Mokhani. He, the heir apparent, was the only obstacle in the way. Once, a good friend of his, Ross Sunderland, looking uneasily at Robyn, had suggested he watch his back. "Robyn likes shooting things, Cy," he'd said.

Cy had responded with a practiced laugh. The reality was he'd been watching his back for years. Right from the beginning, Robyn had been a strange one. Cy had divined even as a boy that in Robyn he had an unscrupulous rival.

But for once, he and Robyn had joined forces against B.B.'s decision to hire Ms. Tennant. His decision had been based on Jessica Tennant's age and inexperience, not her gender; his own mother, after all, had been a very creative woman. But Robyn was violently opposed to the idea of having another *woman* do the job she'd tried to convince B.B. she could do. She had reacted with the bitterest resentment not even bothering to conceal her hostility from B.B. A big mistake.

"Be careful, Robyn. Be careful." B.B. had turned on her coldly. "I have hired this young woman. I don't want second best."

Finality in action.

THEY WERE MAKING their descent into Darwin airport when the slightly tipsy nuclear physicist beside Jessica leaned into her to confide, "We're landing."

"Yes, I know."

"Darwin airport has one of the longest runways in the southern hemisphere."

"Really? I'm not surprised to hear that." She kept staring out the porthole. The guy had been hitting on her in an inoffensive way ever since they'd left Brisbane. At one point she'd even toyed with the idea of asking the flight attendant to move her, but the plane was full. In a few minutes she'd be able to make her getaway from Mr. Intelligence.

It was not to be. He followed her every step of the way into the terminal, making like an overzealous tour guide, pointing out areas already clearly marked. He topped it all off by offering to give her a lift to wherever she wanted to go.

"Thanks all the same, but I'm being picked up."

"You never said that." He turned to her with such an aggrieved look the image of Sean floated into her mind.

"No reason to," she smiled. "Bye now." If her luck held…

It didn't. "At least I can help you with your luggage."

Drat the guy! He was as hard to brush off as a bad case of dandruff.

"So what say we meet up for a drink sometime?" he suggested. "I live here. I can show you all the sights."

"That's kind of you, but I'll be pretty busy."

"Doin' what?" He looked at her as though she were playing hard to get.

Irritation was escalating into her as much as the heat would allow when she suddenly caught sight of a stunning-looking guy, head and shoulders over the rest, maybe twenty-eight or thirty, striding purposefully toward her.

It *was* to her, wasn't it? She'd hate him to change his mind. What's more, the milling crowd fell back as though to ease his path. How many men could carry *that* off?

"For cryin' out loud, you *know* Bannerman?" Her companion did a double take, his gravelly drawl soaring toward falsetto.

Bannerman wasn't Count Dracula surely? She nodded. "He's a *friend?*"

This was starting to belong in the too-hard basket. "He's meeting me," Jessica said.

"Well, I'm movin' outta here." Her annoying companion, a full six feet, all but reeled away. "I wouldn't want to get in *that* guy's way. Good luck!"

Jessica held her breath. So *this* is Cyrus Bannerman, she thought tracking his every movement. This was as good as it gets. The fact that he was so striking in appearance didn't come as a surprise. Broderick Bannerman was an impressive-looking man—she'd seen numerous photos. Obviously good looks ran in the family. What she hadn't been expecting was the charisma, the air of authority, that appeared entirely natural. Obviously Cyrus Bannerman was ready to take over his father's mantle when many a son with a tycoon for a father finished up with a personality disorder. Not the case here, unless that palpable presence turned out to be a facade.

He was very tall, maybe six-three, with a great

physique. The loose-limbed, long-legged stride was so graceful it was near mesmerizing. It put her in mind of the sensuous lope of a famous Pakistani cricketer she'd had a crush on as a child. Bannerman, as well he might be, given his lifestyle, was deeply tanned. In fact, he made everyone else's tan look positively washed out. He had thick, jet-black hair, strong distinctive features, his eyes even at a distance the bluest she had ever seen. "Sapphires set in a bronze mask," the romantically inclined might phrase it, and they'd be spot on. She knew instinctively she had better impress this guy with her professional demeanor. No contract had been signed as yet.

"Ms. Tennant?" Cyrus, for his part, saw a young woman, physically highly desirable, with a lovely full mouth and a mane of ash-blond hair springing into a riot of curls in the humid heat. Her tallish, slender body was relaxed. She had beautiful clear skin. Her large green eyes watched him coolly. Young she might be, but there was nothing diffident about her. She looked confident, clever, sizing him up as indeed he was sizing her up. They could have been business opponents facing each other across a boardroom table for the first time.

"Please, *Jessica,*" she said. Her voice matched her appearance, cool, confident, ever so slightly challenging.

"Cyrus Bannerman. I usually get Cy."

"Then Cy it is." Though every instinct shrieked a warning, she offered him her hand. It was taken in a firm, cool grip. Jessica let out her breath slowly, disconcerted by the thrill of skin on skin. "How nice of you to meet me."

"No problem. I had business in Darwin." The startling blue eyes continued to study her. She had already grasped the fact that, despite the smoothness of manner, he hadn't taken to her. Was it wariness in his eyes? A trace of suspicion? More the pity! Anyone would think she had coerced his father into hiring her. Not that it mattered. She didn't altogether like him. She did, however, like the *look* of him. A teeny distinction.

Baggage was already tumbling onto the carousel. He looked toward it. "If you'll point out what's yours, I'll collect it. I'd like to get away as soon as possible. We're going by helicopter. Hope that's okay with you. You're assured of a great view."

So much for the big dusty Land Cruiser complete with a set of buffalo horns she'd been expecting.

THEY LIFTED OFF, climbing, climbing, into the blue June sky, climbing, climbing. Jessica tried to stay cool even though her heart was racing. This was a far cry from traveling in a Boeing 747. Outside the bubble of the cockpit, a mighty panorama opened up. Jessica caught the gasp in her throat before it escaped. Below them was the harbor. The immensity of it amazed her. She hadn't been expecting that. Aquamarine on one arm of the rocky peninsula, glittering turquoise on the other. She knew from her history books that Darwin Harbour had seen more drama than any other harbor in Australia. The Japanese Imperial Air Force had bombed it during World War II turning the harbor into an inferno. Every ship, more than forty, including the U.S. destroyer *Peary* that had arrived that very morning, had been destroyed before the invaders had turned their attention to the small township itself, standing vulnerable on the rocky cliffs above the port. The invasion of Darwin had always been played down for some unknown reason. The town had been devastated again by Cyclone Tracy, Christmas Day 1974. Even her hometown of Brisbane, over a thousand miles away, had suffered the effects of that catastrophic force of nature.

Today, all was peace and calm. Jessica's first impression was that Darwin was an exotic destination. A truly tropical city, surrounded by water on three sides, and so far as she could see the most multicultural city in the country. The Top End, as the northern coast of Australia was right on the doorstep of Southeast Asia, and there was a lot of traffic between the two. She was really looking forward to exploring the city when she had time. The art galleries, she'd heard, particularly the galleries that featured the paintings of the leading Aboriginal artists were well worth the visit.

The helicopter trip was turning into probably the most exciting trip of her life. As they banked and turned inland—Mokhani was a little over 140 kilometers to the southeast—just as Cyrus Bannerman had promised, she had a fantastic view of the ancient landscape. Such empty vastness! So few people! She'd read recently, when she'd been researching all she could about Broderick Bannerman, that although the Northern Territory was twice the size of Texas, it had one percent of the population. She'd also read that the population of Darwin was less than eighty thousand, while the Territory covered over two million square kilometers, most of which lay within the tropics. The Red Centre, fifteen-hundred kilometers south of Darwin and another great tourist mecca, was the home of the continent's desert icons, the monolith of Uluru and the fantastic domes and minarets of Kata Tjuta, which had thrown such a scare into Brett and Tim. She realized in some surprise she knew more about overseas destinations, London, Paris, Rome, Vienna, New York on her last fabulous trip, than she did about the Top End and the vast interior of her own country.

That was about to change. She watched the rolling savannas and the vivid, vigorous pockets of rain forest give way to infinite flat plains, the floor of which was decorated with golden, dome-shaped grasses she knew were the ubiquitous spinifex that covered most of the Outback. The great glowing mounds made an extraordinary contrast to the fiery orange-red of the earth, and the amazing standing formations, she realized, were termite mounds. From the air, they looked for all the world like an army on the march.

Silvery streams of air floated beneath them like giant cushions. At one point, they flew low over a herd of wild brumbies, long tails and manes flowing as they galloped across the rough terrain. It was such a stirring sight, the breath caught in her throat. She wouldn't have missed this for the world.

"Camels dead ahead." Bannerman pointed. A very elegant hand, well-shaped, the artistic Jessica noticed. Hands were important to her. "Very intelligent animals." Despite himself, Cy was mollified by her high level of response to the land for which he had such a passion. She was young enough to be excited, and that excitement was palpable, indeed infectious. His own blood was coursing more swiftly in response. She didn't appear in the least nervous even when he put the chopper through its paces, whizzing down low. There was much more ahead for her to enjoy. Falling Waters, a landmark on Mokhani, looked spectacular from the air. He planned a low pass over the gorge. It would allow her to see the wonderful, ever-changing colors in the cliff walls.

THE FLIGHT INSIDE the magnificent canyon, carved by count-less centuries of floodwaters, was the ultimate thrill. Here below her was a verdant oasis in the middle of the desert. The colors in the cliff walls were astonishing. All the dry ochers were there, pinks, cream, yellow, orange, fiery cinnabar, purples, thick veins of brown and black and white. She felt a strong urge to try to paint them. Tier upon tier like some ancient pyramid was reflected perfectly in the mirrorlike surface of the lagoon. To either side lay broken chains of deep dark pools, but it was the main lagoon with its flotilla of pink water lilies that held the eye. It directly received the sparkling waterfall that cascaded from the plateau-like summit of the escarpment, littered with giant, orange-red boulders in themselves marvelously paintable.

"Beautiful, isn't it," Bannerman said, his voice betraying his pride in his Outback domain.

This was one lucky guy, Jessica thought. He appeared to have it all. Looks, intelligence, a vibrant physical presence, a rich if ruthless tycoon for a father, and one day all this would be his. Some three million glorious savage acres, and that was only Mokhani. She knew from her quick study of Broderick Bannerman's affairs that several other stations made up the Bannerman pastoral empire. It had to be an extraordinary experience to have millions of acres for a backyard, let alone a spectacular natural wonder like the gorge. Both sides of the canyon were thickly wooded with paperbarks and river gums; the lagoon and water holes were bordered by clean white sand.

"Can you swim there?" She pointed downward.

He nodded. "I have all my life. The pool is very deep at the centre. Perhaps bottomless."

A little frisson ran down Jessica's arms.

FROM THE AIR, MOKHANI STATION was an extraordinary sight, a pioneering settlement in the wilds. Bannerman's ancestors had carved this out, living with, rather than conquering, the land. Jessica, with her capacity for visualization, saw monstrous saltwater crocodiles inhabiting the paperbark swamps and lagoons that were spread across the vast primeval landscape. Not for the first time on this adventure did she consider the fate of Mokhani's governess who had vanished without a trace all those years ago. It was, after all, a haunting tale that had never found closure.

The station was so large it sent a shock of awe through her; miles of open plain interspersed with large areas of dense scrub, through which she could see the sharp glitter of numerous creeks and lagoons. It would be terrifyingly easy to get lost in all that. The table-topped escarpment that towered over the canyon and dominated the landscape was another major hazard. Although she didn't suffer from vertigo, Jessica was certain one could easily become dizzy if one ventured too near the lip of the precipice. It would be all too easy to topple over. Easier still to get pushed.

I've got an overactive imagination, she thought, a strange taste of copper in her mouth. Could it be that was what had happened? A young woman, too frantic to be afraid groping at thin air, skin ripped as she bounced off rock to rock. Did Moira go into the water alive? A body carried into the deep lagoon would make a succulent meal for a man-eating crocodile. Surely no one could say for sure that one didn't lurk there....

She was rather ashamed of her lurid thoughts. There were always suspicions when no body had been found. But if she'd been pushed, it would have been murder.

She longed to question Cyrus Bannerman about the unsolved mystery, but sensed she would only anger him. Such tragedies, though never forgotten, would have resonated unhappily down the years. He could well have been the butt of a lot of taunts in his school days. Like most Outback children, he would have been sent away to boarding school at around age ten. Looking at him now, she felt, boy and man, he had coped.

They flew over a huge complex of holding yards where thousands and thousands of cattle were penned. Probably awaiting transport to market by the great road trains. Clusters of outbuildings surrounded the main compound like a satellite town. The silver hangar with MOKHANI emblazoned on the roof was enormous. It looked as if it could comfortably house a couple of domestic jets. Two bright yellow helicopters were on the ground a short distance from the hangar, as well as several station vehicles. Up ahead, across a silver ribbon of creek, she could see the original homestead, very large as even large houses go, and some distance away what appeared to be a great classical temple.

Broderick Bannerman wanted her to furnish *that?* Hat-shepsut, queen of ancient Egypt, no mean hand at decorating, might have called in the professionals. Should she, Jessica, return to ancient Egypt for inspiration or settle for pre-Hellenic? Smack-bang in the middle of the wilderness, either option seemed a mite excessive, not to say bizarre. Obviously Broderick Bannerman, like the kings of old, had built his temple as a monument to himself. She wondered what role his son had played in it. There was an elegant austerity about Cyrus Bannerman that suggested *none.*

Another employee was on hand to drive her up to the house.

"I'm needed elsewhere, but Pete will look after you," Cy said, his eyes resting on her with what seemed like challenge.

"Many thanks for such an exciting trip," she responded, giving him her best smile. "I feel like I'm starting a new life."

"And yet at the end of a few weeks, you'll return to your old life." He sketched a brief salute and went on his way.

THEY DROVE PAST THE MULTITUDE of outbuildings she had
seen from the air, then topping a rise, she had her first view
of Mokhani homestead. The original homestead that had
withstood the fury of Cyclone Tracy, being miles from the
epicenter. It was a most impressive sight, approached by an
avenue of towering palms. Jessica wondered why Bannerman had wanted to build another. Two-storied, with a grand
hip roof and broad verandas on three sides, the upper story
featured beautiful decorative iron-lace balustrading. The
extensive gardens surrounding the house no doubt fed by
underground bores, were full of trees: banyan, fig, tamarind,
rain trees, the magnificent Pride of India, flamboyant poincianas and several of the very curious boab trees with their
fat, rather grotesque bottle-shaped trunks. Tropical shrubs
also abounded. Oleanders and frangipani, which so delighted the senses, agapanthus, strelitzias, New Zealand
flax plants with their dramatic stiff vertical leaves, giant ti-
bouchinas and masses of the brilliant ixoras. The slender
white pillars that supported the upper floor of the house
were all but smothered by a prolifically flowering white bell
flower.

She had arrived! It all seemed wonderfully exciting,
dramatic really. And Cyrus Bannerman had had a considerable effect on her when she'd grown accustomed to dis-
tancing herself from any physical response to men, as it
made her job easier.

As Pete collected her luggage, Jessica walked up the
short flight of stone steps to the wide veranda. It was obviously a place of relaxation, she thought looking at the
array of outdoor furniture. Low tables, comfortable chairs,
Ali Baba–style pots spilling beautiful bougainvillea. A
series of French doors with louvered shutters ran to either
side of the double front doors, eight pairs in all. She hoped

she looked okay, though she was well aware that her hair, which had started out beautifully smooth and straight, was now blowing out into the usual mad cloud of curls. She was wearing cool, low-waisted Dietrich-style pants in olive-green with a cream silk blouse, but no way could she put on the matching jacket. It was just too hot! Her intention had been to look businesslike, not like a poster girl for amazing hair.

Jessica hesitated before lifting the shining brass knocker with the lion's head. Wasn't anyone going to come to the door? They had to be expecting her. Just as she reached out her hand, one of the double doors with their splendid lead-light panels and fan lights suddenly opened. A tall, gaunt, ghost of a woman, with parchment skin, violet circles around her sunken eyes and as much hair as Jessica, only snow-white, stared back at her. The vision was dressed in the saffron robes of a Tibetan monk, an expression of dawning wonder on her face.

"It's Moira, isn't it? *Moira?* Where *have* you been, dear? We've been desperately worried."

The extraordinary expression on the old lady's face smote Jessica's tender heart. She took the long trembling hand extended to her and gave it a little reassuring shake. "I'm dreadfully sorry, but I'm *not* Moira," she explained gently. "I'm Jessica Tennant, the interior designer. Mr. Bannerman is expecting me."

"Jessica?" Recognition turned to frowning bemusement. "Absolutely *not.*"

"Lavinia, what are you doing there?" A young female voice intervened, so sharp and accusatory it appeared to rob Lavinia of speech. "Lavinia?"

Lavinia feigned deafness, though Jessica could see the little flare of anger in her eyes. She leaned forward, clutching Jessica's hand to her thin chest and whispering into her face, "Always knew you'd come back." She grinned as if they were a couple of coconspirators.

"Silly old bat! Take no notice of her." An ultraslim, glamorous-looking young woman, with her glossy sable hair in a classic pageboy, and the long, dark brown eyes of an Egyptian queen, came into sight.

"Silly old bat, am I?" the old lady shouted. "You just leave me alone, Robyn. I'm the Bannerman, not *you!*"

The young woman cast Jessica a long-suffering look. "Excuse us. You forget, Lavinia, Dad adopted me. I'm as much a Bannerman as the rest of you. Perhaps you could do us all a favor and retire to your room. I know how much you like to read. What is it now? Let me guess. Gibbon's *The Decline and Fall of the Roman Empire?*"

"Bitch!" the old lady muttered sotto voce.

"So nice to have met you, Miss Lavinia," Jessica smiled into the troubled old face. What was it, Alzheimer's, dementia? The bane of old age. So sad. Lavinia had to be well into her eighties, though she didn't look in the least demented. More an eccentric living in the past.

Lavinia kept hold of Jessica's hand as though unwilling to let her go. "You've not come near the house for years and years," she said, looking as though she were about to weep.

"I expect I had to wait for an invitation," Jessica whispered back.

"My dear, don't you care that you put us through such an ordeal?" The sunken eyes filled with tears.

"I didn't mean to," Jessica found herself saying. Anything to calm the old woman.

"Livvy, that's quite enough!" The young woman swooped like a falcon. Her long-fingered hand closed over Lavinia's bony shoulder. "You're embarrassing Ms. Tennant. I suggest you go to your room before Dad finds out."

Lavinia threw off the hand with surprising strength and adjusted her robe. "It was Broderick who brought her here," she said. "I've never liked you, Robyn, though I tried hard. You were a frightful child and you're a frightful woman. She pinches me, you know."

"Lavinia, dear." Robyn Bannerman smiled tightly, obviously trying to retain her patience. "If I've hurt you, I'm sorry. Your skin is like tissue paper. Now, Ms. Tennant is here to see Dad. He's not a man to be kept waiting."

Lavinia nodded fiercely, setting her abundant hair in motion. "Dear me, no."

Robyn Bannerman lifted beautifully manicured hands. "She's quite gaga," she told Jessica softly.

There was nothing wrong with Lavinia's hearing. "Not gaga, Robyn. Ask me who the prime minister is. I'll tell you. John Howard. I didn't vote for him. Ask me about the war in Iraq. I guarantee I'm better than you at mental arithmetic, let alone music, the arts and great literature. I speak fluent French. I had to give up on Japanese. I'm not reading *The Decline and Fall of the Roman Empire* by the way. And it's *The History of the Decline and Fall of the Roman Empire*. I'm reading *My Early Life* by Winston Churchill. Quite delightful!"

"I couldn't imagine anything worse," Robyn sighed. "Please go to your room, Livvy. You'll be happier there."

Looking quite rebellious, Lavinia spun to face Jessica who said in a soothing manner before the whole thing got out of hand, "I'm looking forward to seeing you later, Miss Lavinia. I hope I may address you that way?"

The old lady gave her a startlingly sweet smile. "You always *did* call me Miss Lavinia. I have trouble sleeping, you know. But you always come into my dreams. I've had no trouble remembering you. Until later, then, dear."

Lavinia moved off serenely, while Robyn Bannerman stood, rather inelegantly biting the side of her mouth. "I'm sorry about that," she said after Lavinia had disappeared. "Poor old dear has been senile for years. She usually stays upstairs in her room, rereading the entire library or listening to her infernal opera. Some of those sopranos know how to screech, or it could be Lavinia. She had a brief career on the stage. She only ventures down for dinner, thank God. I'm Robyn Bannerman, as you will have gathered. Come on in. My father is expecting you." Robyn's dark eyes swept Jessica's face and figure. "I must say you look absurdly young for such a big project."

Jessica frowned and was about to respond when Robyn continued, "What you want to do is enjoy yourself for a few days, then head back to Brisbane. My father rarely if ever makes mistakes, but there's a first time for all of us. Though I must say, I'm dying to hear what you come up with."

A lot better than *this,* I hope, Jessica thought, glancing around in surprised disappointment. Although opulent, the interior of the homestead did not so much impress as overwhelm. The furnishings were far too formal for the bush setting, the drapery, though hellishly expensive—Jessica knew the fabric—too elaborate. This was, after all, a country house. It didn't look lived in. In fact nothing looked even touched. There were no books lying around, no flowers, not an object out of place.

The air-conditioning, however, was a huge plus, utterly blissful after the blazing heat outside. Jessica felt that given what she had seen so far, she wouldn't be right for the job. Not if Broderick Bannerman wanted more of this.

Brett wouldn't be happy, either, unless Bannerman gave her carte blanche. The homestead had a vaguely haunted air about it, or so it seemed to her, but she could see how it could be brought back to life.

"I see you're admiring the decor," Robyn said, as though they were gazing at perfection. "I did it all a couple of years back. I hoped to do the new place, but I can't be expected to do *everything!* I practically run the domestic side of things here and I have businesses in Darwin that have to be looked after. If I do say so myself, I'm a hard act to follow."

Jessica managed a smile, but she couldn't for the life of her act impressed. In fact, she could hear Brett's voice saying, *Dump the lot!*

CHAPTER THREE

SHE WAS SHOWN INTO A LARGE, luxuriously appointed study. There was no one inside.

"That's funny. Dad was here ten minutes ago. I'll go find him," Robyn said, giving Jessica another of her dubious looks. "Take a seat. Won't be long. You'd like tea or coffee?"

"Coffee would be fine. Black, no sugar."

"Looking after your figure?" Robyn asked with a slightly sarcastic smile.

"I do, but I've grown to like coffee that way."

Alone, Jessica stared around the room, thinking how one's home environment reflected the person. It had to be the one place from which Robyn Bannerman's decorating talents had been banned. It certainly looked lived in. Going by the faint film of gray on the wall of solid mahogany bookcases, Jessica doubted if anyone was game to go around with a feather duster. Behind the massive partner's desk hung a splendid three-quarter portrait of an extraordinarily handsome man, *not* Broderick Bannerman, though the resemblance to Cyrus Bannerman was striking. He was painted in casual dress, a bright blue open-throated bush shirt the color of his eyes, a silver-buckled belt, just the top of his riding pants, the handsome head with crisp dark hair faintly ruffled by a breeze, set against a subdued darkish-green background. The eyes were extraordinary.

Because of her own deep involvement with art, she stood up for a closer look, wanting to study the fluent brush strokes, which she had the strangest feeling she'd seen before.

"My father," a man's deep, cultured voice said from behind her. He startled her, as she felt sure he had meant to.

She turned quickly toward the voice, surprised he was standing so close to her. She hadn't heard him come in. "It's a wonderful painting," she said. "I was just going to check on the name of the artist. I've a feeling I've seen his work before and—"

"You couldn't have," Broderick Bannerman cut her off, his appraisal of her intense, as though he wanted to examine every inch of her. "The artist was a nobody. Just a family friend."

"He may have been a nobody, but he was a very good painter," Jessica said, determined not to be intimidated by the great man. "Excellent technique."

"Would you know?" His icy gray eyes beneath heavy black brows didn't shift. Had he been a horse fancier, he might have asked to check her teeth.

"I think so. I have a fine-arts degree. I paint myself. I started with watercolors, which I love, but I've moved on to oils and acrylics."

"It's a wonder you've found the time," he said. "You're twenty-four?"

"Yes, but you already know that, Mr. Bannerman." Jessica held out her hand. "A pleasure to meet you, sir," she said, though aspects of the man had already started to worry her. His gaze was so piercing, she felt she needed protection.

Bannerman took the slender hand, thinking most people

had to work hard at containing their awe of him, but this chit of a girl showed no such deference. He stared into her large green eyes. Memories speared through him, for a moment holding him in thrall. "Please, sit down," he said after a moment, his voice harsher than he intended. On no account did he want to frighten her away. "Has Robyn organized some coffee?" With an impatient frown, he went around his desk, sitting in the black leather swivel chair.

"Yes, she has," Jessica answered, thinking intimidation was something this man would do supremely well. He had been born to power. Clearly, he took it as his due. Broderick Bannerman had to be nearing sixty, but he looked at least ten years younger. He didn't have his son's amazing sapphire eyes, but his icy glance was remarkable enough. His hair was as thick and black as his son's with distinguished wings of silver. All in all, Broderick Bannerman was a fine figure of a man with a formidable aura. Why in the world would a man like this choose her to handle such a big project? Brett would have been the obvious choice.

"Speaking of watercolors," he said, "my aunt Lavinia loves them. She's a very arty person, so you should get on well."

"I had the pleasure of meeting her momentarily," Jessica said, thinking it best to say. It would come out sooner or later.

"Really? When was this?" The frosted gaze locked on hers.

"She happened to be in the entrance hall when I arrived."

"Good. I don't want her to hide. Then you'll know she's somewhat eccentric?"

"I found her charming," Jessica said.

"She can be a handful," Bannerman said, with a

welcome trace of humor. "Most people think she's senile, but she's not. She likes wearing weird costumes. She had a brief fling as an opera singer in her youth. Still daydreams about it. You'll no doubt get to see the costumes. Tosca's my favourite. She's a Buddhist at the moment. She's actually had an audience with the Dalai Lama. Regretfully she has arrived at the point where we can't let her go out alone, though she managed to get to Sydney recently—but I'd sent along a minder for her and she stayed with relatives. Don't be too worried by anything she says. Livvy never really knows what time frame she's in."

Wary of his reaction, Jessica didn't tell him Lavinia had called her *Moira.*

Bannerman was still talking when a middle-aged woman in a zip-up pale blue uniform wheeled a laden trolley into the room without once lifting her head. Robyn was standing directly behind her, looking very much as if one false move and the tea lady would get a good rap on the knuckles.

"Thank you, Molly," Bannerman said. "This is our housekeeper, Mrs. Patterson, Jessica. You'll be seeing quite a bit of each other."

The two women exchanged a smile, Jessica saying a pleasant hello.

"I'll pour, shall I?" Robyn asked.

Bannerman looked back at her coolly. "This is a private conversation, Robyn."

Jessica felt mortified on Robyn's account. Was this his normal behavior?

Robyn colored, as well she might. "I thought you might need a little help."

"Thank you, no."

Not the nicest man I've ever met, Jessica thought.

In the end, she poured the coffee, which turned out to be excellent. To her surprise, instead of getting down to business, Bannerman began to question her, albeit in a roundabout way, about her family, listening to her replies with every appearance of interest. One might have been forgiven for thinking before matters progressed any further she had to establish her family tree. Surely he didn't talk to everyone this way, did he? Not everyone would expect to be quizzed about their ancestors, unless they were marrying into European royalty.

In the middle of it all, the phone rang. At least *she* was off the hook for a while, she thought wryly. Bannerman turned his intense pale gray stare on the phone as though willing it to stop. Finally he was forced to pick it up. "I thought I told you to hold the calls," he boomed into the mouthpiece.

He certainly has a way with the staff, Jessica thought. That sort of voice would make anyone gulp, let alone damage the ears.

"All right, put him on."

Jessica made to jump to her feet to give him privacy, but he waved her back into the seat, launching into a hot, hard attack on the poor unfortunate individual on the other end of the line. How people of wealth liked to make lesser mortals quake! Afterward, satisfied he had made himself clear and beaten one more employee into the turf, Bannerman centered Jessica with his lancing eyes. "Look, you haven't had time to settle in and I have to attend to some fool matter. You have no idea the amount of nonsense I have to put up with. Some of my people can't do *anything* on their own. What say we met up again at four? It will be cooler then. I can take you on tour of the new house."

"I'm looking forward to it, Mr. Bannerman," Jessica

said. He might be shaping up to be an ogre, but no need to call home yet.

"You're hired, by the way." He flashed her an odd look, impossible to define.

"Wouldn't you prefer to wait until I submit some designs or at least hear my ideas? They'd be off the top of my head, of course. Better, when I've had time—"

"No need," he said dismissively. "You'll do very well."

It was the first time she'd been given a commission on the basis of her looks and ancestors.

UP IN HER BEDROOM, Robyn paced the perimeter of the Persian rug, as a lioness might pace the perimeter of her cage. She was utterly enraged. For B.B. to humiliate her in front of a complete stranger left her wanting to kill someone. Though she had done everything in her power to fit into this family, she fumed, she would *never* be regarded as a true daughter of the house. Like that old witch Lavinia, who smiled so lovingly on Cyrus, had said, Robyn wasn't a *true* Bannerman. No unshakable bond of blood; the belonging was only on the surface. Scratch the surface and it was as clear today as it had been from the outset when she'd first come to Mokhani with her mother, she was an *outsider.* Her mother, not capable of getting both oars in the water, had nevertheless shoehorned herself in, always sweet and unassuming, dutiful and deferential to her rich and powerful husband.

Their marriage had been a big lie. B.B. had married her mother, an old school chum of the incomparable Deborah, only to beget more sons. But poor Sharon couldn't rise to the challenge, though she had looked like "lust on legs," as a guy she knew put it. The sad reality was that Sharon hadn't been very fertile, and her marriage to B.B. seemed to render her completely barren. Her daughter, Robyn, her only child, was her sole achievement. Needless to say, B.B. was bitterly disappointed in her mother and had all but ignored her, unceremoniously bundling her out of the master suite and into a room on the other side of the house, causing Sharon to curl up and simply fade away. B.B. had wanted a long succession of heirs, not just Cy, the son of the only woman he had ever loved, that paragon Deborah who, for all the cups and ribbons she'd won, had gone hurtling over the neck of her horse.

Robyn had sensed quickly, as an animal might, B.B.'s deep-seated fear of his own son, as though one day Cy would overshadow him, and hell, wasn't it already happening? Though she hated to have to say it, Cy was remarkable. Cy was the *future*. She didn't know anyone apart from B.B. who didn't wholeheartedly admire Cyrus. As for how people regarded B.B., they mostly feared him, called him a *bloody bastard*—but never within B.B.'s hearing. B.B. would regard such a thing as a declaration of war, then order a preemptive strike.

But he *was* a bastard, nevertheless. A ruthless bastard. It was that more than anything that kept Robyn in line. In the odd moment when she choked up on memories of her mother—she really had loved her, or at least as much as she *could*, given Sharon's single-digit IQ—she realized with great bitterness just how badly B.B. had treated her mother. Sharon had had everything *material* she'd wanted, but she had missed out totally on what she really wanted—tenderness and affection. Sharon had realized from the beginning there was no way she was going to get love.

Ironically, this beast of a man seemed to inspire all kinds of women, from the innocent needy like her mother to gold diggers, to give matrimony with him their best shot.

B.B. hadn't married any of them, but he certainly hadn't been celibate since her mother's death. Lord, no! There had been various affairs, all very discreet. Even with young women, who found the sexiest thing about a man was his bank balance. The one thing Robyn hadn't been prepared for when B.B. had announced he was calling in an interior designer to decorate the mansion, was that she would be so young and ravishingly pretty. Attractive would have been okay, but not a bloody aphrodisiac for men.

The shock had been ghastly. She didn't think Cy had expected it either, nor had he been pleased. But here she was among them, this Jessica Tennant.

B.B. had first seen her on national television. Robyn had missed the program herself, as had Cy, so they'd had no warning. They knew only that she was shortlisted for some big prize, which meant she had to be good at what she did, but at twenty-four she couldn't have had much experience. Add to that, she was a bloody siren. Robyn had seen the look B.B. had given the woman. It had been as rapt as a sixteen-year-old boy's.

Robyn halted in her frenzied pacing, and her blood turned to ice water. What if B.B. had it in his head this time to take another wife? Why should that shock her? He had plenty of money, after all. So what if they were decades apart in age? B.B. was a secretive man, but he didn't do anything without a reason. No one had ever seen him make a false move. Now Ms. Jessica Tennant, in the guise of an interior designer. What had seemed incomprehensible started to appear perfectly clear.

I have to protect myself, Robyn thought. *I'm no* loser *like Mum.*

A FEW MINUTES BEFORE THE TIME scheduled for the grand tour, Jessica made her way downstairs. Best not be late, when Bannerman was famous for bawling people out. Robyn had dropped out of sight, no doubt slamming her palm against her forehead in mortification, but Mrs. Patterson, who turned out to be a very pleasant woman, had been on hand to show Jessica to her room.

There, she had changed her outfit, settling for something cool, cotton pants with a gauzy multicolored caftan top decorated with little crystals and beads over with tiny buttons down the front. Usually she did up just enough to cover her bra, but with the way Broderick Bannerman had been looking at her, she decided to do them all up.

The dazzling play of late-afternoon light falling through the beautiful leaded panes and fan lights on the front door held her immobile for a moment. The kaleidoscope of color unlocked some lovely fragment of memory from her childhood. Before she could move, the door opened, letting in a wave of hot air.

And Cyrus Bannerman. The look he gave her held her transfixed.

"Hi!"

"Ms. Tennant. We meet again."

At first glance, he could have been a particularly sexy and virile escapee from the TV show *Survivor.* His darkly tanned skin glowing with sweat and grimed with red dust gave him a startlingly exotic appearance. Red dust had thrown a film over his jet-black hair, which was tousled and fell onto his forehead. There was a stain of brownish-red—blood—across his bush shirt, and his eyes seem to blaze a hole through her.

They continued gazing at one another for what seemed an inordinate amount of time. Was it the atmosphere?

she wondered. The old homestead certainly had an air about it.

"Sorry," he said finally. "I must look a mess. One of the men took a bad fall off his motorbike. Head injuries. We didn't want to move him. I had to call in the RFDS. That's the Royal Flying Doctor Service, as I expect you know. God knows what we'd do without them. They didn't take long."

"Is he going to be all right?" Only now could she take a few more steps down the stairs, reassured that an injured employee so clearly mattered to him.

"We have to wait and see with head injuries. I'm worried about him." Cy's remarkable eyes made another sweep over her. "Meanwhile, what have you been up to?"

"Why, nothing." She stopped where she was on the stairs. "Change of clothes is all," she said sweetly. " Now your father is taking me on a tour of the new house."

"I see." He pulled at the red bandanna at his throat, exuding so much powerful masculinity she felt in need of oxygen.

"That's good. For a moment I thought you'd missed something along the way. Your father *has* hired me to handle the interior design."

"Indeed he has. Forgive me if it takes a little time to get used to it." He came close to her, so commanding a presence, Jessica remained where she was, two steps above him. A dubious advantage.

"You must be extremely clever, Ms. Tennant. Dad was compelled to hire you after seeing you for about ten minutes on a TV program? Have I got that right?"

He was suspicious of his father's motivation, she suddenly realized. It was emblazoned on his smug, handsome face. "You have. What's so amazing?"

"The pure chance of it." His eyes shifted to the little beads and crystals on her top and he gave a leisurely verdict. "Very pretty." He paused, then said, "Look, Ms. Tennant, I'll level with you. I'm concerned about this. I'm sure you're talented, but it doesn't automatically follow you should be given such a big commission. At this stage of your career anyway."

She leaned forward slightly, her voice mock confidential. "Be that as it may, it was your *father* who hired me, Cyrus. He's the man I have to answer to. Not you."

"Say that again." Suddenly he smiled into her eyes. Night into day.

"I'm sure you took it in the first time. Your father hired me—"

"Not *that!*" he scoffed. "The *Cyrus* bit. I really liked the sound of my name on your lips."

She knew she blushed, but she couldn't control it. "Calling you Cyrus *is* the easy bit. Getting on with you appears to be quite another. What exactly is it you and your sister—"

"I don't have a sister," he corrected.

"That's odd. I've met her."

"You've met Robyn," he pointed out suavely. "Robyn is my father's adopted daughter."

"Which surely means legally she's your stepsister?"

"Ah, you're turning into a hotshot lawyer before my very eyes. Robyn is my stepsister, forgive me. She must be. She lives here."

"Not your average loving family, then?" She forced her breath to stay even.

"Unfortunately, no."

"I'm sure there are reasons."

"There always are. Are you going to come down from those stairs?"

"Not for the moment. I like us to be on the same level." She was attracted to this man. *Powerfully* attracted. It was the very last thing she needed or wanted. She was here to do a job, not play at a dangerous flirtation.

"That would never be unless you grow a few inches."

"Or own some very fancy high-heeled shoes, which I do. Well, it's nice chatting with you, Cyrus, but I'm supposed to meet your father."

"I'm not detaining you, surely?" He made an elaborate play of backing off, his ironic smile putting more pressure on her. She felt slightly giddy as she descended the last two stairs to pass him. Something he undoubtedly noticed and chalked up as a small victory.

Her nerves were stretched so taut she actually jumped when Broderick Bannerman, a look of barely suppressed impatience on his face, suddenly appeared in the entrance hall. He looked from one to the other as though they were conspiring in a plot against him. "There you are, Ms. Tennant. I did say four o'clock, didn't I?"

"I'm so sorry—" Jessica was tempted to mention it could only have been a few minutes after four, but Cyrus intervened.

"She was chatting with me, Dad. Okay?" He lifted a hard-muscled arm and glanced at his watch. "How time flies! It's three minutes past."

"And you're back early," B.B. clipped off.

"Surely there's not a note of disapproval in that. I don't clock on and off, Dad. Eddie Vine took a bad spill off his motorbike. He's been airlifted to the hospital."

"I'm not surprised to hear that," B.B. said with a frown. "He's a bad rider."

"No." Cyrus jammed his hands into his jeans pockets. "*You're* the one we all have to get out of the way for, Dad. Now, I'm off for a good scrub. Enjoy the tour."

"We shall," his father replied curtly.

At that moment, a middle-aged attractive woman with soft gray eyes and long dark hair pulled back into a severe French twist hurried into the entrance hall. "Excuse me, B.B. I'm sorry to interrupt, but Mr. Kurosawa is on the line. I know you want to speak to him."

B.B. all but snarled. "Dammit!" Then, more mildly, he added, "Okay I'm coming, Ruth." He turned back to Jessica with a surprisingly charming smile. The many faces of Broderick Bannerman in less than half a minute she thought. "I'm sorry, my dear, this is going to take time. I'll have to postpone our tour until tomorrow."

In the background, Cyrus Bannerman spoke up. "If Ms. Tennant will give me ten minutes, I can show her around the place."

"I prefer to do it, thank you, Cyrus."

"No trouble, Dad," Cyrus insisted smoothly.

There was a silence as B.B. responded to what seemed like a challenge.

"Very well," he barked, turning abruptly on his heel.

Cyrus Bannerman stood, lean elegant frame propped against the cedar post of the staircase. "By the way, Jessica, you haven't met Ruth, have you? Ruth is Dad's secretary. Ruth this is Jessica Tennant, Dad's new interior designer."

"Pleased to meet you, Jessica." B.B.'s secretary gave Jessica a sweet, flurried smile, clearly anxious to follow her master. "I must go. B.B. might want something."

"Best not keep him waiting, Ruthie," Cyrus warned, his blue eyes full of mischief. "Now suddenly it's up to me, Ms. Tennant, to give you the grand tour."

"Why is it I'm thinking you're trying to score points in a competition with your father?"

"God, is it that obvious?" He shook his head. "Why don't you wait for me on the veranda? It's nice this time of day. I'll only be ten minutes."

"I beg you. Don't hurry on account of me."

"You should thank me for rescuing you," he said blandly.

CHAPTER FOUR

HE WAS BACK ON THE VERANDA in fifteen minutes flat. "Did you time me?" he asked. "I'm a bit late."

"Actually I'd forgotten you," she said casually, which was a long way from the truth. "I was breathing in the air and the exotic scents. It's another world up here. I've never felt so connected to the earth. It's rather a profound experience. Thanks again for the helicopter trip. It was a revelation, and one of the highlights of my life."

"I think you mean that." There was an appraising look in his eyes.

"How could you doubt me?" Jessica stood up, trying to hide the excitement he engendered in her.

"There's plenty more I can show you," he said. "How come you've never visited the Red Centre?" Something she had mentioned. "Or Kakadu, which is the jewel in the Top End crown—maybe a little off the beaten track— but Alice Springs? It's quite a tourist destination these days. Our desert monuments, Uluru and Kata Tjuta, are world-famous."

"Maybe when you have the time you can take me." She gave him a sidelong glance.

"Jessica, we don't know yet if you're staying."

"Why does it bother you so much? My staying, that is."

"I have my reasons."

"That sounds intriguing. So what are you going to do to frighten me off?"

"Whatever it is I have to act fast." He met her eyes, a gleam of mockery in his. "No. It's going to be your decision."

"Your father's, surely," she said. They walked down the flight of stone steps together, Jessica acutely conscious of his height and pure, animal magnetism.

"He's already made up his mind," he clipped off. "My father isn't an easy man to know." His tone indicated he wished things could have been different.

She gave him a wry, understanding smile. "I can see that."

"So you can see we're not the best of pals."

"Why is that?" she asked gently.

"Long story." He glanced away.

"I can listen."

"Not right now, Ms. Tennant. Seriously, apart from my dysfunctional family, you don't have the feeling this job might be too big for you? It's a helluva place. Helluva size."

"Your father has a helluva lot of money," she reminded him dryly.

"Doing things right takes a lot more than money."

"I know that. I'm good at what I do, and I can count on my Uncle Brett for all the help and advice I need. Brett's my rock. You mustn't be so skeptical of me. I have skills to put to good use. No job is too big to handle, given ability, time and money. You have to take one thing at a time not tackle it all at once. Then it *can* become too confronting."

He shook his head. "Trouble is, there seems to be more going on here."

"Meaning what, exactly?" She was truly puzzled.

"I'm damned if I know. It's just a hunch backed up by observation. This family has a haunted past. It makes people *different,* for better or worse. No way you're not going to hear about it, if you haven't already, though it's way before your time and mine."

"You're talking about the old Mokhani Mystery?" She headed him off. "The disappearance of the governess?"

There was a decided glint in his eyes. "So you *do* know."

She nodded. "Only because I did my homework." They were walking along a lush avenue of tropical palms and ferns, on one side bounded by a four-foot-high stone wall. Around the base of the ferns grew beautiful soft creamy lilies that gave off a perfume not unlike gardenias. *Exquisite!* She bent to pick one, twirling it beneath her nose.

"I suppose you'd have to," he conceded. "Have you met my great aunt Lavinia yet?" He held back a palm frond that partially blocked their path. "Livvy claims to have seen her, *heard* her around the place."

"The governess?"

"Of course the governess," he said shortly. "Her name was Moira. Livvy was dreaming or having one of her visions. Living in the past is so much richer for her than the present. She's got a fantastic imagination. She's always said Moira would come back one day, and we'd all have to fall on our knees in welcome. People think Livvy has gone around the twist, but they're making a big mistake. A lot of it she does deliberately. It's the thwarted actress in her. But in many respects, she's still as sharp as a tack."

Jessica laughed quietly. "I can believe that. I've met her. She greeted me at the front door. It must have been in the middle of one of her fantasies, because she called *me* Moira. I tried to assure her I wasn't, but I don't think she was entirely convinced."

He stopped dead on the path, forcing her to do the same. "Well maybe that's your trump card, is it, Ms. Tennant?"

"Trump card?" Anger rose. "You sound as though you've caught me out at something."

"I'd really appreciate it if you were straight with me," he said crisply, his gaze very direct. "You've never met my father before? Even fleetingly?"

She frowned and resumed walking. "I think I'd remember. He's not the sort of man you'd miss. *I* would have thought my trump card was the fact I'm in line to win a big award. No point in being modest. Not around you. That's quite an achievement in our business, especially for someone my age."

"Hell, I'm sure there's no question you'll win it." He was brusque. "But I'm not referring to your artistic abilities." He made a frustrated gesture. "As I said, Moira has haunted this family for over half a century. You'd swear she wanted to have some kind of vengeance for God knows what! For all the various articles and versions of events, I've never been able to find a photograph of her. The only one on record is a grainy one supplied by her parents, but then she was only a child. Someone in the family either destroyed what we had or whisked them out of sight. But I do know she was an ash-blonde with green eyes, which might explain my father's attraction to you. Livvy obviously was drawn to you, as well. My great aunt had a soft spot for Moira, so she took it very hard when she disappeared."

"Surely everyone did?"

"That goes without saying," he said tersely.

"I'm sorry. It must have been a bad time for the family," Jessica said. Suspicions, speculations, the police and newshounds coming after them.

"It's bad enough hearing about it all these years later," he said, pulling a sharp twig off a hanging branch and throwing it away. "Even her name causes distress. Can you understand that?"

"Of course I can," she said. "I'm not an insensitive person."

"I don't know yet what you are," he said. "I got hell at school until I was driven to shut my tormentors up. The entire family was badly affected. My grandparents in particular, Steven and Cecily. My dad, who was only a kid, and my dad's twin, Barbara. Aunt Barbara won't come near Mokhani except for the obligatory Christmas visit. She's married to a brilliant academic. Unforunately no one can understand a word he says—we might if he threw in some normal everyday language now and again. They live in Sydney with a magnificent view of the harbor. No children. Barbara used to say she didn't want to pass on a bad gene, whatever the hell that means. Livvy divides her time between them and us."

"I see."

Brilliantly plumaged parrots flashing an array of the most beautiful vivid colors appeared above their heads, several turning somersaults like an aerobatics display before diving into a spectacular flowering plant with huge scarlet flowers and iridescent violet-striped leaves. Jessica looked up, engrossed and entertained. "Does Miss Lavinia haunt art galleries?"

"Yup," he said laconically. "I suspect you do, too."

"I *am* an artist. Would she have attended a Christie's auction lately?"

"Ms. Tennant, I wouldn't know. Why don't you ask her?"

"I will." Who knows where such a question might lead?

For a scary moment, Jessica felt as if she had entered a tortuous maze.

"What's with the *Miss* Lavinia?" he asked presently. "A bit quaint, isn't it?"

Jessica reached out to touch a prolifically flowering truss of bougainvillea somewhere between deep pink and cerise. "It just came to me. It seemed respectful, okay?"

"Respectful, certainly. Maybe contrived. I happen to know Moira called Livvy Miss Lavinia." Outright suspicion glittered in his eyes.

"Surely you don't think there's some kind of conspiracy going on here, do you?"she asked uneasily. "One wouldn't have to be the smartest person in the world to realize your family might have become a bit paranoid about Moira and her sad story. The fact I called your great-aunt Miss Lavinia means absolutely nothing. I'd feel a lot happier if you'd put it down to good manners."

"That's it, good manners?" He glanced at her as if he had considerable difficulty accepting that.

"Of course." Jessica met his gaze squarely. "I told you I came across the old mystery in the course of my research into the Bannerman family. It's been the subject of numerous articles on and off over the years. The mystery has never been solved. That alone would keep it alive."

"I hope you're not implying anything sinister there," he said, warming to the challenge.

"Certainly not." She shook her head. "It's exactly as I've told you. My desire to understand my commission led me into researching the Bannerman history. I'm sure your father had my professional credentials thoroughly checked out well before I arrived. He's since questioned me at some length about my family background."

"Obviously he wants to learn more about you," Cy said, his scrutiny, like his father's, too intense for her comfort.

"I admit I was surprised. I couldn't see what a lot of it had to do with my design skills. But I could say my family is highly respectable."

"Thank God there are a few of us left," he said acidly.

Jessica didn't bother replying. She knew he was seeking answers to what bothered him, but how could she supply them when she didn't even know the questions? But he had made her uneasy. *Was* there more to discover as to why Broderick Bannerman had chosen *her* for this project? Even Tim had found it hard to believe.

Jessica's ponderings were diverted as up several hundred yards ahead rose the soaring white edifice Broderick Bannerman had caused to be erected as a monument to himself and a celebration of his wealth.

"This is it!" Cy announced as if they'd arrived at a great circus tent. "Home sweet home! I might mention I had no input whatever so that gets me off the hook. My idea of Mokhani is the *ancestral* home of the Bannermans. I plan to keep the original homestead intact for my son. Families die out without sons. But my dad isn't circumscribed by those sentiments. He thinks Mokhani is his entirely. It isn't. A lot of my mother's fortune went into keeping it going during the hard times. We've had them like everyone else."

"It's quite extraordinary." She shielded her eyes with her hands, staring up.

"A masterly understatement. It's bizarre."

"Don't shut your mind on it altogether," she said, realizing the original homestead had great significance for him. Probably because it was not only the Bannerman ancestral home, but also the place his father had brought his mother to as a young bride. There had to be many reminders of his mother at the homestead, indeed all round the station. "You must miss your mother," she found herself saying.

He looked at her sharply, his tone cool. "At least I know what love is," he said.

"You've never been *in* love?" she asked, putting a hand to her hair as the wind gusted.

"Have you?"

"Sort of," she said smiling, "but no one I found irresistible."

"While you, no doubt, were adored."

She heard the sarcasm; responded to it. "The question is not whether I was adored, but given your need for heirs, why *you* at the very least aren't engaged?"

"Hey, ease up!" He threw up his hands. "I'm not going to do anything to jeopardize my bachelor state at the moment, Ms. Tennant, if that's what you want to know."

"I'm only making conversation." She shrugged, pausing to take in the magnitude of her commission.

"Wait until you get inside," he softly jeered. "If the Shah of Iran were still around, he'd love it."

"Good grief, it's immense." She was genuinely stunned.

"Well, I suppose it has to be big," he said carelessly. "B.B. does a lot of entertaining. He hosts many important overseas guests. Things quieted down a bit when Sharon, that's Robyn's mother, became so ill. She died two years ago. She was a good, sweet woman."

"Robyn doesn't take after her?" Jessica asked wryly.

"Well, I never!" He did a mock double take. "Are you saying Robyn's neither good nor sweet?"

She colored a little. "I only meant she isn't overly friendly. Shall we go in?"

"Of course. After you."

Just being with him was exhilarating. She felt as though she could go on talking to him forever.

They entered through a huge gabled portico supported by monumental Ionic columns that led directly to the twenty-foot-high double doors. Beyond, a space nearly as big as a football field culminated in an equally monumental staircase. After the first breathless shock, Jessica saw it as a wonderful multipurpose area. All the same, she didn't know whether to applaud or hoot. As a public building, it would have been splendid. As a private home it staggered the imagination.

"We had an army of builders and workers on site forever." Cy groaned at the memory. "They lived in row after row of tents just like on an archeological dig. Dad strode around like a pharaoh bullying and threatening. I'm only surprised he didn't carry a whip. An old quarry had to be reopened in North Queensland for all the marble—lots of columns, as you can see. B.B. loves columns. God knows what his mausoleum is going to be like."

"You're joking!" She turned to stare at him, relieved to catch a smile on his lips.

"Probably. But I can't entirely rule it out."

"This is fit for Prince Charles," Jessica said solemnly.

"Perhaps he'll come a-visiting. Do you wonder why I much prefer the old homestead? It's plenty good enough for *my* castle. It stood firm through Cyclone Tracy, though it has to be said we didn't bear the brunt of it. This place is apocalypse-proof."

"I guessed that." She stared up at the double-height soaring ceiling with its great cupola letting in streams of light. "I think I'm going to need a team."

"Around two hundred might be good," he said. "I hope

they enjoy living in tents. How come your uncle didn't get the commission? I don't want to hurt your feelings, but I had him checked out and he's the best. For that matter, how come he didn't want the job? From what I've seen no one is ever *too* rich."

"Isn't there something you're forgetting?" she asked, starting to pace round the huge area, staring up at the dome with its splendid yet restrained plaster work that bore the imprint of artisans.

"God, you're right. Dad wanted *you*. All we've got to discover now is why. Is it possible you remind him of someone? Someone dead these many, many long years?"

She drew a deep breath; slowly released it. She knew he was baiting her. "Oh come on, *say* it. Why beat about the bush? I made a mistake telling you your great aunt called me Moira."

"Well, she's never called anyone else that," he said, his voice flat. "Not in fifty years. Now, isn't that something that absolutely sets you apart?"

"It would seem so," she conceded. "It's certainly very unusual, but if there is a resemblance, it's sheer coincidence." Jessica walked quickly away from him to regain her composure, entering one of the huge reception rooms off the great hall. "Why don't we just stick to the grand tour instead of trying to figure out odd coincidences?"

"I thought we were doing both," he said blandly. "Perhaps you're Moira in another incarnation."

"Perhaps you're a reincarnation of the guy who chucked her in the lagoon," she retorted recklessly.

He frowned. "Is that wise saying something like that?"

"I usually give as good as I get." She felt anger and excitement in equal measure. "Why is it so difficult for you to accept me at face value?"

"Maybe that's it. The *face*." His tone was light, but with a sharp edge.

"I'm the interior designer your father happened to hire."

"And you haven't wondered at all why *you* in particular?"

"Maybe I have," she admitted irritably, "but unlike you, I haven't credited—or discredited him—with ulterior motives, whatever they might be. I know nothing of the situation between you and your father except what you've told me. So it's difficult? I sympathize, but don't bring me into it. As you pointed out when we met, I'm just passing through. I can handle this job. I know it's huge, but I'm not overwhelmed. If your father's ideas and mine don't mesh or he wants me to do it *his* way entirely, then I'm not the person for the job. He'll have to find someone else. While we're on the subject, why not your stepsister, Robyn? Why did he overlook her? I understand your father gave her carte blanche to refurbish the reception rooms of the old homestead."

"And have you ever seen such a disaster? If my poor mother were around she'd cry buckets." He didn't bother to keep the disgust out of his tone. "It was all done when I wasn't around. Downright sneaky, I call it. Robyn thinks good taste and wild extravagance go hand in hand. Dad gave her the go-ahead—maybe to get square with me for some imagined slight—then went away on a long trip. When he got home and saw what Robyn had done, can you image the furor? Bellowing by the hour. Even great men like B.B. make at least one mistake in a lifetime. I don't want him to make another."

"He won't with me!" she answered, her voice brisk.

"If only we could be sure." He stared at her. She was as beautiful as she was potentially a threat to life as they knew it. Not that that was all good. He knew his father too well not to intuit that B.B. had a consuming interest in this particular young woman, and it wasn't for her creative skills. He'd stake his life on that. Did she remind him of that sad little phantom of his childhood, Moira? There was no doubt his father had been deeply affected by Moira's mysterious disappearance. It was all so damned odd. Cy had all the proof he needed that Ms. Tennant had a certain fascination for his father. His father still had an eye for a beautiful women. But this one was way too young. Hell, she was five years younger than *he* was. Maybe his father's interest had been so captured when he'd seen her on that television program that he'd felt compelled to work out a way to get her here. He knew more than anyone that when his father resolved on something, it happened.

"Why don't we see what's behind this?" Her voice broke into his ponderings. She was waving a graceful arm toward the adjoining room.

"Why not?" He followed her in, both of them moving across the space of the room. Brilliant rays of sunlight fell through the tall windows, holding her as if in a spotlight. They illuminated her very feminine slender figure, the lovely face, the cloud of ash-blond hair, setting a-sparkle all the little shimmering ornaments on her emerald blouse. Beauty like that packed a powerful punch. He had never before seen anyone that beautiful *and* sexy. He could easily imagine what it had been like for his father. A man of strong sexual appetites. Cy was reaching in his deductions, of course. But over the years he had learned how to read his obsessively secretive father.

Jessica turned her head, giving him a small sidelong glance. He was as edgy as she was. Both of them were too aware of each other and showing it. "What are you thinking?" she asked. "You've gone quiet."

"I'm still in pursuit of answers," he said.

"Please don't continue to look at me," she begged. "The sort of answers you appear to be searching for are beyond me. I have no connection to the Bannerman past, even if I do have a passing resemblance to your father's governess."

"Which, like Lavinia, he would have seen immediately."

She reacted with an admonition. "That would scarcely prompt him to hire me to decorate all this. That's just plain crazy."

"Not just crazy, it's completely bloody insane. Look, it's entirely up to you and Dad if you stay or go," he told her. "I'm not asking to be your friend, Ms. Tennant. I've got too much else on my mind."

"When I would have treasured your friendship." She lifted her green eyes to his, not bothering to hide her interest.

He returned her gaze. "It's not mandatory to seduce the clients, is it?" he asked.

She shook her head, her cheeks flushed pink. "I'd have to be very foolish indeed to try to seduce *you!*"

He gave a cracked laugh. "You might enjoy it."

"It's a trap, isn't it?" she asked, her eyes narrowing. "You want me to make one big mistake."

"Damn, you're on to me," he said with a low laugh.

Then he shocked her. His arm snaked out to lock around her waist, sending streams of sensation into her body and down her legs.

"Think before you go any further." She couldn't keep back the faint tremble in her voice.

"Don't guys around you tend to lose it?" He gave her a taut smile, but he didn't take away his arm.

Unconsciously, she ran the tip of her tongue over her dry lips. "Some do. But you're just playing games."

"That's so." He pulled her in and put his mouth against her ear. "I don't get much fun around here."

She stiffened in his arms, alarmed at how easily he was thrilling her. "You're going to be difficult about this, are you?" she asked sharply. Something potentially damaging to her position in this family was whipping up between them. It was like being out in a yacht in a high wind.

"Just testing, Jessica," he drawled, though in reality he was having difficulty taking his arm away. Her body alongside his made him wonder what it would be like for them to become entwined.

"Well, I'm not about to fall into the trap." She pulled back and looked at him. He was so close, if she relaxed against him he could bring his other arm up and lock her in an embrace.

"Do you know how good you feel?"

"Stop it." She felt weak, her limbs swept by a warm languor.

"Hell, I *ought* to."

She thought he was going to release her, but instead he spun her right into his arms, bending his head and finding her mouth.

She saw stars. Other sparkling shapes. The whole world fell away to a roaring in her ears. Only sensation was left. Sensation so violent Jessica could barely stand. She had to cling to him as the only thing that wasn't moving.

When he finally let her go, she had to remain where she was, unable to move until her balance was restored. He *knew* how to kiss a woman. How many other women had he kissed? She put a hand on his chest and pushed.

"I can't believe you did that," she said.

His answer came right away, his tone not a lot different from hers. "I can't believe I did, either." His laugh held a trace of self-disgust. "I hope there aren't any hidden cameras around here."

She pushed tumbling locks of hair behind her ear. "Too bad you didn't have time to get them in place. You'd like to discredit me with your father, wouldn't you?"

He shrugged. "I'm not that kind of guy, Jessica. Truth is, you threw me momentarily off balance."

"Sorry, you're too smart for that. It's obviously much better for you if I get kicked out before I have a chance to get underway."

"Did you think I was counting on Dad turning up?"

"Weren't you?" Excitement turned to anger. She wanted to hit him.

Take that challenging look off his face.

"It scares me to tell you, Jessica, but I never gave my father a thought."

"I don't believe you!"

They were so engrossed in confronting each other, it took a few moments before the clack of boots across the marble floor penetrated. Cy turned immediately, while Jessica froze. "Talk of the devil and you conjure him up. That'll be Dad now. We both better cool down. You can bet your life he's come to check where we're at."

Her agitation increased. She was flooded by embarrassment and panic. "God, have I got any lipstick left?" She was forced to appeal to him. That kiss had been deep and prolonged.

For answer, he whipped a handkerchief out of his jeans pocket. "How could you? It's on *me*." He drew the white linen across his mouth, stuffing the handkerchief back in his pocket. "What are you waiting for? Go into the other room. Come on, *move*."

Jessica didn't need to be told twice. She'd only been on

Mokhani a day and already she was waist-deep in trouble. She bit down hard on her bottom lip—it was still throbbing from his kiss—in an endeavor to color it pink. Her heart was beating a rapid tattoo—which was fast becoming a routine around Cyrus Bannerman. She knew her face was flushed. She could still feel the *heat* of that clinch all through her body. It was the most explosive thing that had ever happened to her.

"Settle down, you look great," he reassured her, crossing the room swiftly on his long legs. He lifted his resonant voice so it rang around the empty space. "This is obviously intended to be the library. Of course you and Dad might have other ideas for it. An auditorium maybe? Dad loves giving speeches."

In another second, Broderick Bannerman appeared, his nostrils flared like an animal trying to pick up a scent. "I expected you'd be a bit further along than this," he said in an accusatory voice, looking from one to the other.

"I had no idea we had to rush," Cy responded, totally unfazed. "Surely Ms. Tennant needs *time* to take in all this magnificence."

Jessica felt as nervous as if Broderick Bannerman had caught the two of them in bed. "I had no real idea of the scale of the mansion, Mr. Bannerman," she said. "The great hall is awe-inspiring."

"My father loves grandeur," Cyrus told her.

Bannerman's smile came close to a snarl. "Thank you, Cyrus. I'll show Jessica the rest of the house."

"Glad to be of assistance." Cy sketched a brief, ironic salute. "See you at dinner, Ms. Tennant."

"Please…Jessica." She gave him a quelling glance. It was obvious he liked to get a rise out of his father, and she couldn't in all fairness blame him.

"Jessica. Thank you. Feel free to call me Cyrus," he invited.

"Don't take any notice of my son," Bannerman warned after Cyrus had gone. "All he cares about is goading me. It's not so surprising, I suppose. He's always lived in my shadow. Makes it hard for him to grapple with. Our relationship is far from easy. Now, what are your thoughts so far?"

The intensity of his gaze made her uncomfortable. She could only hope she wasn't betraying the turbulence that was inside her. How could she have let Cy Bannerman kiss her? Not that she could have offered resistance—he moved so fast. She had to assure herself that's all it was. "You've set me quite a challenge, Mr. Bannerman," she said, getting full control of her voice at last. "It's a massive job. These are great architectural spaces. We'll need to separate the public from the private. The great hall could be used for any number of purposes—functions that I'm sure you have in mind. I know you're looking for a sense of luxury and opulence in keeping with the building, but I see it through the framework of the environment. I don't have to tell you that's quite unique. What we're doing is reconciling classical architecture with modern sensibilities and needs. I don't know if you want to make the public rooms a showcase for art, some sculpture… I'm sure you'll want the latest technology. Equally sure you already have it at the homestead. Why don't we continue our tour? You can tell me your likes and dislikes along the way."

They walked into another room that could be used for banqueting. "What do you think of my son?" he asked with such harsh abruptness she almost jumped.

She knew she had to play it safe. "I haven't really had the time to form an opinion." What could she say? That he was as arrogant as Lucifer and, by the way, the best kisser in the world? That would go over well.

"He's quite a catch."

"I imagine he is," she answered in a calm, composed voice.

"*I'm* bigger," he told her, with what she could only describe as fierce triumph.

CHAPTER FIVE

AUNT LAVINIA CAME TO DINNER in costume.

"Tosca," Cyrus Bannerman told Jessica in a swift aside, an indulgent look on his face. It was obvious he was very fond of his great aunt. They had met on the stairs. Jessica hoped her face hadn't flamed, but his voice when he greeted her had been dead casual, as though absolutely nothing had passed between them. The best way to go, she thought, matching his nonchalance. Now they watched Lavinia, not without anxiety as she tottered down the staircase, one frail knotted hand trailing along the banister. Lavinia must have been beautiful when she was young, Jessica thought. She still retained glimmerings of it.

"Tosca. I guessed as much." Jessica, an opera buff, watched the old lady's gown swish around her ankles. The navy sneakers she wore only slightly detracted from the dramatic effect. In her copious white hair she wore an elaborate high-backed ebony comb studded with pearls and rhinestones. The bodice of her gown fell flat and low due to the fact her bust had diminished with age. Some underwear was showing. Around her neck she wore a shagreen choker from which was appended a great stone that had to weigh ten or twelve carats. It couldn't be a diamond, surely. Whatever it was, Jessica's eyes were dazzled by the bounce of light.

"Don't you look lovely, Moira!" Lavinia called, her watery eyes studying Jessica with pleasure before shifting to her great-nephew. "Good evening, my darling. Didn't I always tell you she'd come back?"

So this is what dementia is, Jessica thought sadly, feeling a prickle run up and down her spine.

"Like my dress?" Lavinia's expression indicated there was no possible answer but yes.

"Love it." Cyrus's smile was a little strained. "Not that I haven't seen it a million times. And it's Jessica, Livvy. Not Moira. Moira has ceased to be."

"Good evening, Miss Lavinia," Jessica spoke quickly to get over a sticky moment. Lavinia continued to stand on the bottom step, posing. "Don't tell me. You're Tosca."

A big smile covered Lavinia's face. "So you still love opera! That was one of the reasons I loved you. You *are* Moira, aren't you? There's no use Cyrus shushing me. Turn around, would you, dear? What a lovely, lovely dress." She smiled and nodded as Jessica twirled. "You always were ravishing."

"*Ravishing* is too tame a word," Cyrus said, his tone sardonic.

"Miss Lavinia, I'm not Moira," Jessica insisted, thinking she was becoming immured from further shocks. "I'm Jessica, remember?"

"Child, what's wrong with you?" The old lady, who had been executing a few dance steps, broke off to stare into Jessica's face, incredulous. "You can't have forgotten your name? Are we dealing with amnesia here?"

Cyrus intervened. "We're dealing with age and submerged grief. Come on, Liv. Give it up. It's a wasteland. Besides, you know you'll push Dad over the edge if you start this Moira stuff."

"His story and my story don't tally," Lavinia said.

"How could they?" Cyrus put a hand to his head. "Dad was a child."

"Broderick was *never* a child," Lavinia said, her voice sinking a whole octave. "And that's the truth."

"Oh, hell, Livvy, have a heart." Cyrus appealed to her. "Meal times are never easy, but we do have a guest. Two guests actually. Jessica and Robyn's boyfriend Erik Moore is here."

At the news, Lavinia began to beat her arms like chicken wings. "Oh, I don't like him!" she wailed. "Started up an affair behind his poor little wife's back. He always looks at me as though I should be locked away somewhere. I don't worry about that, though. If I'm so stupid, why do I know more than anyone else?" She danced a few more steps before tripping over her long velvet skirt. "Bother!"

Both Cyrus and Jessica came to her aid, each taking one of the old lady's arms. "Isn't that costume a little hot for this evening?" Cyrus inquired.

"So far so good." Lavinia gave a little laugh that turned into a cough. "I couldn't decide between it and *La Traviata.* I was such a success as Violetta." She turned her puffed white head toward Jessica. "I would have been a big name, like Sutherland. I could have had the adoration of millions, only the Honorable George Fairweather came into my life and wrecked it."

"At least you had the sense not to marry him," Cyrus comforted her.

"His dragon of a mother, a terrifying woman, insisted he break things off. His father really liked me, but he was no help at all. Mother had the power. I'm constantly astounded at the power of women."

"You can say that again!" Cyrus seconded. "A beautiful woman has all the power in the world."

THE OTHERS WERE ASSEMBLED in the opulent drawing room Robyn had spent so much of her stepfather's money on. As Cyrus, Lavinia and Jessica entered, those waiting looked up with varying expressions. Broderick Bannerman's intense scrutiny gave Jessica goose bumps. She thought he might have been seeing *through* her, then shook her head in dismay; this Moira business was getting to her. Robyn, looking very glamorous as she perched on the side of her boyfriend's armchair, showing off her long elegant legs, said, "Hi!"

Erik, so unpopular with Lavinia, smiled pleasantly and stood to attention. He was good-looking, slightly overweight, a full head of thick brown hair, hazel eyes, well-dressed. A lot older than Robyn. Married *and* divorced? Jessica wondered if he had children. Robyn wouldn't make the sweetest stepmother in the world.

"Sorry to keep you waiting," Lavinia trilled radiantly. "Don't worry. I'm safe with these two." She bestowed her sweet smile on first her great-nephew, then Jessica. "And you needn't look at me as if I've gone mad, Erik," she chided. "I love to keep my heyday alive."

"Tosca," B.B. informed Erik briefly. "You're all having a drink before dinner? Jessica, what would you like?" Again his rapier gaze swept over her face and body, taking in her cool, very pretty minidress, in layered swirls of deep pink and mauve. *Surely he can't have any sexual interest in me,* Jessica thought. If so, she might have to abandon a marvelously challenging commission. *And,* she was forced to admit, getting to know Cyrus Bannerman better.

When she glanced briefly in Cy's direction, she found his expression a touch severe. Had he recognized the sexual component in his father's stare? If he had, he bore *no* sympathy for it. Jessica shifted her gaze to Robyn, who was nursing a half-empty champagne flute.

"Champagne, if I may. That would be lovely."

"Cyrus, would you mind? Sherry for you, Liv?" B.B. asked.

Lavinia reacted with the little trill that fell so softly on the ears. "I'll join Moira in a glass of champagne," she said happily. "After all, it's a celebration. She's come back."

"'Struth!!" Robyn groaned, putting one expensively shod foot to the floor. "That's *Jessica*, Liv. Jessica Tennant, Dad's new interior designer." She'd raised her voice, perpetuating the myth Lavinia was stone deaf.

Lavinia remained oblivious to Robyn's scorn. "Why must you screech, Robyn? No one in the world yells at me like you do. That includes Broderick. I know what I'm talking about, thank you very much. *You* know, too, don't you, Broderick?"

Jessica felt herself go cold, but Bannerman's stare directed toward his aunt didn't waver. "I know you're talking nonsense, my dear," he said suavely. "That's a bit of a worry."

Oh, dear, Jessica thought. *He can't be implying Livinia is due for a nursing home, can he?*

"Ignore that, Livvy," Cyrus instructed, returning with two glasses of sparkling champagne. He gave one to Lavinia, the other to Jessica. "There's no worry. Trust me."

"Oh, I do, my darling." Lavinia's eyes flew to his after a few seconds of rapid blinking. "Every day you're alive is a miracle. The angels are looking after you."

Behind them, Robyn gave another protesting moan. "For God's sake, have we got to listen to this stuff, Dad? What Liv's got packed inside her head isn't entirely harmless. Why did you give her that glass of champagne, Cy?"

"Mind your own business, Robyn," Cyrus answered pleasantly enough. "Livvy has a perfect right to say what she likes."

Broderick Bannerman, who was standing in a cloud of preoccupation, now collected himself. "You must forgive us, Jessica. It's always a circus around here. Belatedly, I present a friend of Robyn's—Erik Moore. Erik's a property developer. I've no doubt he'll want to tell you all about his latest project. Erik, meet Jessica, who has come to take over the job of furnishing the new house. She's young, but she has a great deal to offer. I was very impressed with her ideas as we were touring the house. Off the top of her head, too, but first class."

"Delighted to meet you, Jessica." Erik didn't approach her, perhaps fearing Robyn might kick him in the shins. Instead, he executed a smooth Euro-style bow.

"Well, drink up," B.B. said briskly, throwing back his handsome head and draining the last of his drink. "My afternoon tour has made me hungry."

THEY ATE IN THE FORMAL dining room, occupying one end of the long polished table.

It was beautifully set and Jessica commented on it.

"Molly," B.B. said. "She's so much better at it than Robyn."

"I don't have to prove myself setting a table, Dad." Robyn's voice betrayed no resentment, but her eyes reflected her hurt. "The fact I'm a very successful businesswoman says all that needs to be said about me. Isn't that right, Erik?"

Erik answered the only way he possibly could. "Indeed it is, my love. You're going from strength to strength."

"She'd have been going nowhere without my support,"

Broderick Bannerman cut in like a master stroke. This evening he looked very distinguished at the head of the table, his jacket emphasizing his broad shoulders. Although Jessica hadn't taken to Robyn—the woman had scarcely been friendly—she was starting to feel sorry for her. It couldn't have been easy growing up in such an intolerant household.

It had been the very helpful housekeeper who had knocked on Jessica's door earlier in the evening to inform her with a smile that Mr. Bannerman liked everyone to dress for dinner. There was no slacking on Mokhani.

"Not *formal,* dear. You know what I mean. A pretty dress."

Jessica had thanked her for being so thoughtful. She had an ally in Molly if not in Robyn, who had probably been hoping she would turn up in a T-shirt, shorts and thongs. She had, in fact, laid out a simple yellow dress cut like a slip, but had quickly changed it for something a little dressier. One wouldn't want to offend B.B.'s sensibilities.

All three men were wearing lightweight linen jackets. No ties, but fine-quality shirts open at the throat. A concession to the heat, though the air-conditioning kept the house at a constant twenty-four degrees Celsius. It had to cost a fortune, Jessica thought. But what was a fortune to ordinary folk would probably be B.B.'s notion of small change.

Given the deep undercurrents, dinner went off well. The food was delicious—Jessica vowed there and then to get Molly's recipe for the baked barramundi for which the Territory was famous. Chili obviously, lemongrass, coriander, Kaffir lime peel…and what else? Thai shrimp paste, coconut cream and some other spices she couldn't name. The bouquet of the superb chardonnay mingled with the light scent of the bowl of white, cerise-veined Asian lilies. At one time, B.B.'s hand touched hers where it lay on the tablecloth of starched white damask. Inside, Jessica froze, but tried extremely hard to convey unawareness.

Cyrus continued talking—it seemed to Jessica the conversation eddied around him—but from the blue flash in his eyes he had seen the touch and continued to draw his own conclusions. Robyn, thankfully, was staring across the table at her stepbrother, apparently totally focused on what he was saying. Something about Jabiru, one of the four major mining settlements in the Territory, the other three, Ranger, Kabiluka and Koongarra, all uranium mines, all within Kakadu National Park, World Heritage listed. Although the Commonwealth government imposed a high level of environmental regulation, the issue of mining versus environment was one of bitter controversy. It was clear from what Cyrus was saying that he was firmly on the side of environmental preservation. Robyn, apparently, wasn't. Neither was Broderick Bannerman, with his extensive mining interests. Erik Moore sat uncomfortably on the fence. Australia, the most ancient continent, was an incredibly rich repository for valuable minerals, polarizing both sides.

"What do you think, Jessica?" B.B. asked, putting her on the spot.

No point in shirking it or trying to be diplomatic like Erik. "I'm on the side of the environment," she said quietly.

"Don't go to Jabiru and tell the miners and their families that," Robyn said, happy to entangle Jessica in the controversial issue. "Don't go to the Tasmanian forests either, and tell the forest workers to pack up their chain saws and go home."

"I understand both arguments, Robyn," Jessica said,

"but I believe preserving the great wilderness areas of the world is far more important than the short-term fueling of the economy. Take Greece. Do you think farmers of ancient times realized that their olive crop, their liquid gold, was undermining a fragile ecology and turning their once-lush land barren? They didn't, but I've read that their great writers delivered stern warnings. Sophocles for one. Most trees have a branching network of roots that hold the topsoil, but olive trees don't. It has a taproot that burrows deep. Once the topsoil has gone, it can't be replaced. That was Greece's tragedy."

"That's all news to me." Robyn brushed it aside. "The olive crop is still of great commercial importance, surely."

"Of course. But what was not known *then,* or largely disregarded, is known now. We have to act on the mistakes of the past."

"That's all very noble, Jessica," Broderick Banner said. "But people and governments live in the present. Mining in the Territory is overtaking cattle. *I* should know. Now, why don't we put the subject behind us?"

"With that attitude, Dad, nothing will change," Cyrus said quietly.

Lavinia, who had over-imbibed under cover of the conversation suddenly piped up with, "Mining isn't the *worst* thing Broderick has done."

"Thank you for that, Lavinia." B.B. turned his striking profile toward her. "You'll need help to get up the stairs."

If that wasn't a dismissal, what was? Jessica thought.

Only, Lavinia wasn't going to be deflected from speaking her mind. "What did you do with all the old photographs, Broderick?"

B.B. threw down his damask napkin. "What old photographs, my dear? There are scrapbooks all over the house."

"None of Moira," Lavinia snapped back like *Take that!*

"That's ancient history, Livvy." Cyrus touched his grandaunt's arm in a gentle warning.

Lavinia swept on single-mindedly. "Where are the paintings? The paintings Hughie did."

B.B. smiled at her. "I have emptied the homestead out myself, Liv—which hasn't stopped *you* from foraging around all these years. There *are* no photographs. No paintings. Do you think I wouldn't know?"

Cyrus took a long hard look at his father. "But you *would* know, Dad. You know everything. By your own admission."

"Please don't try to annoy me, Cyrus," B.B. returned. "You do it so often."

"Hear, hear," Robyn raised her wineglass, her rivalry with Cyrus springing to the fore.

"You can't hide things forever, Broderick," Lavinia warned, seemingly unaware of Cyrus's continuing warning touch.

Broderick Bannerman set his two palms down heavily on the table. "Listen and listen carefully, Lavinia. You've had too much to drink." The piercing gray gaze moved on to Robyn. "So have you, Robyn, for that matter. In my view, women should stick to one drink. No more. They have no head for alcohol. I want all this Moira business stopped. If you can't or won't stop, Lavinia, I'll have to speak to your doctor about it. He might well want to put you into a nursing home for a spell."

"You call a doctor and I'll *kill* you, Broderick." Lavinia bunched her frail, knotted hands into fists.

"All right, that's enough!" Cyrus stood up. "Why bait her, Dad?"

"I'm serious," his father said. "She's getting much worse."

Any sense of shyness in Jessica, amid such a family, had to be cast aside. She understood, like Cyrus, that Lavinia had to be protected from B.B.'s wrath. "Would you like to go upstairs now, Miss Lavinia?" she asked, rising to her feet, too. "I'm feeling a little tired myself. That was a beautiful meal."

"Molly is an unsung heroine," Lavinia said. "I *am* a little tired, dear. Don't think I don't know you want me to keep my trap shut, Broderick." She shot a glance at her nephew. "There's always been too much to hide." Unsteadily, she rose to her feet, wincing a little as the blood returned to her legs.

Cyrus took her arm. "Think you can make it up the stairs, Tosca?"

Lavinia giggled like a schoolgirl. "I may be a bit slow."

Erik Moore, who looked as if he'd been hoping against hope it would all blow over, rose courteously to his feet. "Good night, Ms. Bannerman. Sleep well."

"Good night, Erik," Lavinia replied graciously. "You seem like a nice person. Unfortunately I can't seem to like you. Oh, Moira, dear, aren't you sweet! You're coming, too."

Broderick Bannerman wasn't going to suffer that. "Stay here, please, Jessica," he said, gray eyes cold.

Dared she disobey? Jessica thought she could. She stepped forward, hoping her guardian angel was right behind her. "I'll only be a minute or two, Mr. Bannerman."

"Love to you all," Lavinia caroled wickedly over her shoulder, giving Cyrus a woozy smile before Jessica came to stand at her other side.

It was Jessica who helped Lavinia undress, while Cyrus waited in the adjoining sitting room. This was more like it, Jessica thought, looking around the beautiful, slightly theatrical bedroom and what she could see of the sitting room beyond. Robyn had no hand in decorating this. It truly expressed the essence of Lavinia, even if she *had* lost much of her substance. The color scheme was the blue and white of Chinese porcelain. Filmy white draperies adorned the large four-poster bed. Beautiful blue-and-white fabric was used for the curtains at the French doors, the upholstery of the daybed and the two armchairs. An exquisite blue Venetian writing table—Timmy would love it—stood proudly in a corner. There were two lovely flower paintings on the walls, a collection of miniatures, and dominating one wall, a full-length portrait of Lavinia in her heyday dressed in an extravagantly beautiful white ball gown, clusters of pure white camellias tucked behind her ears.

Violetta, the Lady of the Camellias.

Jessica took a long, admiring look. Just as she thought, Miss Lavinia had been a beauty.

"Yes, that's me," Lavinia confirmed. "I was *glorious* in those days. No big fat diva about me. And my soaring voice! I could hit F above top C no trouble at all. Don't know where I got it from. No one else in the family had a voice unless one counts good speaking voices. We all have those. Come back in, Cyrus, darling," she called. "I'm decent."

Cyrus reentered, vibrantly male in that ultrafeminine room. "That's news to me."

"Don't be naughty, darling." Lavinia was tucked up under the covers now, her abundant white hair pulled back in a plait.

"If I had some watercolors handy, I would paint this lovely room," Jessica said. "I adore the portrait."

"Of course the artist was in love with me," Lavinia said.

"Of course," Cyrus smiled. "That was to be expected."

"You'd really like to paint my room, Moira?" Lavinia asked, motioning to Cyrus to come sit on the side of her bed. "I didn't think young artists did that anymore."

"I do," Jessica smiled. "I took it up in my student days. My uncle Brett encouraged it. I've had quite a few commissions."

Lavinia patted Cyrus's hand. "Get Moira some watercolor paints when you're next in Darwin," she said.

"No problem." The sapphire eyes moved to Jessica, standing beneath Lavinia's portrait. "You'll have to come with me to get exactly what you need."

No second invitation needed, Jessica thought.

They were almost at the door when Lavinia said, "Don't go away again, Moira. Promise?"

Jessica appealed to the formidable man at her side. "What do you want me to say?" she whispered.

"This whole bloody thing is totally insane," he retorted quietly with intense irritation. Then, "Make her happy."

"You don't think I should stop it right now?"

"Do you *want* to?" he asked tightly.

She tried to rein in her temper. What game did he think she was playing? And how could it possibly be an advantage to her? Jessica turned her head over her shoulder. "I promise, Miss Lavinia," she said.

Cyrus lifted a hand and turned off the light. "It doesn't matter, anyway. She's asleep now. Bizarre as it may seem, Jessica, your chance resemblance to our resident ghost has brought shock waves into our already disordered lives. Time has stopped for Lavinia. Even my father seems suspended in a past only he can see."

"Well, let me assure you yet again this has nothing to do with me. We don't even know if I actually do look like Moira or if it's simply a matter of coloring."

"What I should do is conduct a hunt of my own," Cyrus muttered, almost to himself. "There are a million places to hide old photographs, even large paintings."

"But your father has denied their existence. Rather strenuously, I thought."

"Which doesn't mean he's not lying. The hell of it all is no one *knows* what happened to Moira, and your resemblance to her is keeping the whole bloody thing alive."

"Has anyone ever thought about reconstructing her last days? The last days she was seen alive?"

"For God's sweet sake, of course they did," he said, none too politely.

"Only making a suggestion. No need to bite my head off."

His eyes flashed. "Jessica, don't expect anyone around here to keep calm on the subject of Moira. She's been dead for a half a century, yet sometimes it seems like only fifteen minutes ago. Now we've had a visitation—you." His eyes rested on her face. "Can you blame me if I'm suddenly very anxious about what it all means?"

CHAPTER SIX

THE NEXT MORNING in her bedroom, Jessica had a long conversation with Brett on her mobile phone, conveying her excitement while answering his many questions. She carefully refrained from saying anything that would make him in the least bit worried, such as Great-aunt Lavinia's memory playing tricks and making her believe she was Moira. She'd rung Brett briefly the moment she'd touched down in Darwin as promised, but a scant, incident-packed day later there was so much to talk about that her side of the conversation continued nonstop.

"Then you think you can cope?" Brett asked when she took a breather. He might have been sitting in a Darwin office rather than his office more than a thousand miles away, Jessica thought. Darwin was, in fact, closer to Asia than it was to any other Australian capital city.

"I'll need help," she told him. "A lot of help. I can't carry it all. It's an immense project. Far bigger than we anticipated."

"You'll get all the help you need on this, Jass. Take plenty of photographs. I need to know the layout."

"I'll draw up floor plans. That should keep me busy. I'll need to ask Mr. Bannerman's secretary, a nice woman called Ruth if I can load them onto one of the office computers. They have all the latest technology here."

"A man in his position, with his vast interests, would need to," Brett said. "How are you supposed to get around?"

"I'm sure I'll be provided with something. A nice spirited horse, maybe a camel. There are thousands and thousands of them roaming around. Kangaroos by the millions. I never knew it but there are twice as many kangaroos in Australia as people. That means roughly forty million."

Brett laughed. "And to think I've never come face-to-face with one. Don't get burnt in that tropical sun," he warned.

"I won't. I've bought lashings of sunscreen. There are plenty of station vehicles, by the way. Helicopters, a Beech Baron and a Lear jet."

"When you're filthy rich, nothing is unobtainable," Brett said dryly.

"I prefer to think *some* things are."

"What is that supposed to mean?" Brett picked up on her tone.

"Nothing. B.B. has his own pilot, but I understand he and Cyrus are licensed to fly the jet. He goes over to New Zealand a lot. He has interests there. Apparently the jet can fly to Auckland without refueling."

"Marvelous! What else does it do?"

"I'll tell you when I'm in it."

"The son, what's he like?"

Jessica twisted a long curl around her finger. "Very lordly. His father's manner veers more to severely autocratic. Cyrus is the only one who doesn't jump at his father's command, anyway."

"Princes are like that," Brett said. "Just don't become his willing subject. What's the father-son relationship like?"

Jessica eased back on the bed. "Not good. I think they've had some terrible clashes in the past."

"That's awful!" Brett sounded appalled. "You be careful, Jass," he warned. "Enmity between father and son is not to be dismissed. Whatever you do, don't get between them. You're there in a strictly professional capacity. Don't let the heir-in-waiting turn your head. Sounds like Tim will play a role in this. He can take a few quick overseas trips if necessary. Source out antiques."

"Good idea. Has Timmy found out anything more about the portrait he bought at Christie's?" she asked.

"Not as yet."

"She looks so much like me. Don't you think that's odd?"

"It *is* odd, but it's not like it doesn't happen, Jass. Remember the portrait we had of the woman in the red dress? She was the spitting image of the Lady Mayoress. What about the governess who disappeared? Any mention of that?"

Brett always had been on her wavelength. "The subject is taboo."

"I guess so," Brett said in a somber voice. "Can you imagine what it must have been like for Bannerman growing up? At least he had an alibi," he quipped sardonically.

"Why would he need an alibi? Why would anyone need an alibi?" Jessica felt an icy finger down her spine.

"Bannerman's father might have had an obsession with the girl, for all we know. He could have seduced her. The wife found out. The kids found out. The servants were agog with gossip. If I were writing a movie script, it would be a life-threatening situation. Listen, I have to go. Becky is signaling me. Clients have come in. Ring me every day and take care."

BRODERICK BANNERMAN INSISTED on coming with her while she took her photographs. Surely, she thought, such a high-pressured tycoon would have something more important to do. But no. It seemed nothing would suit him better than to walk around with her while she shot off hundreds of photographs of the exterior and interior of the new homestead, although *homestead* was far too modest a word for this modern palace. There were six guest suites contained within the main building, all with their own private porch. She would have a lot of fun decorating those. She took shots of the surrounding garden, well-nurtured by bores: sweeps of lawn like a vast green plain, towering palms and banyans, the boabs and poincianas, native frangipani that had grown into huge trees, the mango, coconut and the giant tree ferns that formed such a lush oasis in an arid land.

"We could do with a water feature," she said, removing a memory stick from her digital camera and inserting another. "The sight and sound of water is very cooling. I'd make it a focal point. Keeping to the classical idiom would be crucial. Who was your landscape gardener?" They might have to call him or her back.

"A fellow called Alan Jensen," B.B. answered, his sunglasses making his piercing gaze unreadable.

"I knew it had to be someone good," Jessica said, instantly recognizing the name. Jensen was very highly regarded in the field.

"I only deal with the best."

She took her shot, then smiled. "Then you're taking a chance on me."

"I don't think so." His deep voice was very measured, very sure.

"Well, I'm very happy about it, Mr. Bannerman."

"Broderick. Call me Broderick," he said with a smile. "I don't want B.B. or Mr. Bannerman from you. Broderick is my name. I liked the look of you, Jessica, and the way you expressed yourself on that program. I liked your beauty, your polish, your style. I like grace in a woman. My first wife, Deborah, had it in abundance. I lost her far too early. I was beside myself with grief. Then I had to put her firmly out of my mind. The Bannerman empire had to come first. The fact you're in contention for a big design award helped. The young should be given every chance."

Jessica's mouth quirked. "I'm firmly behind that." She was touched by the way he had spoken about his wife. It showed a more sensitive side of him. It was all so sad. "Thank you for your faith in me. I'll do everything in my power to make you happy you chose me."

He looked at her standing there, flashing her lovely smile and brimming with life. The sun made a glory of her cloud of ash-blond hair, her green eyes shone like jewels, and her skin was shimmering. For a moment, he thought he was dreaming. In this young woman's presence, nothing seemed normal. "I'm not used to happiness," he said, and abruptly turned away.

Jessica stood rooted to the spot for several moments, staring after him as he headed down the path. His progress was unhurried but purposeful. There was a lot of darkness and misery in Broderick Bannerman, she thought, relieved she could now continue on her own. She didn't feel comfortable with the man. She doubted anyone would. She realized, too, Cyrus wouldn't like her calling his father by his Christian name, taking little account of the fact that she, too, preferred not to. But having been *told* as opposed to *invited* to call him Broderick, she would be giving offense if she didn't.

Robyn wouldn't like her calling her father Broderick

either. Both son and stepdaughter were seeing concerns further along the track. Broderick Bannerman was still a handsome virile man. He had obviously taken a fancy to her, which was the very last thing she'd expected. Surely they all knew that. She was making her own way in life. The old rule about never mixing business with pleasure had its history in experience. Her position had already diminished, simply by allowing Cyrus Bannerman to get under her guard. She should have known better. Sexual attraction swept away good judgment. What she needed was a good shot of self-control.

Slowly, she walked back into the house, filled with a desire to capture and send just the right images back to Brett and Tim. She had already made her request to Ruth, B.B.'s secretary, for the use of a computer.

"Whatever you want, my dear, B.B. has given me my instructions."

It was abundantly clear Ruth craved her boss's approval. Jessica also had a strong sense Ruth secretly craved a lot more.

She spent until lunchtime, which Molly had told her was one o'clock sharp, getting her feel of the dimensions of the various rooms and their outlooks. She made some quick sketches of floor plans for her own benefit, having already asked Broderick—why was it such a hurdle to call him that—if she could make copies of the original house plans. The architect, not surprisingly, was of Greek extraction currently living and working in Brunei, no doubt building more palaces.

They were in fact waiting for her when she finally made it to the informal dining room situated at the rear of the homestead. It could be, and probably had been at one time, a lovely room, floor and ceiling dark gleaming timber with contrasting chalky white walls crying out for decoration. Paintings, mirrors, surely they had them? Probably Robyn had had them stored away. The hard question was, if Robyn owned an art gallery, what made her shun putting paintings on her own walls? Jessica had seen lots of superb antique silver, fine china and beautiful glittering crystal, but the house was devoid of artworks and some fine pieces of antique furniture. She wasn't thinking of all that many, but certain focal pieces from China or Japan.

Entering the room, her eye carried to the huge turquoise swimming pool in the garden beyond. She had already taken a quick look at the intricately carved ceiling of the pagoda covering it, which Robyn had told her had come from an Asian temple. It struck her, not for the first time, that the original homestead with its wonderful high-hipped roof and deep overhangs was far more appropriate to the climate and its extraordinary setting than the palatial new building, which would have looked great among the mansions of the very rich rising above Sydney Harbour.

"So sorry," Jessica made a quick, smiling apology. "The time simply flew."

Ruth, who ate with the family during the working day and sometimes at night—she had her own self-contained bungalow on the grounds—acknowledged that with an empathetic smile. Robyn remained silent. Her friend Erik Moore gave Jessica a smile full of interest. Very daring of him, with Robyn sitting by his side. B.B. gestured Jessica into the empty chair to his right. "Wondered what kept you," he said, as though that now she was present they could get underway.

No sign of Lavinia.

No sign of Cyrus. Big disappointment. Again her powerful attraction to him hit her like a blow.

Lavinia would be in her room listening to her favourite CDs of Tebaldi and Callas. Cyrus would be working hard around the station. Being a cattleman was a tough seven-day-a-week job. His father, having done it all in his time, presided at the lunch table.

"So what *were* you doing with yourself?" Robyn was in interrogation mode. She started to help herself to a very small portion of coconut chicken salad sprinkled with toasted sesame seeds and piled high on a large lime-green-and-white platter.

It looked good. Jessica found herself hungry.

"Taking photographs, mostly," she replied. "I've e-mailed a lot of them back to my uncle. He's taking a great interest in the project, which as you can imagine is a considerable coup for our firm."

"Why does everyone go in for designers?" Robyn's voice was laced with scorn. "*I've* never seen the need for calling them in. Obviously a lot of people lack self-confidence and taste."

"For which you qualify on at least *one* count," her step-father commented in a level voice that sat oddly with the barbed remark.

Naturally Robyn protested. Jessica didn't blame her. "Oh, Dad, that's a bit cruel. *You* mightn't have been entirely happy with what I did a couple of years back, but most of our friends love it. *You* do, don't you, Erik?"

"Well, he would, wouldn't he?" her stepfather retorted before the embarrassed Erik could speak. B.B. inclined his handsome head in thanks as Ruth, having piled a plate with the delicious-looking salad, rose and set it before him.

Now that's service, Jessica thought. Ruth was not only the loyal devoted secretary; she was the hired help.

"Robyn and Erik are in partnership building an indigenous art gallery and adjoining boutique hotel on the coast a few miles out of Darwin city," Bannerman said, turning to Jessica. "At least Erik had the sense to call in a good architect, a very clever young Malaysian. Construction has only just started, but there's a chance for a good interior designer." He patted her hand.

For one shocking moment, Jessica thought Robyn would explode; instead, she threw down her fork, which bounced off the table and fell to the floor. "Ms. Tennant will have more than she can possibly chew trying to meet the challenge of the Big House, Dad."

Ruth, whose blush at being thanked by the great man still hadn't subsided, now sat so still and so quiet she might have been trying to make herself invisible.

"I hope you weren't thinking of doing the job yourself, Robyn," Broderick Bannerman said, again in that mild tone. "If so, I have to tell you, if Erik won't, you're not competent."

Robyn flushed but fought back gamely. "That's what *you* say, Dad."

Inside, Jessica applauded. *Good for you!* The nicest person in the world would have been adversely affected by a lifetime with the hypercritical, acid-tongued Broderick Bannerman.

"If you don't want to listen to good advice, Robyn," he replied, "Erik will have to. Remember, I have some stake in this."

Ah, the iron fist in the velvet glove. Jessica watched Erik surreptitiously rub Robyn's back to calm her. "You're being a little hard on Robyn, aren't you, B.B.?" he asked, keeping his tone respectful. Clearly it didn't pay to get on the wrong side of Broderick Bannerman.

B.B. suddenly looked bored. "Well, *you* can't risk the truth, Erik, can you? Erik is hoping to marry my step-daughter," he turned his head to inform Jessica, who, had she been Robyn, would have run from the table, having first slapped B.B. over the head with her napkin. "It isn't particularly good news. Erik made his first wife—a very nice little thing—extremely unhappy. She could have had her revenge for that, but she didn't."

"Actually, B.B.," Erik spluttered, his affable face turning brick-red, "she finished with more than her fair share. Elizabeth deliberately tried to turn our friends against me. She wanted to protect her own reputation."

"Which was blameless." Bannerman gave his judgment. "God knows why Robyn is determined to have you. You won't make her happy, either." He broke off to examine Jessica's plate. "You're not eating?"

She contemplated the chicken dish before her. "Yes, I must start. This looks delicious." Dutifully she picked up her fork before she was force-fed.

"I've organized a vehicle for you to run around in," B.B. told her presently. "A four-wheel drive. You can take it out anytime you like. But unless you have company, I'd like you to keep in sight of the outbuildings and the airstrip. It would be very easy for someone like you, a city girl, to get lost. There's no need for you to spend all your time on the job. I want you to enjoy your stay on Mokhani."

He threw her another one of his rare charming smiles. If only the man would lighten up a little! Even the odd kindly word seemed to exhaust him. If only he'd show some loving kindness toward his son and his stepdaughter. Maybe kindness wasn't in his disposition, and his wealth no doubt had played a large part in solidifying his autocratic manner.

"Thank you…Broderick," Jessica murmured, keeping an eye on reactions around the table.

If looks could kill, she would have been dead in her chair.

"That's a bit presumptuous calling Dad by his Christian name, isn't it?" Robyn spoke emotionally, blindly ignoring Erik's hand at her elbow. Even the deeply reserved Ruth looked shocked.

Bannerman's voice was as dry as ash. "The fact is I *asked* Jessica to call me by my Christian name, Robyn. She isn't taking liberties. I don't hear my name enough. In fact, I don't hear it at all."

Everyone fell silent, embarrassed. Robyn, dark head bent, lifted her eyes just long enough for Jessica to see their glare.

How to make friends and influence people, Jessica thought.

CHAPTER SEVEN

JESSICA FOUND HERSELF working so feverishly on the layout of the Big House, as the family called it, she had little time to go exploring on her own or indeed with anyone else. B.B., too, was extremely busy, for which she was grateful. The very last thing she wanted was that he should follow her around. She couldn't help but be aware that she had captured his eye. Approaching sixty or no, the libido had definitely not been drained out of the man. Besides, he was very rich, and Jessica's experience of rich people told her they thought nothing impossible. Courting and capturing a woman young enough to be one's daughter might be viewed as a piece of cake.

The only time all of them met up was at dinner. As the weeks passed, Jessica had come to think of it as the time that really counted. She got to see Cyrus. Cyrus with his brilliant, mocking eyes resting lightly on her, his attentions friendly but in no way sexual. Yet when he was around, the very air sparkled, her perceptions intensified. It might have been champagne running in her blood. Only, with his punishing workload, she didn't get to see him half often enough. He was up and away at dawn, only returning to the homestead at dusk. His absence *should* have kept her in check, but it didn't. She felt him there even when he wasn't, which she concluded was one of the side effects of such attraction.

Erik Moore had long since returned to Darwin, inviting Jessica to look over his and Robyn's latest development whenever she came to town. Needless to say, Robyn wasn't there at the time he issued the invitation. Aunt Lavinia kept mostly to her room, out of harm's way. Probably that bit about the nursing home had frightened her. Which was cruel. Robyn continued to be unfriendly to the point of being rude. She seemed quite unable to say a single thing with grace. Jessica realized Robyn had convinced herself there was some mischief afoot that included her stepfather's designer. Not that Jessica could blame her when B.B. persisted in treating her, Jessica, with a gentleness and attention he bestowed on no other. Jessica might well be thought to be a rival for Robyn's stepfather's affections. Perhaps a mistress in the making? Whatever the thinking, Jessica was becoming more and more aware that her arrival at Mokhani had produced much the same effect as a bomb going off.

She tried not to let Robyn's manner upset her. Robyn clearly had problems. Although she was by all accounts a successful businesswoman, a mega-rich man's stepdaughter, Jessica had come to appreciate that Robyn's life wasn't easy. Accepted though she was as a Bannerman, she wasn't by *birth*. Jessica could quite understand how Robyn had struggled with that all her life, since blood was so important in this family. So much of her prickly manner could have its basis in insecurity. Odd she had never sought complete independence. Obviously money was the key. Robyn might find separation from the *money* unbearable. Money compelled people to stay when they really wanted to run.

Overnight, Mokhani had become the center of Jessica's world. She felt a powerful affinity with it. Every day she rose with the birds, awakened by the stupendous outpouring of song. A veritable opera she had come to think of as an homage to the sun. She lay in bed each morning, her arms stretched above her head, enthralled. The legions of birds lent the choir great power. She supposed the rest of the household was used to having the world's greatest orchestra in the backyard, but she found the depth and the volume of sound quite impossible to sleep through. And who would want to?

She longed for the weekends to come, for then she had her best chance of seeing more of Cyrus. Neither of them could turn their backs on that kiss. She supposed that's what kisses were for—to bring an attraction right into focus. Not all kisses left one with a feeling of falling into the unknown. Falling into *love?* Sometimes something he said or the way he looked at her built on her own yearnings. Other times, she told herself she was dreaming. Or simply she was far more impressionable than he was. She had never been so impressionable before.

One Saturday when she was well into her second month at Mokhani, Jessica lingered at the breakfast table, saying she'd like to pay Aunt Lavinia a visit afterward. B.B. had left the table only a few minutes before to take an urgent phone call, leaving Jessica and Robyn together. Not a comfortable situation when Robyn was in one of her abrasive moods.

"I wouldn't bother if I were you," Robyn told her shortly. "Livvy likes her own space." She raked her nails over some little bump on her arm, leaving a red weal. "Why the heck are you so bent on ingratiating yourself around here?" she asked, making no effort to hide her resentment. "Don't you think you're exceeding your brief?"

Jessica had been waiting for some sort of attack; still, she was taken aback. "Gosh, I'm certainly not ingratiating myself with *you*, Robyn. Can't we be friends? It would make life so much easier. I can't overlook your rudeness anymore. I know I don't deserve it."

"Well, you'll damned well have to put up with it," Robyn said, a glimmer of tears in her eyes.

Immediately, Jessica backed off. "You're upset. Please tell me why. I want to help."

Robyn didn't answer, but bit down hard on her lip.

"Do you see me as some kind of threat, Robyn?" Jessica persisted, trying to clear the air. "I'm no possible threat to you. How could you think it? I'm here to do a job, then I'll be gone. Out of your lives."

Robyn snorted. "As far as I'm concerned the job is simply a ploy. You're like every other female Cyrus or B.B. meet. They've all got getting bedded on their minds. Who knows? Getting bedded could be a first step to marriage."

For a moment, Jessica saw red. She counted to ten, tempted to bop Robyn in the nose. "Don't be so ridiculous," she said crisply. "If you believe that, you'll believe anything. No wonder our friendship is doomed. You couldn't be more wrong. In fact, you're downright insulting. I'm here in my capacity as interior designer. You must have missed it, but I've been working extremely hard."

Robyn gave a brittle laugh as she demolished a piece of a freshly baked roll in her fingers. "Look, Jessica, I'm the victim here, not you. Dad is paying you so much attention it's sad to see. I wouldn't care if you were one of his old girlfriends, his own age. But you're not. You're a bloody love goddess. Cyrus thinks so, too. Both of us are convinced you have a far bigger coup in mind than pulling off the Big House. *I* haven't seen anything you've done so far."

"Robyn, you haven't shown the slightest interest."

"Why should I? All the money Dad's paying you, I would have done it for nothing."

"I'm sorry, Robyn, but it's not as easy as you think. I have a lot of training behind me."

"Big deal!" Robyn returned rudely. "There's something wrong with this whole thing. Are you going to tell me?"

Jessica sighed. "Robyn, there's nothing *to* tell."

Robyn studied her with narrowed dark eyes. "Obviously, you remind poor old Livvy of that dreary skeleton in the closet, Moira. That being the case, Dad must see something of her in you, too. Maybe *that's* the big fascination. Seeing you on that television show freed up a lot of stuff in Dad's head. Moira still stands for something in Dad's life. *I* rate a lot lower than her. I don't really matter to him, however hard I try. I'm not his blood, after all. I'm not a bloody Bannerman, I'm a lousy stepdaughter. I've been trying to get his attention all my life, yet you sashay in with your blond hair and your big green eyes and you get it right away. It must be a pleasure for men just to look at you. I see Cyrus taking his fill over the dinner table. Dad can't take his eyes off you, either. I've never seen that before. Ever! And I've been watching him for most of my life."

Jessica, staring with a mix of dismay and sympathy into the other woman's eyes, saw genuine fears. "Look, I'm sorry for all this and your problems with your stepfather, but you've just said, they started long before I came on the scene. Don't blame me for being blond, either, or for a chance resemblance to your stepfather's childhood governess, which could be very slight. What you're saying is wrong and damaging to me. Your fears are quite without foundation. Your stepfather is old enough to be my father. Don't you think twenty-four and sixty is a no-go?"

Robyn stood up so violently she sent her chair flying.

"Try twenty-four and sixty million!" she cried, curling her lip in scorn. "You're no different from any other female. Your big dream in life is to land a millionaire. The older the better! You won't have to wait that long to get the money."

Jessica pushed her plate away. "Speak for yourself, Robyn. I'm not another version of *you*. I haven't got anything against Erik, but isn't *he* middle-aged? You could well be chasing a father figure."

"*Bitch!*" Robyn smarted.

Jessica, too, stood up. "You're not the only one who can take cheap shots, Robyn. I'll go and see Lavinia now. Unlike you, she enjoys my company."

Jessica tapped lightly on Lavinia's door. Her little spat with Robyn had upset her. Her hands were shaking. She needed to calm down.

"Miss Lavinia?" She hoped the old lady would speak to her. She'd missed her, although Molly had assured her Lavinia was perfectly well. Her meals were being taken to her room, Molly always returning with an empty tray. A surprise, considering Lavinia looked as though she hadn't eaten in more than a half century!

No sound inside. Disappointed, Jessica was about to withdraw when she heard a scurrying on the other side. The door opened a fraction, a tiny face covered in thick white makeup peered out, then on seeing Jessica, the door opened right up.

"Moira, dear." Madame Butterfly showed her pleasure. "I was wondering when you were going to come and see me."

Jessica was so enchanted, she forgot to correct the old lady. "I've been very busy, Miss Lavinia, but I've been asking about you." She smiled, her eyes ranging all over the elaborate costume so completely different from Violetta's ball gown. No wonder Lavinia could stay in her room, never bored.

"Well, come in, come in," Lavinia invited happily, adjusting the wide red silk obi that had slipped from her waist to her nonexistent hips. Her kimono, red and white silk, was exquisite, the scarlet panels embroidered with white peonies. Lavinia, the purist, had arranged her hair in a loose puff with a thick topknot, various gold and pearl baubles holding it in place. "Shall I send for tea?" she asked. "I know exactly how to perform the tea ceremony."

Jessica would have agreed, only there wasn't time. "That would be lovely, Miss Lavinia, but perhaps some other time. I've just had breakfast."

"Of course you have." Lavinia tottered on her wooden clogs into the sitting room, and Jessica followed.

"Well, sit down." She waved Jessica to a comfortable armchair, taking one herself by falling back into it. "Tell me what you've been doing. I've been keeping to my room out of harm's way. I've found I can only take Broderick in small doses, anyway. As for Robyn! All she does is torment me. She was such an unhappy little girl. Never laughed, always glowering. She wants Mokhani, you know." The faded eyes, set in their violet sockets, were shrewd.

"But Cyrus is the heir?"

Lavinia wriggled in her chair. Jessica, familiar with such wriggles in the elderly, got up to push a little cushion behind her back. "Better?"

"Thank you, Moira, love." Lavinia patted her arm. "Everything fell apart in this house when Deborah was killed. Even then Broderick was a hard, strange man, but he had a horrible time trying to get over Deborah's death.

He neglected Cyrus terribly. I used to think it was because Cyrus is so much like her. Not in looks, so much. Cyrus is a Bannerman, with his grandfather's blazing blue eyes, but his nature. Cyrus is a very fine young man. He's caring and thoughtful and everyone loves and respects him. They *fear* Broderick. Quite a different thing. Since he's become a man, Cyrus has shown his own brilliance. He could take over from his father any day. That's not just me saying that. The people who know agree Cyrus is *The Man*. That hardly makes Broderick happy. It must be a terrible thing to be jealous of your own son—jealous of his *youth*. Aging isn't easy, Moira." Lavinia shook her head dolefully. "Someone said—I just forget who—it was a whiplash in the face of the human spirit. I totally agree."

Jessica felt very disturbed by Lavinia's insistence on calling her Moira, but equally she felt powerless to do anything about it. "Why does Cyrus stay?"

Lavinia shrugged. "His father can't last forever. Broderick can dispose of all his other assets as he pleases, but Mokhani and the ancestral home belong to Cyrus. Even Broderick knows he has no right to deprive his son of that. Cyrus is standing in line to inherit just as Broderick inherited from his own father, Steven. My God, there was a man! But tormented, too, just like poor Broderick."

"I've admired his portrait in the study."

"Doesn't do him justice!" Lavinia delicately snorted. "As *you'll* know." She looked sympathetically into Jessica's eyes. "Madly in love with him, weren't you?"

"Oh, Miss Lavinia!" For an instant Jessica had a powerful attack of vertigo. She lowered her head until the dizziness passed. She despaired she would never get the old lady to recognize her for who she was, but she had to continue to try or slip into a similar kind of madness. "I'm Jessica, remember?"

But Lavinia's brain had an infinite number of interlocking caverns where the past and the present flowed together. She laughed softly. "It's all right, love. I was so worried about you, but now you're back. I'm not mad, you know. I know I make a lot of people uncomfortable, even my darling Cyrus. He doesn't like me talking about Moira."

I don't blame him, Jessica thought. She was feeling spooked herself.

Lavinia's tiny face contorted. "Any talk of Moira always has started such a *fuss!*" Her thin knotted hands began to twitch. "Do you know how many years have passed since you've been gone, child?"

"Moira's been gone over fifty years," Jessica said gently, leaning forward in her chair. "I must look like Moira. That's why you've made the mistake."

"Shh!" Lavinia said, holding a finger to her lips. She didn't look in the least grotesque with the white theatrical makeup plastered all over her face and her lips painted a bright red. The fine wrinkles on her face covered, she looked an echo of her far-off heyday when she had stolen an English aristocrat's heart. "Just between you and me, I think I know where Broderick hid your portrait," she whispered, as though her nephew were standing listening just outside the French doors. "Always said he destroyed it, but he tells lies. Have you ever been into the big storeroom?" she asked.

Jessica was galvanized by that piece of information. "The attic?"

Lavinia shook her head vigorously, setting her pearl-and-gold baubles dancing. "No, the big storeroom is a separate building. You must know it. It's at the rear of the kitchen complex, the old servants' quarters. It's where Robyn, bless her, emptied out all Deborah's things. Graceless creature! Shoved them in there. The nerve of her!" Hostility burned from Lavinia's eyes. "If you manage to get in there—it will have to be when Broderick is away— you can do a search. I failed, but *you* won't."

Suddenly a light went on in Jessica's head. "Have you seen another portrait of Moira lately?" she asked. "At an art auction, maybe? When you were in Sydney?"

Lavinia frowned, at first looking as if she didn't understand but then she responded indignantly, "Some bloody man bought it. Needless to say he was not a gentleman, because he wouldn't let me have it. I thought he would if I offered him a lot of money, but he wouldn't be persuaded, waffling on about how it was the image of a dear friend. Of course I didn't believe him."

Jessica was shaken. Very shaken. So it *was* a portrait of Moira. Moira who had disappeared in 1947. Moira, who had, in fact, looked very much like *her.* It was an incredible coincidence, the resemblance, but the sudden appearance of the portrait after half a century's obscurity surely wasn't. Was someone pulling strings and for what purpose? Had B.B. put it on the market? Maybe even his twin, Barbara?

"Did your niece, Barbara, go with you to the auction?" she asked.

"Skipped off without her," Lavinia said confidentially. "Ferris, their driver, took me in. Babs doesn't like sitting around auctions like I do. As it turned out it was a great blessing she didn't come. She'd have been tremendously upset to see the portrait, and I simply couldn't tell her about it."

No, but it set you off, Jessica thought, appreciating that the portrait had had a considerable effect on the old lady. "Do you know the name of the artist?" she asked.

"Of course," Lavinia's jet-black brows, painted in a high arch, rose farther toward her hairline. "Why are you asking me? It was Hughie."

"Hughie, of course." Jessica murmured, piecing the story together.

"He had a great deal of talent," Lavinia said, sunken eyes gazing into the past. "He painted that wonderful portrait of Steven that hangs in Broderick's study. But Hughie never had a chance. He was a pansy, you know, poor old Hughie. He tried to kill you, didn't he?"

Brilliant sunlight poured across the veranda, but Jessica felt so cold she might have been caught in an icy draft. "Why ever would you say that?" She had to force the words out.

"He was in love with Steven, of course," Lavinia tutted, "but unable to ever speak of it. There was something utterly shameful about being homosexual in those days. A man's reputation would be stained forever if he was suspected of being one. You would never pick him. Looked perfectly normal. But what did F. Scott Fitzgerald call it? An aberration in nature, that's it. Cecily was terribly cruel to Hughie, though they were cousins. Perfectly understandable. Steven was her husband. She worshipped him. People said it was the war, but I think it was poor old Hughie's forbidden love that made him drink. Killed himself in the end. I know I saw the body. I believe he intended to hurt you, Moira. He couldn't stand the fact Steven loved you. It laid him waste."

BY THE TIME HER CHAT with Lavinia was over Jessica's brain felt fried. She crammed a sun hat on her head, shoved on dark sunglasses, then took a brisk walk around the homestead and the extensive gardens. It might calm her, though she'd gotten into the habit of taking a walk every morning after breakfast. Moving about the main compound also gave her a better feel for what she was doing. The landscaper would have to be contacted again. His work on the complex of gardens had been completed before the Big House had gone up. Now a new layout would be required to complement the classical lines of the house. She had in mind a broad expanse of fine gravel the length of the portico bordered by white marble, with perhaps a few of the wonderful upright plants, such as miniature date palms, planted into the gravel. For comparison, perhaps some rounded cushion plants. The contrast would work well.

She had no idea when she would get the opportunity to check out the old servants' quarters. She'd circled the building many times with only a passing thought as to what it was used for. Now that she *knew,* she had a mission. To find another one of Moira's portraits. What she had learned about Hughie had shocked her. Not that he was homosexual, scarcely that, but that Lavinia had thought he had wanted to kill her. For God's sake, kill *Moira,* she berated herself. Lavinia's habit of calling her Moira was really getting to her, the way a role, if taken very seriously, got to an actor.

When she returned to the homestead some forty minutes later, she found Ruth, who didn't appear at weekend meals, bustling about in the great hall. Several pieces of very expensive luggage were stacked at the foot of the staircase.

"Oh, Jessica!" Ruth's furrowed brow cleared. "B.B. asked me to find you. He's been called away unexpectedly. We're off to Hong Kong until at least the end of next week. A development B.B.'s involved in. I'm going with him. I'll be needed."

"Is there anything I can do to help?" Jessica asked. "You look a little flustered."

"I am," Ruth freely admitted. "I've often had to pick up and go at a minute's notice, but I didn't foresee this. How do I look?"

"You look fine."

"Sure?" Ruth's insecurities were deep.

Jessica smiled. "You always do." Jessica guessed Ruth was a very efficient woman to remain in B.B.'s employ, yet she seemed so vulnerable otherwise.

A little distance off, they heard B.B.'s voice, raised in anger. Did the man ever relax? He was a prime candidate for a heart attack or a stroke. "No, Robyn. I won't let you come with me. I want you here."

Robyn's voice, wonder of wonders, sounded young and beseeching. "But why, Dad? I want to do some shopping. You've taken me at other times."

"You'll be company for Jessica," B.B. snapped. "I don't want her here on her own."

"Cyrus is here," Robyn protested. "So's Liv. And Molly. She's not alone. Pl…ee…ze, Dad," she implored.

"I don't want to talk about this!" B.B. strode into the entrance hall, a little startled to see Jessica standing there. "Ah, Jessica!" He recovered quickly. "Ruth's told you the news."

"Yes, she has." Jessica spoke with respectful regret, though in reality she was thrilled the household would be out from under for a few days. "I hope everything goes well for you. I'm quite okay. I have so much work to do I'll be kept very busy until your return. I couldn't help

overhearing you were concerned I might feel lonely.
Thank you for that, but there won't be enough hours in the
day for all I've got to get through. I'm not surprised Robyn
wants to do some shopping. Hong Kong is a wonderful
place to do it."

For the first time since they'd met, Robyn shot Jessica
a friendly look. "See, Dad? I won't take a minute to get
ready." She was, in fact, already prepared, hoping for the
ride but never sure of her stepfather and his unpredictable
moods.

At that moment, Cyrus strode through the front door,
his tall, lean body outlined against the brilliant sunshine.
"Got your message, Dad," he said. "I thought I'd come in
and drive you down to the airstrip."

"Very thoughtful of you, Cyrus," B.B. answered in his
habitually sardonic tone.

"Think nothing of it." Now it was Cyrus's turn to be sarcastic, though initially he had spoken as a devoted son
should. What deep rifts lay between father and son resided
within Broderick Bannerman's complex personality,
Jessica thought.

"Well, Dad, what's the decision?" Robyn asked eagerly,
only to be admonished by an emphatic, "No!"

A lot of friendships must have crumbled around Broderick Bannerman. Jessica felt Robyn's disappointment.
Who knew? Robyn might have become a pleasant person
had B.B. been a different kind of stepfather.

"No, what?" Cyrus asked, looking from one to the other.

Robyn turned to him, desperate to enlist support. "I'm
trying to cadge a ride on the jet. It's ages since I've done
any real shopping. I love Hong Kong."

"So?" Cyrus shrugged. "What's the problem? There's
plenty of room."

"The problem *is,* Cyrus," Bannerman said testily, "I've told Robyn I don't want her along."

"So much for optimism!" Cyrus gave a lopsided smile. "That's a bit mean, isn't it? It's not as though she's going to bother you." He was watching his father closely, long used to picking up on hidden motivations. "We'll look after Jessica if that's what you're worried about."

It was Jessica's chance to step in. She caught Cyrus's eye. "I've already told…Broderick—" just the slightest hesitation "—I have a big job to grapple with. I don't need looking after."

"That's wonderful news," Cyrus said suavely. "Your work is your pleasure. So, Dad, can Robyn go?"

Any other father, no matter how grumpy—including even Jessica's father, not the easiest man in the world—would have said, after a beat or two, "Oh, very well!" But Broderick Bannerman was in many ways the father from hell.

Robyn on the other hand, pleasantly stunned by so much support rushed toward him to peck his cheek. She wasn't going to give him the chance to refuse. "Thanks, Dad. I'm all packed."

For a moment B.B. looked as though he would explode, but Cyrus laughed. "There's something you can do for me, Robyn, if you would. Drop in on my tailor and get me a stack of shirts. You know, smart, casual kind of thing. They know what I like by now. I'll attend to the bill at this end."

"No problem," Robyn said quite cheerfully for her, and danced off.

It was a wonder she didn't blow him a kiss, Jessica thought sardonically.

WHEN CYRUS RETURNED to the house thirty minutes later having seen his father off, he found Jessica, Lavinia and Molly sitting out on the rear terrace enjoying morning tea.

"When the cat's away the mice will play," he observed dryly.

"Want some tea, darling?" Lavinia asked in a wonderfully jovial mood. She had changed out of her Madame Butterfly costume into her monk's habit. Traces of white paint lingered around her ears.

"Why not?" Cyrus pulled out a chair and sat down beside Jessica. "And how's our lady interior designer?" he inquired, looking into her eyes.

He seemed to have a hundred different expressions when he looked at her, each more heart-stopping than the last. She commanded her pulses to stop racing. "Fine," she smiled. She had expressions, too.

"I'll make fresh tea," Molly said, jumping up.

"Goody." Lavinia clapped her hands. "You can bring back some more of those lovely cookies. Cyrus will enjoy them."

"Will do." Molly smiled, as happy as a kid let out of school.

"You're not thinking of working today, are you?" Cyrus asked Jessica.

Excitement soared. Hadn't she wanted and waited for this? "I should."

"Nonsense!" Lavinia broke in. "What is the weekend for if not to relax? Broderick's gone." She grinned. "Why else would I be sitting here? Robyn's gone with him. Something I was counting on, so there's just you two. And me, of course. And Molly. But we old girls don't count. Show her around the place, Cyrus. There's so much that's new for her to enjoy."

Me or Moira? Jessica thought, but dared not ask.

"Do you ride?" Cyrus asked, looking a shade doubtful.

"In a fashion," Jessica answered, resting back in her rattan armchair. If she levered herself forward a little, she could brush his throat with her lips. She knew how warm his skin was. She knew the touch of his mouth. It seemed an awfully long time since he had kissed her and in doing so changed her life.

"Perhaps we should take the Jeep then," he said, continuing his own exploration. "I was planning a fairly long trip, and if you're not a seasoned rider you'd finish up very sore and sorry."

"No, we'll go riding tomorrow," she said blithely, rather enjoying keeping him in the dark. She was, in fact, an excellent rider, but it was plain he had branded her a city slicker.

"Don't go near the escarpment," Lavinia suddenly moaned.

"Now, now, Livvy." A flicker of irritation was in Cyrus's eyes.

"When I go there I always hear her cries."

"It's the waterfall," Cyrus clipped off in a way meant to shut Lavinia up. "I've told you that."

But Lavinia thought she had something important to say.

"Never!" She shook her snow-white head. "It could never be the cry of falling water. It's a woman. The sound haunts me, it's so piercing."

"Oh, for God's sake! If you're going to start, Livvy, I'll have to bolt."

"No, no, sit there." She reached out to detain him. "Have your cup of tea. You understand, don't you, Moira?"

"Miss Lavinia, please let it go," Jessica urged gently, and caught the old lady's trembling hand. "It's all in the past."

If only it would stay there.

CHAPTER EIGHT

IT WAS UNLIKE ANY OTHER day trip Jessica had ever taken, one filled with tumultuous fun and excitement. It seemed a marvelous thing to have Cy's company, and she wondered if her happiness showed. The breadth and grandeur of the landscape was enthralling. The sky above them was a bewitching peacock-blue, the arid earth supporting little vegetation but the ubiquitous spinifex, colored a bright rust-red, which made a brilliant contrast with the sky. The heat haze ran before them in shimmering parallel lines of silver-blue, suggesting far-off lagoons. She could readily understand how the early explorers had been fooled into thinking the mirage was real.

The vibrancy of the colors—the burning reds, the bright yellows, the dark greens and all shades of the color purple—had been captured wonderfully by the great Aboriginal artist Albert Namatjira. To Jessica's artistic eye, too, they were an extravagance of inspiration. This was *her* country, too. She felt a great urge to paint it with the substances she loved: indigo, cobalt-blue, vermilion, lapis lazuli, cadmium, gold. An artist could create any color by blending the three primaries, red, yellow and blue. The whole world *was* color when touched by the miracle of light. She felt saturated in it.

They stopped many times so she could get a closer

view of a particular natural feature. Once, they stopped to watch the antics of a joey only a few days out of the pouch, bounding about ecstatically on its supercharged pogo sticks of legs while its mother kept a gentle eye on it. It was like a frolicking lamb, only on a far more dynamic scale.

"Kangaroos have to breed when they can," Cyrus told her, leaning indolently against the Jeep, yet managing to convey hair-trigger alert. "They can't depend on water in the Dry. That mother has the little fella, another in the pouch and probably an embryo, as well."

"Have you ever seen such joy!" Jessica, charmed by the joey's antics, laughed aloud. Easy to see how kangaroos had evolved in a land where they had plenty of room for their fantastic bounding!

"At certain speeds, kangaroos are far more efficient than horses," Cyrus told her. "There are so many of them they're a damned nuisance, but so much part of the land-scape you have to love them. They can go without water for a while, but they don't stray too far from it. There are billabongs nearby. And all those standing 'monuments' you see around us are termite mounds."

"They're extraordinary." Jessica looked out over the vast terrain where termite mounds sprang up like ancient build-ings. Wide at the base, very narrow at the tip, many of them were nearly twenty feet tall. "Can we take a closer look?"

"Of course. We might even catch a piece of action."

Jessica soon found out what he meant. Fierce little lizards with forked tongues were trying on burrow their way out of one mound, almost twice Cyrus's height.

"Oh, goodness!" Jessica jumped back as several foot-long monsters clawed their way to the surface of the termite walls and clambered eagerly down their length.

"Won't take them long to reach six feet or more," Cyrus told her, amused by her reaction. "Goannas are harmless to man though I'd steer clear of the big fellas. They grow to more than eight feet and have very powerful limbs. I wouldn't want to try outrunning one."

"So they incubate in there?" Jessica asked, moving back cautiously, expecting more to emerge.

Cyrus nodded. "All goannas lay eggs. They've been in there around nine months. The mounds are the perfect protection. By the same token they present a formidable barrier when the newly hatched babies want to get out. Those walls are rock hard."

Jessica stretched out a tentative hand. She had seen the newly hatched goannas formidable claws.

"It's June now." Cyrus raised his face to the cloudless sky. "In another five months, when the monsoon comes, probably the most powerful weather system on the planet, all this—" he waved his arm "—becomes a very different place. The Wet has a dramatic effect on the landscape. Rain falls so hard our creeks, lagoons and billabongs fill to overflowing and inundate the plains. Falling Waters, the waterfall I showed you when we flew in, becomes a mighty torrent. As the rains subside, we have a glimpse of what ancient Gondwanaland—the supercontinent— looked like. Wildflowers bloom in exotic profusion, quite different to the floral carpets of the Red Centre with their endless vistas of paper daisies. These are tropical flowers. This part of the Territory, the Top End, lies in the torrid zone. And abundance of native fruits and vegetables ripen. The land turns lush and green. You get a real feel for the prehistoric past. There's a plentiful harvest for all— humans, animals, birds. We've got more species of animals, most of them unique, than Europe and North

America put together. That happened when Australia broke away from Asia. The water birds have to be seen to be believed. They arrive in their millions. It's an incredible sight. The crocs don't have to swim about in lagoons fast turning to mud or do their extraordinary overland gallop to find a pool that hasn't dried out. It's paradise while it lasts. A few months. Then the dry southeast trade winds arrive. By July, the plains will have started to dry out and all the waterways shrink. We have a few lagoons with deep permanent water like the lagoon at the foot of Falling Waters. By October, every living thing is waiting for the return of the Wet."

"Are we going to the escarpment?" She lifted her gaze to his, feeling the familiar surge of pleasure.

"If you want. We'll drive some more, then have to go by foot." He glanced up at the table-topped mesa. It wasn't particularly high, but the flatness of the giant landscape lent it considerable impact. From this distance, it glowed amethyst. "Tell me, is all the interest because of what Livvy said?" His look was very direct. "Livvy has never been exactly *normal.* Even, I understand, when she was a young woman. She has her own way of seeing things. She gets muddled up between past and present—as you know by now."

"What's normal?" Jessica shrugged.

"I suspect one can't talk to long-dead people to qualify," he said very dryly.

"I suppose not. Has she always talked about Moira?"

He sighed as though bored to death by the whole subject. "Not until *you* arrived, which in itself is quite extraordinary, don't you think?"

"I didn't plan it, Cyrus," she said, not for the first time, aware of his suspicions. "It's quite scary to be confused with someone who disappeared off the face of the earth."

"But she *didn't*." His tone was softly vehement. "Somewhere on this land, in some crevice, in some cave, lie Moira's bones. The number of deaths in the Outback by misadventure is quite frightening. Moira wasn't a good rider or an experienced one. She had, in fact, learned on the station. The horse came home as horses do eventually. Moira didn't." His face hardened. "I find this whole business of Moira, tragic as it is, phenomenally upsetting. For a while, my entire family was under suspicion, despite the proud Bannerman name. My grandfather was a war hero. He flew Spitfires in the Battle of Britain and reached the rank of squadron leader. He was decorated. How would you like it if your grandparents were thought capable of murder?"

"They say we're all capable of murder, given overwhelming circumstances," Jessica said bleakly.

He flinched. "Let's start again. My grandparents were fine people. Highly respected all over the Outback. Everyone was fond of Moira. She loved being on Mokhani. According to Lavinia, a thousand times she said she didn't want to go home."

"Who exactly was Hughie?" Jessica asked abruptly. "What relation?"

"Look—" His brilliant blue eyes flashed.

"Cyrus." She grasped his arm. "I don't want to upset you, but this whole business, the Mokhani Mystery, has never been laid to rest. It haunts Lavinia. It haunts your father. It haunts *you*, fifty years later. There must be something more to it than the tragedy of someone becoming lost in the bush and perishing. I know it's happened many, many times over the years, but with Moira there appear to be so many suspicions. That's why journalists can't leave it alone. Now by some truly bizarre twist of fate, I'm involved in it."

"I don't disagree with that," he said somberly.

"Simply because by some freak of nature I look extraordinarily like her," Jessica went on to say.

His brow furrowed in puzzlement. "But how would you actually *know* that? You can't rely too much on what Livvy says."

"I'm not," Jessica answered quietly, turning her head away. It was about time she told him about the portrait Tim had uncovered, no doubt increasing his lack of trust. "You still haven't told me who Hughie was."

The question did nothing to ease his somber expression. "He was Hugh Balfour, my grandmother Cecily's cousin. Livvy told you about him?"

H.B., of course. "She told me Hugh liked to paint Moira."

"Maybe he did," he answered curtly, "but I've never seen anything he did outside the portrait of my grandfather."

"You're certain?"

"Of course I'm certain." Cy's temper flared. "Finding a portrait of Moira would be a major discovery."

"One has been found," Jessica said, watching him snap to full attention. "It was bought at a Sydney auction by my uncle's partner simply because it reminded him of me."

Cyrus's strong hands grasped her shoulders. "What the devil are you talking about? I think you'd better level with me."

"I'm trying to, if you let me. Tim attended a Christie's art auction a short time back. So did Lavinia, apparently without your aunt Barbara's knowledge. Tim's interest was captured by the uncanny likeness. Lavinia would have recognized it right off. Who knows seeing the portrait after all this time hasn't disturbed the

balance of her mind? She didn't tell your aunt because
she thought it would upset her greatly. According to
Tim, he had a confrontation with Lavinia afterward.
She offered to buy if off him, but he refused. Lord
knows what she intended to do with it. Probably
confront your father with it for reasons of her own. At
the moment, it's hanging in the foyer of our design
studio in Brisbane."

Cyrus's hands dropped away. He wheeled to calm
himself. "What's the time frame here?" He turned back to
face her, looking quite daunting. "When did this mysterious portrait turn up? Before or after Dad hired you?"

She reacted to the hard flare in his eyes. "It would have
been put up for auction some time before your father
offered me the job. Please don't take your anger out on me.
I know nothing about any behind-the-scene machinations,
if indeed there *are* any."

"Of course there are. You're not stupid." Stern blue
eyes stared down at her.

She shrugged. "I admit it all seems very odd. My uncle
and I were discussing the project the same day Tim returned
from Sydney with the portrait. At that time I had absolutely
no idea who the subject was. Why should I? None of us did.
It was simply a portrait given to Christie's for auction. Tim
only bought it because it reminded him of me."

"And there's no connection?"

"Absolutely not!" She reacted sharply to his tone. "I
wonder you ask. Lavinia hasn't laid eyes on Moira for over
fifty years. It's coincidence, the whole thing. Chance rules
our lives after all." So why, then, was she so perplexed and
confused?

"Lavinia's brain might be a little skewed as to time, but
she obviously recognized Moira. She would have known

it was Hugh Balfour's work. *Who* put it on the market. Can you find out?"

"Tim tried, in fact, but got nowhere. A solicitor handled it for a client. The solicitor is not saying."

"I suppose we've all got a double," he said doubtfully.

"So they say. But the portrait gave us all a shock. It would shock you if you saw it."

"Oh, I will see it," he said grimly, beginning to walk toward the Jeep. "All right, I've had about enough of Moira for today."

JESSICA WAS GLAD SHE WAS FIT and took regular exercise, because they had to walk up the track, which was tough going but infinitely rewarding. To one side of them lay rugged bushland, to the other magical glimpses of the lagoon and the multicolored walls of the canyon. By the time they neared the high plateau, her hair was damp with sweat and her pink cotton shirt stuck to her back.

"You okay?" He stretched out a hand to her. The spark where their hands touched wasn't just a physical thing.

"Fine."

"You're doing well. Pretend a dingo is chasing you."

"I think I can make it under my own steam, thank you."

He looked back at her. The flush of exertion in her cheeks only served to enhance the flawlessness of her skin and the clear green of her eyes. She was a beautiful woman. He had to assume her lookalike Moira had been beautiful, too. Hadn't his grandmother Cecily been a little naive bringing a beautiful young woman into the household? The family had lived in such isolation, but paradoxically in close proximity to one another. Beauty made waves. It disturbed the very air. He reached down with fluid ease and lifted this maddening young woman up the rest of the way.

"We're here!" he announced, finding it nigh on impossible to release his hold on her. Her head had sunk against his left shoulder and she was moaning softly at the exertion.

"It better be worth it." Jessica straightened, laughing, until she saw the expression in his eyes. Was it desire?

The raucous cry of a bird broke the spell of the moment.

"I should have brought my camera." She busied herself retying the lace of her shoe, shocked at how quickly he could stir her body to arousal.

"We've got hundreds and hundreds of photographs."

"I'd love to see them."

"And so you shall. We can fit in quite a bit before Dad gets home."

Jessica let out a shaky breath. She started to move off toward the edge, feeling slightly light-headed.

"Jessica, *no!*" His voice cracked out, loud and urgent. He caught her up swiftly, pulling her back. "The lip could crumble at any time. Those rocks and boulders down there in the canyon have come from up here. Never, ever go near the edge."

"It's okay." She tried to soothe him. "I wasn't going to. It's a pretty vertiginous drop, anyway." His cry of *no!* had had the velocity of a bullet. "I just wanted a better look at the lagoon."

"Stay with me." He drew her back against his chest.

"You're the boss." She could have remained there forever. "It must be wonderful to preside over your own kingdom," she murmured, filled with a piercing exhilaration. "This is fantastic. It's like we're on another planet. It's daunting, too, all that empty vastness without end. It would be so easy to die out there."

"Just you remember it," he said, the harshness still

evident in his voice. "Don't go wandering off on your own. We've had seasoned bushmen get lost."

"So not everything's a mystery." The remains of the little governess could be anywhere out there in the wilderness. Moira could have been injured; thrown from her horse, lying helpless, vulnerable to the attack of wild animals. She had heard the dingoes howling at night. The deadliest snake in the world, the taipan, had its home here; marauding camels, wild horses, foxes, wild boar, feral cats as fierce as miniature lions. A massive search for Moira had been mounted. Jessica had read that in all of the articles she had sourced on the computer. The search had revealed nothing. Today, looking out at the ancient land spread before her as far as she could see, she didn't find that so strange.

Her eyes dropped to the deep lagoon. It looked so beautiful, the vegetation fresh and green even in the Dry. The waterfall, which apparently would become a deafening roar in the Wet, was tranquil today, spilling its crystal purity from the top of the escarpment whence it flowed to the water's edge. The lagoon was surrounded by aquatic reeds and grasses of a lush emerald green. The glittering water floated its cargo of magnificent pink water lilies holding their heads high above huge pads. Around the base of the escarpment grew a luxuriant tangle of exquisitely colored creepers that climbed into the stands of pandanus palms decorating their spikes. It was like looking down into an earthly paradise.

"The view from here is magnificent, but is it possible to walk the length of the canyon?" she asked him, eager to try.

He nodded. "Yes, but let's take one thing at a time. There are grottos at the base of the cliffs sculptured by the water over thousands of years. In the Wet, the high waters drown out everything down there."

"So there could be a crocodile still in residence, you're suggesting? Perhaps with a mate or two?"

"No one has sighted one," he answered, frowning at the thought. "Which doesn't mean one isn't there. Aboriginal stockmen take dips in the lagoons—those are the guys with the crocodile totem. We haven't had a fatality at Falling Waters."

One you know about, at any rate, she thought. "But elsewhere?" she asked.

"We've had a couple of stockmen taken over the years. Working dogs. Cattle. Kangaroos, of course. They never learn. This is the Territory. We have to live with the crocs. We respect them."

"No matter how great your detestation?"

"I don't detest them," he said. "I don't trust 'em either. The trick is not to stand near the edge of a river or lagoon where they're known to be. We're not that far from Kakadu National Park and the Alligator Rivers system. The person who named the East and South Alligator rivers thought the prehistoric beasts he saw lining their banks *were* alligators. Of course they were crocs. The rivers should have been named the East and South Crocodile rivers. Kakadu inspires reverence. The Aborigines worship the place. If you're lucky, we could take a trip in. It's only accessible— and then only parts of it—in the Dry. In the Wet, enormous stretches turn into water-lily-covered lagoons supporting phenomenal birdlife. A white mist hangs over the dripping canopy of the rain forest, adding to the primeval look. Waterfalls thunder. Our waterfall is a trickle compared to them. You'd swear you were back at the beginning of time."

"So why can't we pack up and go tomorrow?" She knew they couldn't, but her heart swelled at the very thought.

"Tomorrow's out, I'm afraid."

"I was only joking," she said, shaking her head. "I have a ton of work to get through."

"You've done sketches, that kind of thing?"

"Plenty," she said. "I'm getting close to what I want to achieve. I've designed quite a number of pieces that will be custom-made. The rooms are so huge, but the six guest rooms will be a piece of cake. As will the other bedrooms. I have a good idea what Broderick—"

"Did he ask you to call him that, or was it your own idea?" he cut in.

"Left to myself I'd be calling him Mr. Bannerman for the rest of my life," Jessica retorted crisply, moving away from him a little. "He asked me to call him Broderick. *Ordered* really. Arrogance runs in the family."

"You should be flattered," Cy said. "Dad's a different man around you."

"What are you implying?" Her voice rose.

"I'm not implying anything. It's a simple statement of fact. My father is a different man around you."

"Maybe you should be grateful." She shrugged. "I find calling him Broderick rather embarrassing, but I can scarcely disregard his wishes."

"Of course not," he agreed suavely.

She chose another tack. "The great hall is the biggest challenge. I have to get that right. I have a good idea what your father wants for the conference room and the tele-communications room. I'm in constant contact with my uncle Brett. Nothing will go ahead without his say-so."

"Something wrong with your judgment?" he inquired.

"Not at all. But this is an important project. I work for my uncle, as well as your father. Uncle Brett taught me all I know. Eventually, we'll need a team of people up here, as I've told you. Before that happens, I have to work it all out in my head and on paper. That includes color schemes. I work from the floor up."

"Isn't that a lot to deal with for a relatively inexperienced twenty-four-year-old?"

She knew he was baiting her. "It is. But someone's got to do it. It may seem like heresy, but I prefer the original homestead. Please don't tell your father that."

"Not unless I want to stop your winning streak," he told her with a mocking glance. "I prefer the old homestead, too, as I've said. It looked a million times better before Robyn was let loose on it. Notice the minimalism on the walls? She solved the problem by shoving the paintings my mother had put there away. The Oriental screens and rugs were next. All the touches of Southeast Asia my mother loved and so suited the house. The porcelains and big fishbowls on carved stands. The fishbowls used to be filled with orchids. They stood on either side of the staircase. Robyn removed every vestige of my mother from the house. And my father let her."

"Perhaps he found it too painful," Jessica suggested, hearing the bitterness in his tone. "Didn't you make your feelings known?"

He grimaced. "I did, but it made no difference. I'm biding my time. I could at some time in the future have the mausoleum razed to the ground."

"Oh, don't do that," she advised. "It will have its uses. If not as a residence, than as a conference and business centre. I'm assuming you will take over your father's extensive business interests?"

"You're assuming a lot." He spoke very dryly. "My father is an extremely unpredictable man, a strange man in anyone's judgment. He's become increasingly hard and aloof as he's grown older. You've brought with you a troubling sea change. For all I know he could be planning to start another family. Sire a new heir. He could have met a woman he'd risk his soul to possess. I know he'd like to be young again. He makes no bones about it. He wants to be my age again, wants his life all over again. Dad won't ever be content with his allotted portion. He wants life everlasting. Maybe he thinks a young woman would bring it to him."

She couldn't control a shiver. "That's quite Faustian. I hope to goodness you're not looking at *me* for the job?" Jessica felt the shock break over her.

He stared into her eyes. "A lot of women, young, good-looking women, would fight to the death to marry Dad. Money is the perfect aphrodisiac, didn't you know?"

"Not for *me* it isn't." Jessica said emphatically.

"Really? That's heartening to know. So tell me, what is it you want, Jessica? *Love?*" His blue eyes were melting not only her limbs but her brain.

"Don't you?" she parried. "I thought love is what we all want. And *need*. Why is it every time you mention your mother I can hear the grief? Your father suffered from the loss, too. He'd made a powerful emotional connection with your mother, Deborah, then she was cruelly taken away from him. A man could become very bitter from that experience. Your father is a very rich man, but no one could describe him as at peace, much less happy."

"God, no. His life has been difficult. There's no denying that. The tragedy in his childhood—the invasion of privacy the family suffered—was the start of his misery. He never got over his governess's disappearance. His twin, Aunt Barbara, was adversely affected, as well. Both of them were almost twelve before they were ready to be sent away to boarding school. My grandmother taught them herself. I went to boarding school at ten. Even then the Mokhani Mystery was still alive. I guess we'll never be free of it."

Her answer came out unconsidered and of its own accord. "Maybe that's about to change."

"Why do you say that?" He turned on her.

"Just a feeling I have."

"You're psychic, then? That explains it?"

Tense moments ticked over. "Don't you sense that, too?" she responded to the challenge.

His expression was dark and brooding. "All I know is, when the past intrudes on the present, there can be unwanted consequences."

CHAPTER NINE

JESSICA REMINDED HERSELF SHE had to work even on
Sunday. She would have to have something fairly impressive to show Broderick Bannerman when he returned, so
she sat at her desk working away, though with perhaps not
her usual serene efficiency. Her emotions were in a kind
of turmoil. So many things were happening that her life
had taken on new dimensions, some thrilling, some
ominous and strange. Added to that, she had discovered
within herself a certain recklessness and a taste for danger.
Infatuation, falling in love, was an extreme state, after all.
  Violent delights could have violent ends.
  Hadn't Shakespeare said it all? She was in daily com-
munication with Brett, speaking to him each morning on
the phone, then sending him reams of sketches and information by e-mail. When she was ready, she would make
watercolor renderings of her proposals. She needed to take
that trip into Darwin to stock up on her art supplies. She
supposed she could make the two-hour journey on her
own in the four-wheel drive B.B. had put at her disposal.
There were bound to be plenty of readable signs, preferably the ones not featuring a skull and crossbones. There
was something very daunting about a dead straight road
that ran through endless uninhabited miles of shifting red
sand blanketed with spinifex.

Over dinner, Cyrus relaxed, his heart-melting smile much in evidence as he and Lavinia recounted stories from the family's past—mercifully without the complications of the family ghost. Molly, the housekeeper, joined in, displaying her own puckish sense of humor. Cyrus and Lavinia treated Molly as one of the family; B.B. and Robyn treated her like a programmed robot. There was no question of Molly's sitting down to join them either for a cup of coffee or a meal when Broderick Bannerman was in residence. Servants had their place as far as B.B. was concerned.

Afterward, Lavinia, in high spirits, brought some of her favourite CDs downstairs for the occasion, comparing this soprano against that, turning up the volume so high the station staff in their bungalows and dormitories probably had to shout at one another to be heard. Cyrus indulged her, with only a mild "Turn it down a bit, Livvy," as criticism, but soon Lavinia was up and away, reminiscing about her career.

"I do believe I could have been as great as Sutherland," she told them, not for the first time. "Marvelous voice, marvelous technique, but oh, there was something about poor tragic Callas I adored. The *passion* in her voice! I miss that. No one else has it. I can't hear her without the tears coming to my eyes."

Occasionally, she astonished Jessica, but not the others, who had probably heard these performances many times before, by belting out a top note along with the diva on the CD. Of course Lavinia's voice was being supported by the voice singing with her, but Jessica realized she was hearing however briefly, little patches of what once had been a brilliant coloratura soprano. Molly, having produced another one of her delicious meals, poured more wine. Both ladies sat sipping contentedly while Cyrus and Jessica excused themselves for a short stroll before turning in.

That, too, proved intoxicating, though Cyrus made no move that could have been construed as romantic. Nevertheless, an exquisite tension vibrated between them as if neither knew where or when or even how the tension would manifest itself in action. Jessica looked and listened as he pointed out the stars in the night sky and their spiritual significance to the Aboriginal tribes of the Top End. That in itself provided an element of the romance she was starting to crave. In Aboriginal life over countless thousands of years, when the people slept out beneath the stars, the moon and the stars had assumed great significance.

"They know every star in the sky," Cyrus said, his tone full of appreciation. "There's a legend to explain every origin. Such beautiful myths and legends, too. No matter how many times you hear them, you don't mind hearing them again. I used to find them enthralling when I was a kid around the campfire listening to a stockman—who also happened to be a tribal elder—telling them so soulfully. Aboriginal gods and goddesses are all too human. The sun is a woman—a beautiful woman who spreads light and warmth. The moon is a man. All the stars and planets were at the time of creation, men, women and animals. They flew up to the sky when times were bad on earth. The sky was their refuge. The Gagudju people of Arnhem Land believe a shooting star is a spirit canoe transporting a soul to its new home."

"You were blessed with a childhood out here," she said.

He nodded. "I don't know what I would do if it were taken away. Mokhani is my life."

She could hear the love and pride in his voice. She thought, as she did so often these days, how difficult it must have been for him growing up without the love and support of his mother, especially given his father's unyielding nature. He must have been wounded over and over in the past. Probably continued to be to this day, though he had grown an extra skin. B.B. seemed to be hell-bent on having control and mastery over everyone, but in his son he had chosen the wrong man to try to dominate.

"Home is where the heart and the soul find their most comfortable place," she murmured into the starry night. "I've never seen such a glorious night sky." Her eyes were on the blue-white scintillating broad river of diamonds across the sky. The Milky Way. It shone with great brilliance and luminosity in the pure air of the Outback.

"No pollution," Cyrus explained. "No buildings, no glass and concrete towers, just the timeless land. There's the Southern Cross sparkling over us. It couldn't be clearer. The star furthermost to the south is a star of the first magnitude. It's said the ancient Greeks and Babylonians were able to see it. They thought it was part of the constellation Centaurus, so that's how much the Crux has shifted. The night sky in the Red Center is purported to be the most beautiful sky on earth. There again, it's rarified desert air and our isolation. We might be able to fit in a trip there."

"That would be wonderful." Jessica felt like a plant fast unfurling its fronds. But like tender new fronds exposed to sizzling heat, she could get burned. She had divined that the moment she'd laid eyes on Cyrus Bannerman at Darwin airport.

TO EVERYONE'S DELIGHT, Cyrus returned to the homestead for lunch. Something he rarely did when his father was there, which was perfectly understandable considering the two men were often at loggerheads.

"Darling boy, how lovely it is to have your company."

Lavinia sat up straight in her planter's chair. She and Jessica had been sitting companionably on the front veranda enjoying the brilliant display of strelitzias in the garden. Now Lavinia jumped up, surprisingly spry in the legs when her once-elegant hands were knotted with arthritis. "I'll tell Molly you're here. She'll be so pleased. Broderick could stay away forever, as far as we're concerned."

"Don't go to any trouble," Cyrus called after her, pitching his Akubra into a chair. "Coffee and a sandwich will do.

"So, making progress?" he asked, pulling out a chair and settling into it "You'll have to have lots to show Dad." A lock of crow-black hair fell over his forehead and he put up a hand, raking it back. Jessica let her eyes rest on him. He was wearing his usual working gear, an open-necked pale blue bush shirt, jeans, dusty high boots, a red bandanna knotted carelessly around his throat.

He looked marvelous, so intensely vital he took her breath away. How could any woman ignore a man like that? It took a moment or two for her to answer. "You'll be pleased to hear I've been at my drawing board all morning. Mostly sketching designs for the custom-made furniture I told you about. Regardless of size and scale, the pieces must represent intimacy. It's a private residence, after all. I want to stick to the classical idiom, but obviously with a twenty-first century twist. The furnishings need to be elegant, functional, with pure, clean lines, if you know what I mean. The architecture speaks for itself."

"You're able to do that?" He looked at her as if she might have bitten off more than she could chew.

"Sure. My goal is to push myself to the limits. I have talent. I'd like to do more furniture designing down the track. My uncle Brett has won awards for furniture design. He's been my mentor."

"I'd like to meet him," Cyrus said. "He sounds a very talented guy, and obviously you love him."

"I'm sure it could be arranged. He's gay," she tacked on casually.

He cocked an eyebrow. "So? I'm not looking for a relationship."

"Just thought I'd mention it. Uncle Brett is a very clever, multitalented man. He trained as an architect, which has been an enormous help with his work."

"Tell me, do you see something embarrassing about his being gay?"

"Not at all!" She shook her head "I wanted to see your reaction, cattlemen being such macho types. I love my uncle dearly. He's been very good to me, but he's suffered in his way."

"I daresay," he answered, letting the *macho* bit go. "One can't afford to be different. But tell me about *yourself*, Jessica. I'm all ears."

She found that electrifying. "What do you want to know?"

"Everything. Go on. Give it to me. I know you're beautiful and gifted. You certainly don't lack confidence. You think you can conquer the world. I like that. I've got big plans of my own. Tell me about when you were a little girl. I bet you were adored, with your big green eyes and your blond curls."

She looked out over the garden before replying. "It wasn't quite like that," she said wryly, by now used to the way life really was. "I'm an only child. My father is a high-profile lawyer, senior partner in a firm started by my great grandfather. I think he felt betrayed when my mother couldn't give him a son. Mum always says so, anyway. There was just curly-headed me. To make it worse, I don't look at all like him or that side of the family. I was a good student, at least, so he expected me to follow him into law. Show some ambition. Instead, I opted for a fine-arts degree, which I gained with honors. But it wasn't a degree my father thought much of. He's made no bones about the fact that as far as he's concerned I've let the family down. Especially as I went to work for Uncle Brett. The *different* factor came into play there. Dad is a great one for civil liberties and the rights of minority groups, but he's actually ultraconservative at heart. Needless to say, Brett and my father don't get on. In fact, they avoid one another, which makes it hard. Practicing law in my family is considered by all to be far more important than practicing art of any kind."

"Poor Jessica." He reached out, his palm briefly cupping her cheek. It was a gesture so unexpected, so *tender*, it nearly washed away her hidden tears. "I didn't expect to hear that. You certainly *look* very loved."

"Well, I am." She didn't fully understand why she had told him so much, but he affected her on all levels. "Don't get me wrong. Maybe it's just not in the way I'd choose. I was very close to my maternal grandmother, Brett's mother. Closer even than to my own mother, who likes her own space. Nan was my haven when my teenage world went mad. Sadly, she died some years back, but her memory will always remain with me. A lot of the time I feel she's looking out for me. Brett and I have the same coloring, the same family face. Both of us take after Nan."

"She didn't, by any chance, have a Moira in the family?" Cy's voice had a sardonic edge.

"Good grief, no." Jessica shook her head. "Don't you think Moira would have been mentioned in passing? Especially given what happened to her? Had Moira lived she would have been a couple of years older than my nan. Someone like that would have haunted my family as much as she's haunted yours. Left alone to die—"

"We don't know *what* happened to her," he cut in, his voice hardening slightly. "I'd very much like to see that portrait of yours."

"That can be arranged. I'll ask Tim to e-mail a photograph first. Tim is Uncle Brett's partner in life and business. Once you see it, it'll be your turn to be astonished. Did you ever find out what Moira's parents had to say after she disappeared?"

He sighed deeply. "Jessica, I missed all that, not having been born. Moira belongs to another time, another world. I just wish she'd stay there. My *father* was only a child."

"But you must have heard *something* over the years," she persisted. "I mean, they couldn't just paper her over or abandon her to a deep watery realm. Moira is part of your family's history."

"I assure you there's no need to constantly remind me. All I know is her parents journeyed up here to see for themselves. I believe they were an older couple. Moira was a child of their middle years. Naturally they were filled with grief but compelled to accept, as everyone else did, that Moira had died by misadventure. Either she'd become lost in the bush, fallen from the escarpment or even drowned. Despite an intensive search, she was never found. Have you spoken to Livvy about any of this?"

"Not for now. She knows about the existence of the portrait, of course. She told me about her confrontation with Tim. She claimed he wasn't a gentleman because he didn't give it to her. I didn't tell her of my connection to Tim. Neither did I tell her I'd actually seen the portrait. She thinks there should be others, or at least one, here at Mokhani."

He groaned. "Well she would. Livvy is a creature of the theatre. She loves dramas. My father denies it."

"I recall you said he tells lies."

"Jessica, please."

She searched his face for a moment. Blazing blue eyes. Enigmatic. Maybe a little hostile.

"That's no answer." She knew he didn't trust his father. For that matter, neither did she.

"Perhaps you should ask Dad yourself," he suggested dryly. "Where exactly do you stand with my father?"

Hot color bloomed in her cheeks. She swiped her long beautiful hair over her shoulder. "I scarcely know him— he isn't an easy man to know. As for me, what you see is what you get. Why can't you accept that?"

"Too many coincidences along the way. What do you suppose was my father's first thought when he saw you on that television program? Hey, this is a young designer who could bring off decorating my mausoleum? What could be more B.B. than going with his instincts? They're so sharp they're feral. Or did the image of his former governess block out every other consideration? He may have been a child at the time of her disappearance, but that image has been kept alive. Something has to be feeding it. It's like a fairy tale by the Brothers Grimm. Maybe Hugh's paintings of her were hidden away, but given my father's temperament and his excessive persistence, he would have gone hunting for them. He's the best hunter in the world. Maybe it was *he* who put the painting you've got on the market? It would have been too beautiful to destroy. Maybe it was a member of Hugh's family. Who the hell knows? Maybe one day Dad stumbled upon the hiding place— 'Nice to see you again, Moira!'"

"A bit melodramatic don't you think?" Though she didn't disagree with any of it.

"Hell, Jessica, we're all experts on melodrama with Dad and Lavinia playing the leads." He leaned toward her, unconsciously emanating tremendous male allure. "We could go on a treasure hunt together."

"We should." She was quick to agree.

Lavinia chose that very moment to stomp back onto the veranda in her monk's habit worn with gym boots. Jessica found herself wondering when Lavinia would come down to breakfast in a pink tutu. "What are you two whispering about?" she stared at them with deep satisfaction.

"I've asked Jessica to marry me," Cyrus said calmly.

"When?" Lavinia asked delightedly, turning her head to peer at Jessica, who was past being surprised by anything, however outlandish, that was said.

But shouldn't that *when* been an astonished *What!* or a *Wow!* "I've had to tell him no," Jessica said. "I won't be crowded by proposals. I'm not ready to tie the knot for years yet."

Lavinia hurried over to touch her shoulder. "But darling girl, you have to get on with your life," she protested. "You've wasted so much time already."

Jessica caught Cyrus's searing glance. "You went too far with that one," she muttered.

"You're worried I wasn't serious?"

"To be serious a man has to get on his knees."

Lavinia beamed at him. "*Do* it, Cy! Don't let her get away again."

When he moved, Jessica jumped up, placing her chair in front of her as a barrier. "This has gone far enough, thank you, Cyrus. We're joking, Miss Lavinia. Just fooling around."

Lavinia made a little birdlike cry of pain, tears welling

up in her eyes. "But you're *perfect* for each other! You don't doubt that, do you, dear?"

"Miss Lavinia, I'm Jessica. Moira hasn't come back again."

Lavinia's chin wobbled. "No, of course not."

"You understand that, Livvy," Cyrus said, drawing a great sigh of relief for that chink of sanity. He regretted the fact, however, they had upset her.

"Yes, I do, darling. It's just that…" She turned and stared beseechingly at Jessica. "You *are* Moira, though, aren't you?" she whispered as though Cyrus couldn't hear.

"I'm planning to take you out riding this afternoon, Jessica," Cy intervened in an endeavor to head Lavinia off. "We should be able to find you a nice quiet horse."

"Thank you, thank you," she said sweetly sardonic. "I'm so grateful. This is the happiest day of my life."

"Yes, indeed. It's not every day a girl gets a marriage proposal," Lavinia said, yanking on her saffron robe. "Just wait until Broderick hears about it. He won't be pleased. He wants you for himself." She cackled as though she'd said something very funny.

"The most useful thing about growing old is you can get away with saying anything," Cyrus observed, his tone a little harsh. "Although in all fairness I have to say there's been something to Livvy's revelations in the past."

"Oh, stop. Livvy's revelations are way off this time," Jessica said tartly.

"Just teasing, Jessica," he said. "I really don't fancy you as a stepmother."

"Which part of *stop* don't you understand?"

"I told you I jest. Though deep down—"

Jessica couldn't restrain herself any longer. She picked up a plush cushion and began belting him with it.

Molly, eyes bright with pleasure, came out on to the veranda at a brisk trot. "You're a one, Jessica, so you are!"

"So she is!" Cyrus put his hand very gently around Jessica's wrist and took the cushion from her, throwing it back on the chair. "I'm not used to women who play rough."

"That's hard to believe," Jessica said, "when you're the most infuriating person I've ever met."

"Now, now, my darlings!" Lavinia intervened. "It's only an excuse to kiss and make up. You were doing great, Moira. I think you scared him."

"So there it is!" he declared. "You've become one of Lavinia's incurable hallucinations."

"If you're hungry, and I hope you are, I've set up lunch on the rear terrace," Molly intervened, her cheeks flushed with pleasure.

"Oh, goody, hurray! If only there were more Mollys in this world." Lavinia executed a little pirouette, holding her arms aloft for balance. "If it weren't for you, Molly, we'd all starve."

It wasn't until later in the afternoon when the heat was less oppressive and the fiery exposure to the sun lessened that Jessica made her way down to the stables, where Cyrus had arranged to meet her. He was running a little late, so she had the Aboriginal stable boy, Seth, saddle up a lively looking filly called Chloe. Jessica had taken to the filly, one of obvious good blood, on sight. Chloe in turn appeared to like the smell, voice and touch of Jessica. They made friends over a couple of oatmeal cookies.

"That's pretty damn good." Seth grinned his approval. "Most people have to watch themselves around that one. Chances are she might throw ya."

"I don't think so, Seth." Jessica continued to stroke the filly's sleek neck, making soothing clicking sounds at the same time. Chloe was jet-black, well-groomed, with a white blaze on her forehead.

"She got speed and she got spirit." Seth spoke with love and pride. "A real high stepper and a natural jumper, but she ain't an easy ride." He gave her a black liquid glance. "Threw Miss Bannerman, but then, Miss Bannerman got bad habits."

"Robyn?" Jessica turned to stare at him.

"Yes, ma'am. Chloe here don't like to be pushed around. She's a beautiful sweet girl when you know how to handle her right, but when ya don't…" Seth pulled a face. "Miss Bannerman don't treat the horses right. She think she got to be in control all the time. Thing is, she don't really like horses and they don't like her. Tell you the truth, the boss won't be happy you picked Chloe. He told me to saddle up Manny. A nice sedate horse. I gotta do what I'm told."

Jessica had already met Manny, a bay gelding, as she'd entered the stables. Manny was friendly, extending his silky muzzle to be stroked. She had fed him an oatmeal biscuit before leaving him in peace. "That's okay, Seth. I'll explain to him that Chloe was my choice."

"Manny is the nicest, quietest ride we've got." Seth tried to persuade her.

"I'm not surprised." Jessica smiled. "Manny's just about due for retirement. Chloe and I are a better match. Don't worry. I know how to ride."

"Thought so, seeing how you are around 'em, but Chloe can be full of mischief. Skittish, I call it. Why she has days she gallops off in all directions."

"Don't you worry," Jessica repeated. "It won't take me long to get Chloe to trust me."

JESSICA WAS TROTTING the responsive Chloe around the yard when Cyrus arrived. He stood stock still for a moment watching the proceedings. "Okay, so you can ride," he observed dryly. "Why didn't you tell me?"

"I thought I'd take the mickey out of you," she responded sweetly. "I've been riding since I was a little girl."

"I can see that." He had checked her out automatically, his mind processing all the information that told him she was perfectly at home on a horse. In fact, she looked great, a good seat, well balanced, straight back.

She brought the filly to a halt beside him. "Your automatic assumption I would sit like a sack of potatoes piqued me."

He gave a faint smile. "Oh, well, you are a city girl."

"This city girl lived on acreage. My nan, Alex, bought me my first pony when I was six. My parents didn't really want me to have it, but I was thrilled out of my mind. My father saw to it I was well taught. I joined a good pony club."

"What a piece of luck." He turned back as Seth led out his horse—a gleaming, silver-gray Thoroughbred, clearly no workhorse, but a horse reserved for pure pleasure.

"What a beautiful animal," Jessica said with appreciation. She had an excellent eye and instinct for good horses. The gray was superb.

"Monarch," Cyrus pronounced. With a nod to Seth, he took charge of his horse. "So named because there's nothing comparable in our stables. So don't bother racing me."

"I'm not that foolish. You've got the superior horse. Monarch must be a good sixteen hands high, but then, a tall horse for a tall man. Chloe is only a filly, but I can outwit you."

"You can't. I know this land like the back of my hand." He stared up at her. She had bound her long hair into a thick plait, revealing her very pretty ears. For a moment, he thought he could taste the creamy lobes in his mouth.

"So what are we waiting for?" She didn't know it, but her face was lit with such exuberance, that feeling was transferring itself to him. "Come on," she urged. "You've stared at me long enough. Let's get going. Tallyho!" She clicked her tongue, lightly kicked the filly's flanks and the spirited animal spurted into action.

She was off and away before Cyrus had time to swing into the saddle.

What a surprise packet Jessica was turning out to be! he thought with a mix of amusement and admiration. She even put him on his mettle. She was scooting across the back paddock in a genuine gallop, approaching the white post and rail fence where a short distance off, a glossy-flanked chestnut mare was pacing with her beautiful foal.

No! For God's sweet sake, no! His heart rose to his throat as he saw Jessica lean forward, rising in the saddle as she gave the filly the signal to jump.

"God almighty!" High spirits were one thing, but you had to have nerve and confidence galore to attempt that fence. Robyn always stooped to unlatch the gate. So did most visitors to the stables.

Jessica had both confidence and nerve. Horse and rider soared, clearing the top rail with maybe an inch to spare. That the filly showed a surprisingly clean pair of rear hooves was brought to his attention. Chloe could make a show jumper. He could hear Jessica whooping with delight. He knew the incredible feeling of exhilaration and power, but his moment of fear was legitimate and had its roots in the tragedy that had taken his mother. Yet risk appeared to be a state Jessica happily embraced. Risk, to the point of recklessness. His mother had been reckless. Her dying in a riding accident had left a deep wound that would never heal.

Suddenly he felt mad as hell. Why hadn't he insisted she wear a hard hat? Because she had let him believe she was a novice who could only travel at a sedate pace.

He took off after her, urging Monarch into a gallop before he, too, flew over the fence. At least he knew what Monarch could do and what lay on the other side.

Jessica glancing back over her shoulder, saw him pursue her at a gallop. She took in a lung full of air, almost light-headed with exhilaration. Across the plain to the left of her, a great herd of prime cattle were strung out. She needed fresh territory. This was glorious! She had proved Chloe was a natural jumper. In fact, to her very pleasant surprise, the filly was flying like she was on steroids.

"That's it! Go, girl!" Cyrus would have that much more of a job to catch them. God, she loved racing!

By the time he caught up to her, he was fairly seething with anger. He came alongside, his eyes flashing. "What are you trying to do?"

"That's easy," she called back. "Beat you." Her lustrous green eyes brimmed with life, which in his agitated state he interpreted as having no sense of danger.

"Slow down, Jessica," he thundered.

"Why?"

"If you don't, we won't continue on to the canyon."

Immediately she started pulling the filly back to a fluid bounce, muttering her resentments at the same time.

When the two horses were back to a walking pace, he said tersely, "That was pretty damned risky taking the fence."

She raised her eyebrows. "I know what I'm doing. Chloe was traveling well. She *wanted* to jump the fence. She didn't take much urging."

"If her back legs hadn't cleared it, you'd have taken a tumble."

"I've taken plenty of tumbles in my time. The trick is to get right back up. Whatever is the matter with you, Cy? Why are you so upset?" Now she noticed a definite pallor beneath his deep tan.

"While you're on Mokhani, you're my responsibility."

She was a little startled by the sternness of the rebuke. "Okay, I'm sorry if you got a fright. It was stupid not telling you how experienced I am, but you're being far too cautious."

"That's the way I am." He tried to lighten up, but found he couldn't.

"Oh, God, oh no, how insensitive of me!" Jessica flushed as she belatedly recalled the great tragedy of his childhood. "I am so sorry."

He fixed his eyes on the purple escarpment that dominated the flat landscape. A pulse beat in his temple. "My mother was reckless. Just like you."

Jessica quietly protested. "You could have that wrong, Cyrus, though I do understand how you feel. Your mother could look after herself. So can I. Freak accidents happen. No one can prevent them. For a fatalist that means your number is up." She reached across to briefly touch his hand. "You promised me we'd ride into the canyon. I hope that wasn't a ruse because I looked like giving you a run for your money."

"You'd be still nursing the disappointment." He relented enough to smile slightly. "Okay, Jessica, we'll go explore the canyon."

CHAPTER TEN

WITHIN HALF AN HOUR, they were deep inside the canyon, parts of which had been hidden from Jessica's eyes when she'd viewed it from the escarpment. No matter how beautiful the canyon had appeared from the escarpment, it was pure magic when seen from the ground. An idyllic place lost in time. The walls glowed with such intensity, the very air was shot through with rainbows of color; all the deep terra-cottas, the russets, the rose and pink, the dark purples. What was extraordinary was the way the ubiquitous, indestructible spinifex clung to every crevice in a spray of gold. Cascades of icy cold water tumbled down the tiered rock face supplying moisture to the lush profusion of plants that grew in the shade and shelter of the towering walls. Jewellike greens, tangles of blue-flowered vines, gorgeous little native hibiscus, ferns that could be quite rare, secreted as they were in this far, far away ancient canyon that few people or animals had penetrated. It was so wonderfully unspoiled. A belt of small redbarked trees with shining green foliage lined both sides of the ocher walls, interspersed here and there with what must have been some species of wattle—glowing masses of fluffy yellow puff balls gave off the all-suffusing scent of her childhood, when the lovely Queensland wattle lit up the hills surrounding her home.

Jessica walked slowly, noticing everything. The color effects and the natural beauty of the scene touched every artistic nerve. She and Cyrus scarcely spoke, but they frequently threw smiling glances at one another, each content to be in this wild and beautiful place. Small shrubs were ablaze with a heavy crop of scarlet fruit the size of cherry tomatoes.

"A bush delicacy?" she called to Cy.

"Yes, you can eat them. They taste a bit like loquats."

Jessica popped a couple in her mouth, her taste buds coming alive. They were sweet, a little bit tart. They had a sweet, tangy smell, as well. She knew there were any number of native fruits and vegetables highly prized by the Aborigines and bushmen alike. To her sensitive nostril, everything was so clean and fresh. The sand of the canyon was a radiant white in stark contrast to the deep lagoon, with its tall humming reeds and flotillas of pink water lilies, the sort Monet would have loved to paint. The waters of the lagoon were a milky lime-green in the shallows, deepest cabochon in the center where the spirit of the Aboriginal girl lived. In such a place, if one were listening, one could almost feel her presence, perhaps even hear her voice.

Jessica wandered near the edge of the pool, wondering if long ago Moira had met her fate here. No matter how beautiful, the lagoon had treacherous depths. Here, too, some prehistoric monster could have found its way through the neck of the canyon and into the lagoon to make its home. This was the Dry. What would this place look like in the full swing of the monsoon? This glittering stretch of water, at absolute peace today would the next fill the entire canyon, pounding against the rock walls and carving out the grottos before inundating the valley beyond. The beautiful pink water lilies would be torn away, scattered for miles. Falling Waters would grow and grow, immeasurably wider, thundering down the escarpment. A striking picture began to form in her head. It would be an incredible thing to see from the air, a sight never to be forgotten. She envied Cyrus his wilderness home. There was freedom to think here, to glory in nature, to get a profound sense of oneness with it. Mokhani was having such an effect on her it was difficult to believe she had another life in the city.

A shadow fell over her. Overhead, coasting low, was a powerful blue-gray peregrine falcon with its distinctive blackish-brown bars. Probably it had its nest on a shelf of the cliff face. She knew it was the fastest of all birds, able to swoop in on its prey at incredible speed. Even as she watched, guessing the predatory bird was ready for the kill, it plunged into a patch of thick vegetation and made off with its prey in a matter of seconds.

"Poor little thing!" She saw it was a small bird with azure-blue-and-black wings with flashes of bright yellow. It was slightly unnerving, the speed and accuracy of the attack, but that was nature, after all.

Much later, Cyrus called to her, pointing to the cooling blue of the sky. "Had enough?" He was a short distance down the canyon, picking up and examining some curiously shaped stones.

Jessica shook her head. "I could stay here forever. What about a swim? I'm game if you are." Of course she was teasing. Soaring on horseback over fences was one thing. Sharing a swimming pool with a crocodile was suicidal.

To her amazement, he began unbuttoning his shirt. Jessica gulped for air. This wasn't an ordinary guy from the suburbs. This was a Territorian, probably used to going skinny-dipping. She ran toward him, grasping his arms. "I was fooling, you know."

"What are you worried about?" His blue gaze was deeply teasing. "It's been many years since anyone sighted a croc around here. You feel like a dip. I feel like a dip. What's stopping us?"

She felt herself blush yet again. "I don't have a swimming costume with me."

"So you can swim without one. *I* don't care."

"Sorry, but *I* do."

"I'm amazed to hear that, Jessica, you being such an adventurous girl." He smothered a laugh. "Okay, but hell, it was definitely worth a try."

His skin in the sunlight was enriched to a warm amber. A light mat of hair, as black as the hair on his head, tapered to a narrow V dipping into his low-slung jeans. Her heart catapulted into her throat. The sight of him aroused her like nothing she had known in her life. She could feel the vital heat off his body. Her fingers ached to touch him, to stroke him, to lick the fine beads of sweat that glistened at the base of his throat…

His head snapped up. He leveled her with a blazing blue stare. Sexual tension stretched to the breaking point between them. "You want to touch me, don't you?"

"I was thinking about it," she said slowly, knowing there was a lot of ammunition in her hands. A single move on her part could lead straight into a sexual encounter.

"So what stopped you?" he asked.

"Good old common sense," she said wryly. "I have to obey the red light."

"I thought you liked risk." He covered her shoulders with his hands. Warm, light, but enflaming.

"You're too risky for me," she said in a low voice.

"Also contrary to what you might think, risk hasn't been part of my life."

"It is now," he pointed out. "The two of us are quite, quite alone. No one around for miles and miles."

"Look, I'm shaken enough already!" Her laugh trembled. "What are you trying to do to me, Cy?"

"Charm you, maybe."

"You're succeeding."

His fingers caressed the fine bones of her shoulders. "Is it fate that threw us together, Jessica, or planning?"

She gave a deep sigh. "You won't let it alone, will you. Okay, it *was* planned, but not by me." She was struggling against a need so intense, nothing in her experience had prepared her for it.

"So we all dance to Dad's tune?"

"*I* don't and from what I've seen you don't, either." She tried to step free of his hands, but he preempted her movement, locking his arms around her, trapping her in a cocoon of sensation.

"No, Jessica. You're not going to get off that lightly. The last kiss we shared was so intoxicating, it left me with a driving desire for more."

She abandoned any thought of resistance. At that moment being in his arms was what she wanted most in the world.

Time stood still as he kissed her. Caution was suspended. Desire ran ahead like a flame to a keg of dynamite.

Their kiss was passionate, openmouthed, sumptuous, as though they both wanted as much as they could get in the shortest possible time.

Jessica brought up her hand, breathing hard, to sink her fingers into his black glossy hair, loving the feel of it. Her entire body clutched for his—her breasts, her stomach, her groin, hot and tingling now, her legs.

Still holding and kissing her, he moved them back into
the shade of the towering cliff walls. His hand sought her
breasts, pulling at the buttons of her shirt until it fell loose
and he pushed it off. Immediately, he lowered his head,
tonguing each sensitive nipple through the delicate fabric
of her bra, so it became wet and the engorged buds strained
against it.

"God, I'm *mad* for you." His free hand moved to unsnap
her undergarment. He inhaled sharply as her small breasts
sprang free. "So beautiful!" His hands moved over her bare
skin, his lean fingers, calloused on the pads, positioning
themselves over the pale creamy contours.

"Jessica!" he cried softly, and the sound was so erotic
her breaths came shorter and quicker. Her heart hammered.
She brought up her hand to press his over it. Couldn't he
feel how her heart beat for him? His touch was exquisite,
nothing rough or insistent, but masterful, and meltingly
tender and loving. He took hold of her long hair to release
it from its plait, wrapping it around his hand. His mouth
tasted of salt. From her flesh?

When finally he lifted his mouth from hers, they were
both breathing as if they'd just run a marathon. "Is this a
good time to stop?" he muttered, perversely holding her
closer to him so she could feel his hard arousal. "If we
don't, I mightn't be able to stop later."

"So don't!" She clung to him, afraid of the ease with
which he had dismantled all her defenses.

"But is it a safe time for you?"

She hid her face against his chest, but her voice didn't
falter. "Yes."

"Then I'd be a saint if I resisted you." He made her lift
her head, his blue eyes glowing. "And I'm no saint, Jessica.
Lord, you're so beautiful it *hurts*. I should warn you I'm

the kind of guy who wants it *all*. *All* is something I've never had in my entire life. I guess you could say some part of me has been deprived. I find myself wanting to drown in your body like a man might drown in waterhole out there in the desert."

"But is it *me* you're seeing?" Jessica asked, desperate to be sure he saw her as a *person* rather than the object of his sexual desire before their lovemaking went further.

"Of course it's you." He shook her slightly. "I've had to put up a struggle against you since the moment I laid eyes on you. I'm still not sorted out. Sex isn't all I want, Jessica, if that's what's bothering you. There are worse wants. I want to know everything about you."

"That will come," she said gently. "Everything I've told you about myself is true."

He relaxed his grip slightly, pulling her head back. "Except you haven't told me everything, have you?"

Her expression broke into pieces as if in pain. "Oh, Cy, will I ever have your trust?" At last, she found the strength to step away.

"You have to admit strange things are happening," he countered, "and you're the catalyst. Dad got you here for a lot more than decorating the Big House. What's his real motivation?"

"I don't know." Her voice was very tight. "Ask him."

"I'm sorry. I'm spoiling things."

"You are."

His gaze was intense. "Because you have the power to change my world, I want desperately to believe in you. Surely you know that." He reached out a hand to her, but she drew farther away. "Why does Dad follow you around? It's been a real eye-opener for Robyn and me. What's his plan for you? A portrait of a young woman who disappeared over fifty years ago suddenly turns up in an auction room. Your uncle's partner buys it, though Livvy wants it, too. Livvy claims there are more paintings. When she looks at you, she sees Moira. She calls you Moira and you call her *Miss* Lavinia. Why should that be? Do you wonder I want to know what the hell is going on?" He stood there, gloriously handsome and very troubled.

Jessica lifted her head to stare into the brilliance of his eyes, as her own ripples of anger and confusion washed over her. "You're not the only one who's desperate for a few answers. I'm as much perturbed by your father's attentions as you and Robyn. I came up here to do a job. My expectations in life don't include marrying a man old enough to be my father. And I think there's something evil about too much money—it's such a powerful force it can start wars. I'm genuinely amazed Lavinia calls me Moira, though I have to admit Moira and I share a remarkable likeness. When you see the portrait, you'll agree."

"I can't wait," he said tersely.

Jessica's eyes were very green. "You're right about one thing. I mightn't be here long. You say you want me, yet it will probably be *you* who drives me away." To her horror, she felt like bursting into tears.

"I might have wanted to at the beginning, but I don't now," he protested. He'd been so high a moment ago, and now was plunged to the depths.

"Is that supposed to make me feel better?" The electric tension in him whipped up an answering tension in her. "Because it doesn't." Angry and suffering a feeling of humiliation, she shrugged into her shirt, fumbling with the buttons. "Let's drop this, shall we? All we've got going for us is sexual attraction."

He leaned closer, as if pulled by an unseen hand.

Jessica, too, felt herself swaying into him. She might have been a stringed instrument strummed by a master.

"It's okay, Jessica." He felt the trembling that went through her body, the warring emotions that were in her. "The day isn't ruined. There's no need for you to feel threatened. I'll keep a respectful distance. That way we won't be led directly into temptation. It's not going to be easy, though, when we cued in to each other on sight. But what the hell!" He winced and moved away from her. "Shall we call a truce?" His voice had more than a lick of mockery in it.

"I've no choice," she answered, still fumbling with her shirt. "My job is at stake."

"Dad's your boss. Not me." He shrugged, watching her. Then said, "You do realize you've forgotten your bra. I know how you like to be modest."

"What? Oh, blast!" It came out in a staccato burst.

"Why don't you just leave it off?" he suggested, plucking the scrap of polyester and lace off the bush where it had landed. "You're in no further danger from lustful old me." He twirled the undergarment around his finger. "This'll fit neatly in my pocket."

"Why don't you just give it to me?" Her green eyes flashed as she stretched out a hand.

"In the old days a lady, if she were romantic, allowed an admirer to keep her handkerchief."

Jessica snatched the bra from his finger and stuffed it in her pocket. "Well, I don't have a handkerchief on me right now," she said jaggedly.

His blue eyes burned into her. "Despite that feisty rebuff I'll be seeing you in my dreams. Tonight, Jessica. I have to tell you, I think you'll be seeing me in yours."

Arrogant bastard!

IT WAS MOLLY WHO TOOK the news that B.B. and Robyn would be returning at the end of the week.

"All good things come to an end," Lavinia lamented. "I do so love it when they're not here."

Jessica had to throw off her fluctuating moods and get motivated. Because there was no time to make the trip to Darwin, all the art supplies she'd ordered had been flown in. She had Cyrus to thank for that, but when they came together, the atmosphere between them was so far removed from companionable she never did get a thank-you out. She had no excuse now for not creating a whole portfolio of sketches enhanced by a sensitive wash of watercolors. The last thing she wanted was strong color. The vast landscape was ablaze with it. For the interior she wanted a cool tranquillity. Pristine white with accents of aqua, turquoise, harmonizing greens and maybe a shot of fuchsia-pink in the huge living room. She and Brett had discussed antiques, rugs and artwork over the phone. She had the large, well-equipped office at her disposal, and e-mails and faxes were going back and forth daily. Brett had vetted most of her proposals coming up with some excellent suggestions of his own, which was something she had counted on. Everything was going well. It was a great comfort to know her clever uncle had such confidence in her judgment.

Lavinia took great interest in what Jessica was doing, poring over the sketched interiors brought to life by watercolors. "There's some marvelous stuff Robyn had stored away," she told Jessica, frowning. "You should get over to the old servants' quarters and have a look while you can. It's a very interesting place. Haunted, of course, but that's not going to worry you. Once Broderick and Robyn get back, they'll be following your every move. Robyn is

terribly jealous and it shows. I remember some priceless
things, Persian rugs, *big* rugs, dear. None of your little silk
prayer rugs. Incredibly beautiful, glorious colors and
patterns, a couple of floral Herats of the Isfahan type.
Deborah knew how to display things. Coromandel screens,
porcelains, furniture and paintings galore. Lovely mirrors
in gilt frames. Robyn didn't even leave them up—she has
no taste whatever, but I'm fascinated by your vision. It's
most sophisticated, Moira, very polished. I had no idea you
were such a wonderful drawer. Exciting things going on!
We'll leave these out, shall we?" She indicated the many
sketches spread out all over the table. "Cy will want to see
them when he comes in. It's so wonderful to see the pair
of you together. But don't forget. The two of you have to
face Broderick when he gets home." She leaned forward
and chucked Jessica under the chin.

Talking with Lavinia was like being detached from
reality.

Towards late afternoon on the Wednesday, Jessica
decided to take a great leap into the unknown. She knew
the old servants' quarters were locked, but only ten minutes
before Lavinia had crept up on her as she was working,
dangling something hard and cold against her cheek.

"Oh, goodness!" Jessica gave a start, not knowing
anyone was there.

"Sorry, dear, did I startle you?" Lavinia asked, gentleness surging into her voice. "This will solve the problem
of how to get in." She twirled the large brass key, blinking
coyly. "I found it in Broderick's study. I actually stole it.
Oops. Did I really say that?"

"Yes, Miss Lavinia, you did, you brazen thing! Mr.
Bannerman probably doesn't want anyone to go in."

"I don't care a fig for what Broderick wants," Lavinia

snorted, drawing the gypsy shawl that topped off her Carmen costume around herself. It reeked of naphthalene, but it went wonderfully with all the gold medallions hanging around her neck. She passed Jessica the key. "Now push off," she said behind her hand as though someone was hiding behind the curtain. "I'd come and help you, only dust affects my sinuses. Don't say anything to Cy," she warned. "What's biting you two, anyhow? The air sizzles when you're together." Her voice dripped with interest.

"Nothing," Jessica assured her. "Cy likes to bait me, that's all."

"Works both ways, dear," Lavinia chortled. "You know, Cy hated what his father let Robyn do to the house. You never saw a boy love his mother so much. Broderick, of course, was jealous of his own son, even in those days. He craved *all* Deborah's attention, but she was a mother who loved her son. A mother, I think, before a wife. Broderick couldn't take that. He's such an extreme person."

Jessica wasn't about to argue with that.

INSIDE THE STOREROOM, it took a while for her vision to adjust to the gloom after the brilliant sunlight outside. She had never done anything like this in her life before. In truth, she could have been about to open a Pandora's box, so nervous did she feel. Why hadn't she waited for B.B. to come home and ask permission? To answer her own question, she wouldn't get it. She couldn't for the life of her think of him as Broderick, and calling him that was a jarring note. If a man, however rich and powerful, was starting to develop warm feelings toward her, she'd have to start praying those feelings would fizzle out. She had no ambition whatever to become a rich man's trophy wife,

even if he covered her in diamonds, rubies and pearls. It
was so embarrassing and so totally unforeseen she
couldn't bring herself to tell Brett.

There were several rooms, she discovered. One very
large, all of them crowded with a great collection of things
covered in dust sheets. She turned away to work at a catch
on a window to let in more light. There! It was oppressively hot and still. All these unmoving things towering
over her, and right up the walls gave her the willies. Despite
the size of the main room, which she suspected had been
several rooms knocked into one, she felt strangely claustrophobic.

She nervously looked under a couple of dust sheets. The
whole place was drenched in an atmosphere one could
almost call ghostly.

Settle down, girl!

"Drat it!" she said softly as she stubbed her toe on what
was the leg of a heavy mahogany chair. She could see a
stack of what looked like pictures in frames behind a gray
dust sheet. She'd probably have a heart attack on the spot
if one turned out to be another painted image of Moira. Sad
little Moira belonged in the past but it seemed she wouldn't
stay there. She lifted the sheet and was confronted by a
magnficent oil on canvas of exotic fowl in the Dutch style.
A glorious peacock its iridescent tail spread, its hen, a pink
flamingo, a crane with a golden tuft on its head, several
pheasant, and a bird she couldn't identify nesting in a
branch of a tree. Such a painting had to be extremely
valuable. What was it doing here in the heat? Didn't these
people care? It was so big and so heavy, it was difficult to
see the paintings behind it. Not portraits. Landscapes.
More paintings. Chairs, marble-topped side tables.
Cabinets. High up, rolled rugs. Probably rotting the whole

damned lot. This was frightful! Broderick Bannerman had turned his back on what had to be a large family collection going back generations. In doing so, he surely had turned his back on his wife and son.

There was an instant when Jessica thought she heard a whispering behind her.

Mice.

What else could it be? She stood perfectly still, listening.

When the whispering became a little louder, she swung around to face it. "Is anyone there?" She moved on again, treading warily.

You feel guilty, that's what's wrong with you. You shouldn't be here.

Even that was ridiculous. Why should she feel guilty? She was absolutely certain there was a treasure trove for the Big House beneath all these dust sheets. Why buy expensive antiques, paintings and artworks when you already possessed a valuable collection? she rationalized. She ventured into the other rooms, flinging dust sheets this way and that. Why, they'd scarcely have to buy a thing outside the custom-made sofas, armchairs and soft furnishings. She didn't intend to use draperies at the double-height French doors, but white, brass-bound shutters fitted on the inside.

The whispering started again. Either she could bolt or pay it no heed. Was she going to allow a little family of mice to send her away? Even so, she felt nervous.

Her shoulder bumped against something that turned out to be a splendid eight-panel coromandel screen decorated with birds and flowers and studded with ivory and jade. What a find! She could easily place that and the two majestic baluster vases standing on the floor—both green and gold, with brilliant enameling—without any protection to the right of it. She supposed Robyn would be furious with her for entering the storerooms without permission. But she in turn was furious with Robyn for her wilful disregard of the correct storage and preservation of beautiful and valuable things. Why was such a place made inaccessible?

She patted the curly head of a life-size white marble statue of a little girl carrying a basket of flowers. "At least *you* won't fall apart."

The whispering continued.

"Go away!"

Her words had no effect. She walked toward the sound, thinking she could better cope with an apparition than a gang of scurrying mice.

After a while, hot, dusty, dry in the throat, her toe aching, she'd had enough. She recovered one of a pair of superb tall cabinets veneered with panels of marquetry and turned to leave. Still, she lingered and looked around as though something further was required of her. Finally she made her way between the mounded dust sheets, heading for the main storage room.

As she did so, the whispering increased in volume. It wasn't mice. It was more like a frantic murmur. Something was trying to get through to her. She could feel it in the very air. "Is there anyone there?" she called out again.

Nobody was. She was quite alone, her heart knocking madly. She looked back the way she'd come. Just for a moment she thought she saw a curling *shape* swirling in the dusty air. Suddenly she felt ice cold. The sudden drop in temperature raised gooseflesh on the skin of her arms. She even put up a hand to cover her eyes.

"Jessica!"

She reacted by collapsing against one of the tall cabinets.

A tall figure emerged from the gloom. Cyrus. "God, you scared me."

He walked toward her. "What the hell are you doing here? Dad says this place is off-limits." After the brilliance of the daylight outside, Cy could just make out her cloud of ash-blond hair. As he drew closer, he took in the rest of her, pale face, huge glittering eyes. "Are you okay?" He reached out to her, holding her arm as she slowly straightened up. "You look like you've seen a ghost."

"Frankly I think I have," she said raggedly. "There's something skulking around back there."

"Mice," he said shortly, continuing to stare at her, doomed to be fascinated.

"Mice whispering secrets in my ear? I don't think so."

"What are you talking about?" he asked impatiently.

"God knows! I'm not a nervous person. I don't panic easily—until today. There are bloody ghosts back there."

"Right. Let's go and take a look," he said with some decisiveness. "What's the matter? Chicken?"

"Not with you around. Even a ghost won't want to mess with you."

"Give me your hand." His tone was brisk, at odds with the way he was feeling.

"You know what happens when we hold hands."

"Any excuse will do for me," he told her dryly. "But ghosts are definitely out, Jessica. There's no such thing."

"Tell that to the people who've entertained uninvited guests. Tell me, if there's an afterlife and hundreds of millions of people believe there is, why can't a few souls go missing? For one reason or another, their travel home has been interrupted. They still have business to attend to before they can move on."

"I'm not buying it," he said firmly.

"You haven't got a spark of imagination."

"Whereas you have too much. What exactly did you hear?" He led her through the spectral dust sheets. "This is one of the earliest buildings on Mokhani. The timbers creak."

"I'm not hearing anything now," Jessica said, starting to feel a little foolish. "What are you doing here, anyway? Checking up on me?"

"I might just be," Cy said, staring around him. "I'm really angry with Livvy for encouraging you and giving you that key."

"Why shouldn't she?" Jessica retorted, standing up for herself and Livvy. "What's the big secret about this place? It's jam-packed with beautiful and valuable things. No way should they be here. Certainly not the paintings. Fine paintings should be stored at a certain temperature. I can't imagine why *anyone* would banish the treasures I've seen to a storeroom. They must have rocks in their head."

"Yeah, well you won't get any argument from me."

"Don't you *care?*"

He leaned heavily against a sideboard, giving into sheer need and pulling her taut body alongside. "Oh yes, I care," he said bitterly. "But when I was a kid, after my mother died, when I cared about something my father disagreed with I got whipped."

"You didn't!" The expression on her face mirrored her shock.

"I've still got a scar on my back. Want to see?"

"Yes." Suddenly she was extremely angry. Broderick Bannerman, what sort of man *was* he? She hated physical violence. Abuse of any kind. And on a child, a motherless boy? That was a sin!

Cy released her, pulling his denim shirt out of his jeans, one hand lifting the hem of his shirt.

His skin, even in the poor light, gleamed a dark bronze. She could see the play of muscles across his back. And the long scar that ran from one shoulder blade almost to his waist.

"Oh, Cy!" She couldn't help herself. Tenderly she traced the faintly depressed line. "This should never have happened! I'm so sorry." His pain lacerated her. On an impulse, she leaned forward and pressed her lips to the deepest part of the scar. "I'm kissing it better," she explained huskily.

He took a deep jagged breath. "Then could you do it again? You're turning my legs to jelly."

"We're starting to forget how we decided it should be."

"Relationships are like that," he said, his voice very dry.

"So we've got one?"

"You know we have. Next thing you know, I'll be back to kissing you."

"I might get in first." She slipped her arms around him, pressing her mouth to his puckered skin.

The flame of desire, ever present in him, leaped higher than the rafters. He turned about swiftly, the muscles of his arms quivering, as he caught her face between his two hands. "Abstinence isn't working for me, Jessica." His voice was harsh with emotion.

She stared back at him. "Don't you think I know what it's like to be sick with longing?"

"So what are we going to do about it? I have to tell you sexual frustration is weighing very heavily on me."

"Me, too," she sighed, determined not to say a word out of place.

"I get the feeling you're not on the pill?"

"No." She shook her head. "I wasn't expecting any sexual encounters when I came here," she said wryly, "but boy, has everything changed."

"Maybe we'd better take a trip into Darwin," he said tautly. "Meanwhile I've got protection. I want you but you have to come to me of your own free will. I would never put pressure on you."

She raised her head, giving him a dreamy smile. "You put pressure on me every time you look at me!"

"You've been pretty good at hiding it these last few days."

"I wasn't being my true self. Anyway, you're conceited enough."

"I'm not conceited at all," he scoffed. "This week has been pretty much a torment."

"You wanted pulling into line."

"What I want is to pull you into my bed." His hands ran caressingly down her back.

"Oh, I like that," she murmured. "Your father won't take too kindly to…us." She had a grim picture of what might happen.

"I can imagine," he said. "So what's more important to you? Your relationship with *him* or your relationship with me?"

She looked up to meet his eyes. "I don't have a relationship with him, Cyrus. So quit trying to extract a confession. It's *you* I care about."

"Good." He bent his head and kissed her fiercely. "Because you've got a choke hold on *both* of us," he muttered, as they paused for breath. It was incredible, Cy knew, that he could say such things to her, but the rivalry between himself and his father had been going on for years and years.

Instantly, Jessica felt animosity enter into their passion. "Don't make me another point of conflict between you," she warned. "Lavinia told me there was rivalry between you and your father for the love of your mother."

There was a distinct edge to his voice. "The rivalry was always on Dad's side. I couldn't even recognize rivalry at that stage. I had a wonderful mother. She loved me, Jessica, but she loved my father, too—or she must have at one stage to marry him. He's a striking-looking man now. How much more so in his youth? He couldn't always have been a monster, but the monster began to appear early. God knows what Dad's true nature is. I've given up trying to find out."

"I can understand that." She looked at him with sympathy. "But please don't direct any bitterness toward me. I may have some effect on your father—an aging man's fantasy—but the deep attachment I've formed is for *you,* so don't give me a hard time."

"Blame it on the difficulties of our situation," he said laconically, hauling her back into his arms. "Kiss me."

She reached up to draw down his head.

They kissed with such hectic passion, the very air around them throbbed and whirred and both of them wound up disheveled. Finally, he wrenched back. "We Bannermans are a tortured lot. You have to sleep with me, Jessica."

It was like being offered a passport to heaven. "One day I want you to talk to me about your childhood," she said. "Your precious memories of your mother. I can't imagine what else you're going to tell me about your father, now that I've seen that scar."

"Don't make too much of it." He shrugged the injury off. "I don't think he meant to go as far as he did. Dad was severely depressed for quite a while."

"Yet he remarried quite soon?" There was a subtle look of disapproval in Jessica's eyes.

He drew her down on an old Victorian settee with beautiful but threadbare upholstery. "Dad wanted more sons. One maybe more like him. It was no whirlwind romance with poor Sharon. He didn't love her, but she, incredibly, loved him. Can you beat that? Years of being treated like a piece of furniture, yet Sharon continued to love him."

"It's a wonder he didn't beat *her*," Jessica said, deeply disturbed by what she had learned that day.

"Good God, nothing like that." Cyrus shook his head. "He'd never raise his hand to a woman. *I* was his mark. It made me grow up fast. By the time I was fourteen, I told him I'd kill him if he ever touched me again. I must have sounded like I meant it. By the time he got over the shock, he never tried it again."

"What an awful story!" she sighed with sick disgust. "How am I supposed to work for a man like that? I feel like throwing in the towel."

He replied instantly, "The only problem is, Jessica, you signed the contract, remember?"

"He pressed me into it."

Cy stroked her cheek with his finger. "You can't fight Broderick Bannerman and hope to win. Scores of people could tell you that. Dad has control of everything while he lives. I know the priceless stuff that's here. I know it shouldn't be here. This is my inheritance, too, but sometimes I think my father would like to see me miss out. This can all crumble and decay. He's not dedicated to preserving it for me. He's one of those people who think only of themselves, their own pride and place in the world. Other people aren't important."

"No wonder he's a deeply unhappy man," Jessica said. "Caring about other people brings its own fulfilment." She waved an arm around her. "I'm going to speak to him about all this when the moment is right. All these treasures lying neglected. There's a magnificent painting in the other room. The light was too bad to see the name of the artist, but I wouldn't mind betting it's a Dutch master."

"It is," he confirmed. "One of my mother's family— English originally—worked for the Dutch East India company. He lived in Batavia for many years. He acquired it there."

"So it's yours through your mother."

His expression was grim. "My mother died without a will. Anyone so young and beautiful was meant to live forever. Her premature death was never foreseen. She often pointed out what things were mine. The paintings, the jade collection, the porcelains—all her family stuff. The one time I mentioned it to Dad, he told me to go to hell. He was drunk and in a brutal mood. It was all *his* until he died, and he had no intention of dying before he reached ninety."

"Then he better start looking after himself," Jessica said. "He must have a problem with high blood pressure. He's like a pressure cooker threatening to blow the lid."

"Maybe, but he's never had a sick day in his life. Probably the bad stuff will happen all at once. He survived a plane crash, did you know? Walked away from it with only a few lacerations. The pilot was killed. Dad thinks he's invincible. He thinks he's going to go on forever. Maybe take another wife. Rupert Murdoch fathered a child in his seventies. Men do."

"Lucky old them!" Jessica said tartly, staring toward the back of the room. "Listen…"

"The mice again?" He dropped a kiss on her hair, inhaling its freshness.

"The whispering has stopped. I swear it was real enough. It was like someone trying to contact me."

"Not get rid of you?" he asked, rising and pulling her to her feet.

"Joke all you like." She shook her head. "This place has a strange aura. There's not enough light around here, either. It's dangerous in a way. Any of that stuff up there in the rafters could fall."

"Except there's no wind to move it." He lifted a dust sheet that covered a very pretty writing desk. "My mother's." The expression on his face had grown more intense. "You didn't come across another painting of our resident ghost?"

She shook her head. "It would take a month of Sundays to sort through all this. It should have been catalogued. If there were such a painting, it could be anywhere, even up there." She pointed high up on the wall to what could have been covered paintings secured by an iron brace. "I can't explain it, but I can't help thinking there is one. There are a lot of shadows around your father. It seems to me that the more strident he was when denying the existence of anything relating to Moira, the more I thought he wasn't telling the truth."

"That's a state of affairs that's been going on a long, long time. We'd better go," he said. "And don't say anything about being inside or Livvy giving you the key."

"Of course I won't," she said indignantly. "I'll try to find another way to get in. Your father's tough, but he's not that tough."

"Not when he's in the middle of creating a fantasy." He picked up the white marble bust of a young girl. "Mignon," he read the inscription. "My mother's."

"It's beautiful." She realized just being in here and seeing his mother's things was upsetting him. She was about to turn back when a voice clearly said:

Don't go.

She almost couldn't breathe, stumbling back against Cyrus. "Did you hear that?"

"What? I didn't heard a thing, but I have to say it's a little weird in here."

She caught his hand, holding tightly to it.

He laughed, looking down at her. "I'm starting to see another side of you, Jessica."

"You're not too happy here yourself."

"Then let's get out."

They were almost at the entrance to the main room when there was a blast of wind that rushed at them with surprising force. Then a loud crash.

"What the hell!" Cy swore.

"It has to be the window I opened."

Cy strode into the main room, looking quickly around him. "That makes no sense. No wind has blown up." He crossed to the door. "It's perfectly still outside. The fronds of the palms aren't moving."

"No glass shards on the floor, either." The window Jessica had opened was still on the hook, intact. "So what crashed?"

"Must have been the other room. We must have disturbed something. It could easily have been a pedestal or a lamp." He said it matter-of-factly to counteract the strangeness of the occurrence.

"Time to take our ghost seriously, wouldn't you say?"

"Big girl like you believing in ghosts." But he, too, felt edgy without knowing why. "That's the cause," Cy said when they saw how half a dozen paintings had come down from the wall. "The strap must have broken."

"The ghost got to it," Jessica said stubbornly.

"Doubt it." Cy dropped to his knees.

Jessica joined him, the two of them pulling the pictures

from their coverings one by one. No portraits. A couple of good still lifes. A flower painting Tim would have loved, a beautiful storm scene by a famous Australian artist— Jessica didn't need to see the signature to recognize the work—a forest scene and an abstract that could have represented a star being born. The canvas had come away from the gilded frame in the fall.

"Something has to be done about these," Jessica, the artist and lover of all beautiful things, said. "Leaving them like this is a crime."

"Okay, so we *will* do something about it," Cy said, pierced by her criticisms, which were warranted. "I try to avoid major blowups with my father, but one's long overdue."

"I guess so," Jessica said, rewrapping the flower painting. "He's afraid of you, you know."

"No way!" Cy was startled.

"Oh yes he is," Jessica maintained. "You're everything he's not."

"That deserves another kiss." He put his arm around her neck and kissed the sensitive spot behind her ear.

"You're kiss deprived, that's your trouble," she said.

"I've had hordes of girls chasing me," he said, then continued his inspection of the paintings.

"You never married one. I'll leave you to rewrap the abstract, although it really should be reframed. What do you think?"

"Let's have a look," he suggested. "It's getting dark in here." He broke off abruptly, his fingers slipping down behind the canvas. "There are two paintings here," he said, sounding intrigued.

"What?"

"Take a look for yourself. There's another canvas here."

Cy rested the large painting against himself while she looked.

"Push the canvas backward."

"Right out of the frame?"

"Yes. It'll be okay."

Cyrus obliged while Jessica separated the two paintings. One filled up Jessica's vision.

She rocked back on her heels in shock. "How is it possible this has been hidden for so long?" Momentarily she looked away from the newly revealed painting to stare into Cyrus's eyes. "It's Moira." She started to tremble.

"Who else!" he said in a hard, considering way. "And horror of horrors, a nude!"

"God, yes," Jessica whispered.

Moira was reclining on a couch covered in green silk, her back and shoulders propped by cushions covered in rich fabrics. Her beautiful long hair fell over her shoulders and her white, pointed breasts. She looked extraordinarily vivid yet fragile. Her skin was luminescent. Her eyes glowed. One slender leg was discreetly raised, blocking the pubic area. One lovely hand rested on her stomach, the other was twisted in her hair.

The artist in Jessica bowed low before the artistry, even if she was shocked Moira, the little governess, was the subject of such an erotic painting.

"Poor old Hugh must have been madly in love with her," Cy said, hit by a wave of arousal that had at its center the extraordinary resemblance Jessica bore to the painted image.

"That's Hugh Balfour?"

Cy bent for an inspection. "There's an *H.B.* in the right-hand corner. How did he get an innocent young girl to pose for him nude? I'm not getting any of this."

"It's a tough one all right. It opens up a whole new area

of investigation. At the heart of the Mokhani Mystery, was there a love triangle? A crime of passion?" It stuck in Jessica's throat, but she had to say it. "Yet Lavinia claims Hugh was gay."

He swung his shoulders her way. "Livvy should be arrested," he said with quiet vehemence. "It's best not to believe anything Livvy says. She's outrageous, sometimes even mad. I've never heard anything about Hugh being gay."

"It was probably a big secret."

"Nonsense!" His tone was clipped.

"People were scared to admit being gay in those days. Wasn't it against the law then?"

Cy's expression was disturbed. "Look at this painting, Jessica. Doesn't it look a wee bit erotic?"

"It looks bloody marvelous," she said, suddenly wondering if the artist had painted from life or simply drawn on a fevered imagination. He could have done it from numerous seemingly innocent sketches. Would Moira, fresh out of convent school, really have posed for this? Today it mightn't have been so shocking, but fifty-odd years ago it would have been considered scandalous. And where did that leave Lavinia's claim that Moira and Steven had fallen in love? Conceivably that, too, was nonsense. Perhaps Lavinia made up stories so life wouldn't get boring. One could expect something like that after life on the stage. "Hugh Balfour was really a very fine painter," she said. "Maybe that, too, was frowned on. Painting wasn't considered a serious career, perhaps? Hugh was probably expected to do great things. Lavinia says—"

Cyrus broke in. "No one, absolutely no one, including Dad, has ever been able to get Livvy to shut the hell up." He took a calming breath, still reeling from the stunning resemblance between the painted Moira and Jessica. Of course the longer he looked, the more he could see differences. Moira appeared more fragile, a vulnerable young person. Jessica was a thoroughly modern young woman, very fit, confident, with a promising career. But the coloring, the small features, the full mouth, the luminous skin. It would appear to anyone looking from the painting to the living woman they were somehow related.

Were they? He had to wonder. More to the point, did Jessica know and was keeping it from him for some reason? Was there a conspiracy at work here? Was his father part of it? Someone had taken a punt by putting the other portrait of Moira on the market. To what end?

"Just listen quietly to what I have to say," Jessica began cautiously, anticipating an explosion. "Don't shut your mind to it. Lavinia said Hugh loved your grandfather, Steven."

He coolly scrutinized her. "My darling Jessica, I *know* that. Everyone knows that. Hugh damned near worshipped him—for what he was, for what he'd done. He was a war hero, you know. He remained Hugh's friend from the first to the last. Hugh's own family deserted him. Many men came home from the wars alcoholic. They needed alcohol to deaden the pain of their terrible memories. The world can be a pitiless place. Hugh committed suicide. He wasn't very old at all. I don't suppose anyone told you. He died here on Mokhani. My father was there when they found the body."

Jessica drew in a sharp breath. "I didn't know that."

"It's not the sort of thing one wants to talk about. No wonder Dad grew up the way he is. The events of his childhood permanently scarred him. That's why I occasionally feel pity. I don't know how Livvy came to believe

Hugh was homosexual. Livvy's such a drama queen! She's known for telling howlers. God knows what she'd say if she saw *this!* The poor devil was in love with her. She disappears. Years later, after silently grieving, Hugh finds a way out of all the pain." His voice took on a harder edge. "You'd tell me, wouldn't you, if there's a connection between you and Moira?" He lifted a hand as she rushed into speech. "I know you've denied it, but you could have your reasons. I want honesty between us."

"Of course, honesty. That's all important. I've told you nothing but the truth. There's no connection whatever. Past or present. I expect you to believe me, Cyrus, otherwise what have we got?" She touched his arm briefly. "It's as my uncle says. We all have a double somewhere. If *I* look like Moira, then so does Brett. My grandmother, Alex, looks more like this Moira than I do. But there was no Moira in our family." Her hand dropped away as, acutely attuned to him, she felt a residue of resistance.

He might want her. He might long to have her. But he wasn't *sure* of her.

CHAPTER ELEVEN

B.B. RETURNED MUCH THE SAME as he'd gone away. A difficult, domineering man, surrounded by shadows and given to long bouts of moodiness. At least the trip had gone well. His partners in whatever venture it was—he didn't explain—had come to heel, no doubt with words of contrition. He was, however, generous in his praise when Jessica submitted her conceptualizations for the main rooms of the Big House. He didn't go so far as Cyrus, who on seeing them had remarked they were good enough to be framed, but his opinion was highly favorable.

They were in B.B.'s study with the drawings spread out across the desk. "So you like the idea of rendering the columns that support the dome lapis lazuli?" she asked.

"I can see they'll be striking." Bannerman stabbed a finger at the excellent architectural drawing. "Who is supposed to do the fresco on the cupola?" Jessica had meant to represent a heavenly blue sky with dazzling white puffs of clouds, the edges touched with gold and pink as if from the sun. Had this been glorious Italy, she could have added cherubs for good measure, but they would have looked out of place in such a setting as Mokhani.

"I know just the man," she said. "He's Italian, classically trained. He's never out of work."

"You can't do it yourself?" His glance beetled beneath his heavy brows.

"I suppose I could, but I wouldn't have the time and I'm not as good as Primo anyway. I had been thinking that instead of paintings for the hall, we could use panels. They would go here." She quickly began to draw in several long rectangular panels. "Blue on gold. They would pick up the blue of the columns. There's so much white we need a contrast. It's a pity when the marble floor was laid the architect hadn't thought of a central design. But never mind. Do you like the library?"

"Very impressive," he nodded. "But where are we going to get the leather-bound books in those particular colors?"

"Well, we can't," she smiled, "unless we have the covers specially done. That would cost a great deal of money. Or we could have *some* of them done in order to pick up the turquoise blue. I felt the carpeting should be this very soft pinkish-red. Inviting, nurturing, but not too warm. We'll need a big important painting here." She pointed to the pale ocher wall above her rendering of an antique writing desk flanked by two splendid chairs.

"This is all very palatial," he said, his body a large physical barrier between her and the door.

"Isn't that what you wanted? A modern palace. I had to strike a balance between sumptuousness and classical purity."

"Well then you've succeeded, Jessica," he said, making no attempt to disguise the admiring scrutiny he bent on her. It went well beyond the aesthetic, Jessica thought. In fact, he was thoroughly unnerving her.

"I have some ideas for the front court," she quickly added, beginning to sketch a plan for the landscaping immediately in front of the house.

"We used to have an artist in the family," he commented, staring down at her slender flying fingers. "Name of Hugh Balfour. Ever heard of him?" He lifted his handsome head, shooting her the now-familiar piercing glance. This wasn't a man who indulged in idle conversation. He was pushing her to declare what she knew. Moreover, who'd told her.

Calmly she lay down her pencil. "Lavinia mentioned him. I think in connection with the portrait of your father up there. She's interested in art."

"Not that she knows anything about it," he scoffed.

Again she wondered if he had, through his agents, put Moira's painting on the market. To what purpose? She couldn't figure it out.

The silence stretched, uncomfortably for Jessica, during which time he continued to stare at her. Jessica thought she held up rather well. How many people actually could? Oddly, she had the impression he was not so much staring *at* her, as *beyond* her. As though Moira lived in *her* body and the two of them had metamorphosed right in front of him.

"You got to look around the station, then?" He finally shifted position, moving around the massive desk.

She could see where this was leading. "Not as much as I wanted. I needed to have these drawings ready for you. That was my top priority. I did, however, get to the top of the escarpment and later explored the floor of the canyon for a while. It was a marvelous experience, like seeing a surviving pocket of Gondwana. Before I go home I want to take lots of pictures. This is another world, the Top End. The plant life is unique. I used to think a lot of our tropical plants had their origin in the South Sea islands. Apparently it's the other way around."

He shrugged off the information as of little interest. His

whole life had been addressed to making money. "You didn't go by yourself. Cyrus took you?"

She had already anticipated the question. "He was kind enough, yes," she said with a smile. Broderick Bannerman was indeed in some sort of conflict with his son, conflict that had deep roots in the past. For all she knew, Bannerman could have had problems with his own father, Steven, the man Cyrus resembled so closely. Many factors in Broderick Bannerman's early life could have been in play.

"It must have been really hard work escorting a beautiful young woman around Mokhani," he said, openly sarcastic.

Had he ever appeared in another guise, this severe, controlling man? "There was something I was going to ask you, Broderick." For the first time, she uttered his name with ease. "I understand you have many beautiful things from the family collections stored away in the old servants' quarters."

He smiled, the sort of smile that was almost alarming. "You can't use those," he said.

"I had hoped you would allow me to see them."

Bannerman leaned back in his chair, interlocking his hands behind his dark head with its distinctive silver wings. "I can't have any of my wife's things back in the house," he said.

An aura of pain was suddenly around him. Jessica stared at the handsome features drawn taut. "Oh, I'm sorry! I didn't mean to upset you." Who could begin to understand this complicated man?

"It appears I still haven't dealt with my wife's death," he said. "Perhaps I never will."

"A tragedy like that does strange things to people's lives."

"What would you know about tragedy?" he said.

"I lost the grandmother I adored."

"Ah, yes, the grandmother!"

"Why do you say it like that?" She frowned.

"You resemble her greatly?"

"Well, yes. How do you know? I don't believe I mentioned it at our first meeting, or since."

"I think you did and you've forgotten. Maybe I *will* let you take a look at what's in storage. As an artistic person, you must love beautiful things."

"That would be wonderful. Thank you. I was told there are beautiful paintings. Forgive me, but it's not wise to store them in the heat. Even the furniture will buckle. I had thought there might be a possibility of placing some pieces in the Big House. They could look quite different in such a very different setting."

He looked at her with such a strange expression on his face. "I understand what you're saying, Jessica, about the heat and humid conditions. I can see you *care*." Then, the words rolling like drumbeats, "Who's been talking to you?"

"It's been more my asking questions!" She laughed. "You must understand, I've never been anywhere remotely like Mokhani before. Do you wonder I'm fascinated?"

He seemed to relax, if indeed a hunting hawk ever relaxes. "It pleases me to hear that." He reached out, spreading his large elegant hand over hers. "Speaking of fascination, there's some magic about *you*." His resonant voice dropped low. "I'm already feeling your influence about the place. I enjoy talking to you. In fact, I've so looked forward to coming home. I haven't done that since I can't tell you when."

Jessica made no comment, not daring to inch her hand away. Well, not immediately. It wasn't the first time a

male client had become attracted to her. She had begun to
look on it as an occupational hazard. But this was something else again. She knew women married men old
enough to be their fathers—certainly if they had several-
odd million stashed away—but she thought she'd rather
remain unmarried for the rest of her life than play on the
soft underbelly of an aging man's weakness. Broderick
Bannerman, with his formidable energy, bitterly resented
growing old. He may have come to the conclusion
marriage to a young woman could accomplish the impossible and keep him eternally young.

Jessica swallowed her dismay. Was it possible he was
seriously considering *her?* Dear God, if true, it was a
nightmare, particularly when she was head over heels in
love with his son. Gently she withdrew her hand , starting
to put all her sketches together.

"There's no word yet about your award?" he asked, a
faint flush in his cheeks.

"I expect to hear any day now." She hugged the rolls of
sketches to her. "I don't expect to win. It was an honor to
be short-listed."

"So modest when you're so clever. I like that. The
painter in our family wasn't a success. He was a great
failure." His eyebrows jutted in a frown.

"Hugh, you mean?" Jessica's mind was racing. *Had*
Balfour been gay? The family would have known. Could
a gay man paint such an erotic nude? Silly question. Great
painters had done it in the past.

"Rumor had it he was gay," Broderick said with a harsh
laugh. "But if he were, he was very discreet. Hell of a thing
to be homosexual. Maybe that's why he topped himself."

"Poor man. So he couldn't have been in love with
Moira?"

The handsome, heavy head shot up. "Whatever are you talking about?"

She was almost welcoming a confrontation, but backed off. "I did a lot of research on Mokhani before I came. Many articles have been written about the Mokhani Mystery."

"I expect there'll be lots more," he grunted. "The press is conspicuous for dragging up all the old unsolved mysteries."

"They said Moira was beautiful. Was she?"

"I was only a child, my dear."

"So you never saw the paintings Hugh Balfour did of her?"

He smiled like a man who had nothing to hide. "If I did I've forgotten. I have to tell you I'm not used to being interrogated, Jessica. I can tell you Moira had your coloring. She was tallish like you and exceptionally slender."

"So you do remember some things about her?"

He studied her very gravely. "I suppose, now that I think about it. Few women in my experience have been as beautiful as Moira, though my boyish memories can't be entirely accurate. My wife was a very beautiful women with skin like a pearl. You, too, are beautiful. When I first saw you on that television program, your chance resemblance to my governess stunned me."

"Is that why you hired me?"

"You sound very anxious to know."

"Well, of course I am."

"Let me set your mind at rest," he said suavely. "I paid far greater attention to your qualifications, Jessica. You don't know me if you think otherwise."

I don't know you at all, Jessica thought.

"By the way, Robyn's boyfriend—ridiculous word,

particularly as he's been married and divorced—is giving her a birthday party Saturday night at his home. I'd like you to come."

"Shouldn't I wait for an invitation?" She gave him an uncertain glance.

"You're getting one from me." He spoke as if that was all that was required. "Dress up."

"Is that an order?" On her way to the door, Jessica turned to ask.

There was a flare of amusement in his eyes. "Of course not. I confess I'm looking forward to seeing you turned out for a party. Formal is what Robyn wants. She spent a fortune in Hong Kong. That way no one gets to see her in the same thing twice."

WITH THE MASTER OF THE HOUSE back in residence, Lavinia didn't come down to dinner.

"I've told Jessica about the party on Saturday." B.B. threw the remark at Robyn as though daring her not to catch it. "She says she won't come without an invitation."

"But she must come. Please come," Robyn said as though the invitation had been lost in the mail. "I'm so sorry, Jessica, I was getting around to it. It's going to be a big night."

"She's thirty now, you know," B.B. told Jessica. "Thinking of matrimony. We'll have to make sure there's a prenuptial agreement. No way is Erik getting his hands on my money."

"He's got money of his own, Dad," Robyn was moved to protest.

"Let's face it, my dear, Moore wouldn't have given you the time of day if you hadn't been my stepdaughter."

"I'm truly amazed someone hasn't bumped you off,

Dad," Cyrus drawled. "Erik isn't the only man to notice Robyn's attractions. With or without your money."

"I'm not a very nice person, as you know, Cyrus," Bannerman said.

Cyrus lifted his wineglass in a dubious salute. "Actually I'm not all that keen on going. I think you can do better than Erik, Robyn. He ran out on his wife. He could run out on you."

"He promised me he would never leave me." Robyn was bristling and very much on edge.

"Hell, you couldn't exactly call you a loving couple. My bet is you're desperate to leave home."

Robyn gasped. "How can you say such a thing? Dad has given me a marvelous life. It's as he says, I'm not getting any younger."

"Check with Erik, he wants children," Bannerman slipped in smoothly, turning his head to capture Jessica's gaze. "Robyn could be barren like her mother."

Jessica felt herself flinch. Could Robyn be that desperate to inherit her stepfather's money to tolerate all these cruel, cutting remarks? But it was Cyrus, not Robyn, who came to Sharon's defense. "Sharon wasn't barren, Dad. She had Robyn. That, of course, was long before she met *you*."

"How you love to set me straight, Cyrus," his father answered, brushing that fact aside. Once more he addressed Jessica. "I have a little something for you, Jessica, I bought in Hong Kong. I'd like you to wear it Saturday night."

It was a startling statement that left Jessica greatly worried.

"I really think you should tell Jessica what it is first," Cyrus suggested. "Some things a girl has to refuse on principle."

Jessica felt Robyn's gaze locked on her, but her answer was weighed and controlled. "Goodness, I don't need a present, Broderick. You're paying me extremely well."

"Of course I am," he smiled, "but it gave me pleasure to buy it. I'm sure you're going to enjoy wearing it. I have it in my study. You can take a look after dinner."

"It would be so nice if Robyn and I were invited along, too," Cyrus said, contemplating Jessica's face, a decided glint in his eyes.

"This is *private,* Cyrus," B.B. said. "You and Robyn will just have to wait."

"How do you know you haven't made a big mistake?" Cyrus sat back with indolent grace.

"About what?" B.B. asked in his most aggressive fashion.

"Jessica's mother will have told her not to accept presents from near strangers," Cyrus pointed out.

"I don't think sarcasm is the answer, Cyrus," his father said.

"Of course it isn't. Jessica is shocked, in case you haven't noticed."

"That's not true, is it, Jessica?" B.B. turned to her.

She swallowed, not wishing to insult him but determined to find a way out of it. "I *am* surprised," she said.

"And a little nervous. Don't be, my dear," Bannerman patted her hand. It was getting to be a habit.

WHAT B.B. HAD REFERRED TO as "a little something" turned out to be a pair of platinum earrings, each set with a half carat round brilliant cut lemon diamond and two brilliant cut white diamonds from which was appended a beautiful golden South Sea teardrop pearl of at least fifteen millimeters. Pearls of that size and shape were relatively rare, and so were much sought after by collectors. Jessica knew this from her love of pearls and her own mother's collection. Luster, the single most important factor in determining the value of a pearl, was well in evidence. The nacre was very rich.

It was quite out of the question to accept a gift like this. It was too valuable and too personal. The sooner she made that clear, the better. "Broderick, I can't possibly accept these," she said as courteously as she could.

His piercing gaze rested on her. "That alone makes you different from most women of my acquaintance." Dinner was over. They were alone in his study.

"It's extremely generous of you, but I've done nothing to warrant such a gift."

"Try them on, anyway," he said, pointing to a mirror. Broderick Bannerman hadn't gotten where he was without putting down opposition. "At least let me see them on you. They say pearls are in again."

"They should never have been out." Jessica didn't want to offend him, but she couldn't give him leverage, either. Broderick Bannerman's inch was another man's mile.

"*Please.* I don't often beg." He turned her by the shoulders, looking directly into her eyes.

Yes, she thought. Begging would be grotesque in such a man.

"If you see yourself wearing them, you might want to keep them," he said, reaching for the jewelry box.

"They must have cost a good deal of money," Jessica said. She had a fair idea how much; she looked in the windows of jewelry stores often enough. She would have thought a gift costing a hundred dollars too much, but these earrings had to be worth many thousands of dollars. There was no way she could accept. In her embarrassment, she saw it as a form of prostitution.

"What's money?" he asked, as only a rich man could. "I have all the money in the world, but it hasn't made me happy. Since you've been here, Jessica, I've felt a lifting of the spirit. Do you know what I'm saying?"

She kept her head down, not needing to feign sweet confusion.

"Put the earrings on," he urged, looking as if he wanted to do it for her. "At least give me the pleasure of seeing them on you."

She relented. "Very well." She removed her own earrings, the peridots Tim had bought her, and inserted the pearl drops. "It was very nice of you to think of me, but I know you'll realize I can't accept such a valuable gift—the skin on the pearls appears flawless."

"Would I select pearls with the slightest imperfections when your own skin is flawless?" He came to stand behind her, an imposing-looking man. "I suggest we take one thing at a time."

Jessica vowed he wasn't going to override her decision. "Which I've done. I've shown you what they look like on."

"Perfect!" he breathed, like a connoisseur. "Push your hair back," he instructed.

Though the air-conditioning was working efficiently Jessica felt stifled. He stood back studying her, then he moved to lay a hand on her shoulder. "You can't refuse me."

To her horror, his voice had taken on what seemed to her an ardent note. This was the worst thing that could possibly happen. It would change everything, make her job untenable. With no encouragement whatsoever, Broderick Bannerman had become infatuated with her.

Patches of color stained his prominent cheekbones.

"It's clear to me you're not used to accepting presents, Jessica. A beautiful young woman like you should be showered with them."

The intensity of his expression altered abruptly when a knock came at the door. The next moment, without waiting for an invitation, Cyrus entered the room, his blue eyes flashing over the fixed tableau: his father's hand on Jessica's shoulder, Jessica, her head averted, her face as pale as his father's was ruddy, her cloud of ash-blond hair pushed behind her ears to reveal exquisite drop-pearl earrings.

It was *exactly* what Cyrus had feared. His father had been struck by Cupid's arrow. A man couldn't avoid it any more than he could avoid dying. Approaching sixty—even if he didn't look it—his father was now young at heart. For once, B.B. wasn't thinking with his *brain*. He was endeavoring to romance a woman young enough to be his daughter. He should know better. That's if any man would know better with someone like Jessica around.

Jessica fell back from the blazing contempt in Cy's regard. He was so judgmental! Anyone would think she'd been caught in some odious act.

"So this is the present." Cyrus reached Jessica, standing before her. He put a finger to the beautiful drop pearl, setting it swinging. "I expect you've promised Dad never to take them off."

"Why should she when they suit her so beautifully!" Bannerman exclaimed in a mix of anger and triumph. "Is there something you want, Cyrus?" he demanded. "It's customary to knock and wait for an answer before you barge into a room."

"Sorry about that, Dad," Cyrus said. "I had a rough

childhood. No mother to teach me manners. I just wanted to know if Jessica wanted to go for our usual after-dinner stroll, if that suits her?"

"It suits me," Jessica said, already removing the earrings one by one and laying them back in the satin-lined, polished walnut case. "These are much too good to wear around the garden. They're perfectly beautiful, Broderick, but I can't accept them."

"And I can't take them back. Not *now*." A deep crease appeared between Bannerman's brows. "You've worn them. Pierced ears and so forth. As I've said you'd make me happy if you'd wear them Saturday night, Jessica. I'll leave them in the safe for you. You probably didn't bring much in the way of jewelry and the other women will be dressed up. There's quite a bit of money in Darwin."

JESSICA'S KNEES WERE TREMBLING as they walked down the front steps of the homestead. Cyrus was striding ahead as though he wanted to lose her.

"What's your hurry? Are you so desperate to get back inside?"

Immediately he stopped, swinging around to face her. "What the hell was *that* all about?" He towered over her.

Her temper rose to match his. "Might I remind you we're still within spitting distance of the house?"

"I'm seething, that's why." He grasped her arm, hauling her along the path. They had rounded the end of the veranda, though the exterior lights shone over the path and into several feet of the garden, ablaze with huge birdlike heliconias. "Well?"

"Well, nothing!" Jessica jerked her arm away. "Absolutely nothing. You have a very suspicious, not to say, dirty mind."

"No one has accused me of that before." He swung her back to face him. "There are certain rules of behavior—"

"Never stopped you," she reminded him sharply. "Look, Cy, I don't want to get into an argument with you. It's really your father you should be speaking to. If he sees nothing wrong in wooing a woman young enough to be his daughter, I *do*. It's so damned embarrassing."

"I agree. I told you to tread carefully around him."

"What do you think I've been doing? I've given him no encouragement at all—it simply didn't occur to me. Why put the pressure on me anyway? Go tell your father to lay off."

He laughed, though he was obviously upset. "Hell, I mightn't be seen or heard of again."

Tentatively she reached out to him, trying to read the expression on his face. His striking features, which for all the bad feelings between them bore his father's stamp, were tense. "It can't be that bad." She had a fluttery sensation in her chest as though her heart were missing beats.

"A slight exaggeration," he said in self-mockery. "I've learned how to defend myself." He walked on. Jessica followed, increasing her pace to keep up. "Dad's cracked the whip for so long, he thinks there's nothing and no one he can't get. He could exhaust any woman with his persistence and his money. Dad's not coming to the end of his sex life. It's still all systems go."

"Not with *me,* it isn't, as I've told you a dozen times. What do you think I am, an adventuress?"

"Maybe more of a temptress."

Jessica smarted. "I'd watch it if I were you. Men are all the same. Always bemoaning a woman's power over them. *She made me do it.* Rapists have sworn on their mother's lives that their victims seduced them. It all started with Adam."

"What are you going to do about those earrings? He clearly expects you to wear them."

"He can take the bloody things back. And I don't care if my swearing offends you."

"Don't worry, I'd be swearing, too. I *hated* to see my father's hand on your shoulder."

"Jealous?"

"Yes. That's what you wanted me to say, isn't it? Jealous, angry, sad, embarrassed, deeply concerned, as well. My father is a dangerous man, Jessica. A predator. It would be very foolish to trust him."

"I don't need *you* to tell me that. A little bird told me on day one—he's very cruel to Robyn. I can't help feeling sorry for her."

"So do I, now and again. Only, Robyn has picked up a few too many of Dad's traits, haven't you noticed? She reveres him like some people revere dictators. Like Dad, I don't think she'd have any difficulty resorting to drastic measures. If she could get away with it, she'd push me off a cliff."

"Are you serious?"

He forced a laugh. "If she could get off scot-free. Poor old Robyn craves Dad's love and attention. In that way *only* is she like her mother. Robyn suffered from being adopted. She's never believed she *belonged*."

"Hardly surprising!" Jessica cried. "No one acts as though they like her. Even her husband-to-be."

Cy made a little clicking sound of disgust. "They're a pair all the same. Erik's just as mercenary as she is. Dad's right when he says Erik's real interest in Robyn is the family connection. Being Broderick Bannerman's son-in-law would be great for business. Which is why I don't like him. In fact, I despise him, though he always tries to be pleasant.

As for Robyn, don't think I didn't try quite hard to be friends with her when we were kids. Sharon was a nice woman who deserved better than what she got. Livvy tried hard to be good to Robyn, as well. Neither of us got anywhere. She didn't want us. She wanted Dad. Robyn is her own worst enemy. I've gone way past trying to connect with her, especially when she'd like to see me out of the way."

Jessica's whole body tingled with a sense of danger. "That's a terrible thing to say."

He shrugged. "I'm afraid it's true. Robyn believes that with me out of the way, everything would be perfect. Of course, she couldn't be more wrong. My father and I might be mostly at loggerheads, but he'd scarcely be happy if anything happened to me. At some level, in some deep dark cave, he's buried his love for me. But it's there. He's a tormented, moody, restless man. Robyn could *never* take my place. That's what she can't seem to understand. Dad never gives me a word of praise or gratitude, but he knows and I know he can't do without me. I run Mokhani these days and I've inherited his business brain. It was my mother who gave me the gift of a *soul*. Dad might have had one, but he doesn't own it anymore."

JESSICA WAS IN THE OFFICE reading through a long fax from Brett, which included an architectural drawing she found very helpful, when Robyn came in search of her.

"Hi! Thought I'd find you here." Robyn actually smiled, looking a totally different person in the process. She had beautiful white teeth that showed up well against the pale gold of her skin.

What had caused this huge sea change? Since Robyn

had returned from Hong Kong, she was acting much more human and likable.

"I'm so looking forward to my party!" Robyn laughed excitedly, perching on a desk and placing the envelope she had in her hand beside her. "It's going to be great! I'm very much in love with Erik."

Jessica tried her level best to look as if Erik were among the most desirable of suitors. "I'm happy for you, Robyn. Is there going to be a surprise announcement?"

"Gee, I don't know." Robyn put her elegant, manicured hands to her blushing cheeks. "Erik loves surprising me. Whatever Dad says, Liz wasn't a good wife to him. She never wanted children. Erik is a man who should have children."

"Have you discussed it with him?" Jessica's instinct told her Erik might have been lying.

"Heavens, it's understood. The truth is, I don't want to rush into motherhood. After a couple of years of marriage, maybe. Dad would adore a grandchild."

Jessica couldn't for the life of her fire off a quick answer. She tried hard to see B.B. through Robyn's eyes, but had to leave off. Broderick Bannerman would make her own crusty grandpa seem like a Boy Scout.

"What I wanted to ask you…" Robyn frowned for a moment, considering. "Have you a suitable dress? It's formal, you know."

"Your father told me," Jessica nodded. "I do have one dress I think might do."

Robyn removed some photos from the envelope. "Look, here are some possibilities. I'd like to help. You know I own a boutique in Darwin. Exclusive designer wear. I can tell you're a girl who knows clothes."

"Why thank you, Robyn. You have beautiful taste." It

wasn't a white lie, for strangely enough, Robyn did—with her dressing. She always looked very glamorous, nothing over the top. It was when she had attempted to be her own interior designer she had gone adrift.

Robyn passed the photographs to her. A lovely Eurasian model was wearing a collection of party dresses, all in the height of fashion.

"These are beautiful!" Jessica said with genuine enthusiasm.

Robyn leaned forward. "I had Selina put them on to give you a better idea of what the garments would look like when worn. So much better than showing you something on a hanger. Selina is your size." Her dark eyes ran over Jessica's tallish slender figure. "What do you think? If you like one, I could have it ferried in. Evening shoes to match. What would you be? Size thirty-six, European?"

"Yes." Jessica was starting to feel a little more kindly towards Robyn. "This is very thoughtful of you, Robyn, but—"

"Dad wants you to look your best," Robyn said as though that clinched it.

"That would be my goal in any case," Jessica answered with faint irony. "But you're the guest of honor, Robyn. Not me. My own dress is very pretty."

"As glamorous as these?"

"Maybe not." She smiled. "I didn't come here expecting to be at the ready for formal parties."

"I have a faultless eye," said Robyn, obviously thinking there was nothing to be gained from false modesty. "You'd be pleasing me very much if you would pick one out. You've got a good figure, and a good back—the dresses are cut low at the back. There'll be a lot of beautifully dressed women there. All showing off. The husbands have money coming out their ears. The wives fly off to Hong Kong and Singapore all the time to do their shopping. Some have the most gorgeous jewelry. Hope I'm not boring you. You've heard of Paspaley pearls?"

"Who hasn't? They're the most beautiful pearls in the world."

Robyn gave a throaty laugh. "I know Dad called into their Darwin showroom fairly recently. I happened to run into a friend who let it slip. I suspect he chose something to mark my thirtieth birthday. Dad knows I adore jewelry. He bought my mother a few nice pieces, which I inherited, but I can't get my hands on Deborah's stuff. Deborah died without a will, but her jewelry goes to Cyrus's future wife. That's sure to be Roslyn Newman. They've been on and off as an item for years. Not Roz's fault—Cyrus won't commit. No one measures up to the adored Deborah. That's pretty much it. Cy never got over losing his mother."

"I can understand that," Jessica said.

Robyn's mouth tightened. "I lost my own mother a couple of years back. I've had to get over it. You learn to pack your feelings away in a box. You can't let them influence your thinking."

"Easier said than done, Robyn," Jessica said quietly.

"Some of us are more strong-minded than others." Robyn snapped her fingers. "So what's the verdict? I thought the green myself as you've got green eyes."

"The green is beautiful. I'm a little nervous about the price…"

Robyn laughed. "It would be a pleasure to *give* it to you, Jessica. Good advertising for me, too, if you could just drop the hint it came from my boutique. You're bound to be asked."

The fact Broderick and Robyn wanted to shower her with presents Jessica found more disturbing by the minute.

"I wouldn't dream of taking it for nothing, Robyn, though it's very generous of you to suggest it. How much is it?"

"You'll accept a discount, surely?" Robyn named a price that was practically a giveaway.

"Not *that* much of a discount," Jessica said, looking adamant.

"All right!" Robyn named a price Jessica had never yet spent on a party dress. "But it's worth it."

"Done." Jessica wanted to look beautiful for just *one* man. She put out her hand, but instead of shaking it, Robyn slapped it in a bit of fun. "I'll get on the phone right away. What about evening shoes?"

"I think my own will do."

"There'll be dancing." Robyn executed a few dance steps.

"That's great!" A sexy lambada with Cyrus, Jessica thought.

At the door of the office, Robyn turned, her gleaming pageboy falling in close on her cheeks. She really was very attractive when she managed to unwind. "We must go riding one day. I'd love to show you around. You *can* ride?"

Obviously no one had told her Cyrus had taken her riding on Chloe. "Yes."

"Good," Robyn said, sounding pleased. "I don't imagine you're an expert, but I'll be able to give you a few tips. I'm sorry we didn't exactly hit it off when you first arrived—the fact you're so young was a shock—but if Dad says you know what you're about, who am I to argue? I'll leave you in peace now. Wait until you see *my* dress. It's terrific! I want Dad to be really proud of me."

Jessica was left feeling sad. Robyn measured all her triumphs and failures against what her stepfather thought. A pity when no one could call Broderick Bannerman a kind man.

CHAPTER TWELVE

THE DAY OF THE PARTY Cyrus flew them into Darwin. A stretch limousine was waiting at the airport to drive them to their city hotel. The same limo would be on call to deliver them to and from the party that evening, as Erik's house was a few miles outside the city. It was eight-fifteen before they were ready to leave, although Robyn was the guest of honor. Lavinia had kept them waiting, trying to manage her freshly washed hair. Now it stood out from her head in a pure white pompadour decorated on the crown with a great jewelled brooch. Around her neck she wore a necklace that could have adorned the neck of Queen Nefertiti: multiple strands of turquoise beads caught at intervals with diamond arrows with a large open square of diamonds as the center piece. Lavinia, Jessica had noted, was not short of stunning vintage pieces. Tonight she had abandoned her arresting operatic wardrobe in favor of a classical turquoise toga. Turquoise-and-amethyst pendant earrings circa 1930, now the rage, dangled from her ears, dragging down the delicate lobes.

"Magnificent!" Jessica applauded when they met up in the lobby. "I'm wild about your necklace."

Lavinia advanced regally, putting her arms around Jessica and kissing her with real affection. "How I wish I'd had a granddaughter like you, Moira. If you find my necklace attractive, it's yours. But you must keep your hands off it until I'm safely with the angels. You look glorious. What it is to be young, beautiful and in love. I've never seen you made up. Those *eyes!* Where did you get all your beautiful clothes from? I don't remember seeing any of them." Her eyes swept Jessica from head to foot.

"You know how it is. One always finds something," Jessica joked, forced to accept the fact Lavinia would always confuse her with Moira.

Looking up—hadn't she been anticipating this very moment?—she saw Cyrus quickly descending the stairs with easy male grace. He looked so stunning she thought he would take any woman's breath away. Clothes hung the way they were supposed to on his tall, lean, wide-shoul-dered body, but in a white dinner jacket with black tie he was so sexy it *hurt!*

"Nothing like a family party, is there?" he smiled, his blue gaze moving from his great-aunt to Jessica, where it stayed.

She bewitched him. Her exquisite evening dress clung to her, molding her body before it tapered to her delicate ankles. Her beautiful eyes glowed sea-green. Her hair was even more abundant than he had ever seen it. Magnificent hair, that rare ash-blond!

His heart bucked beneath his ribs. She filled him with such pleasure. All he wanted to do was pick her up and run away with her. Far, far away from his father, who was starting to act like Count Dracula. Of all the scenarios he had calculated had lain ahead when Jessica had first arrived, he had never considered he and his father might want the same woman. It was crazy.

"So where are the others?" he asked, managing to sound relaxed when the sight of Jessica in her finery had nearly robbed him of breath.

Jessica's own light tone covered her heightened emotions. "Your father *was* here, but he went off again with Robyn." She wanted to put out her hand to caress him. It was getting so bad she didn't think she'd be able to hide her depth of feeling for him much longer.

Look at me Cyrus. Look at me in my beautiful dress. I've never had a dress as beautiful as this. And it's all for you.

"I HAD TROUBLE with my pompadour," Lavinia was explaining to Cyrus. "I washed my hair. It was so soft it kept falling down, but Moira loaned me some spray. I never knew spray made it so easy. I must get some."

"Well, you managed in the end, Livvy," he said, kissing her cheek. "It looks marvellous. You both look marvellous. I'm glad you decided to come, Livvy. I find it impossible to believe you're in your eighties."

"I know. I look splendid in my dotage," Lavinia said complacently, rearranging a fold of her toga.

"Indeed you do. Just remember one thing."

Lavinia understood perfectly. "Be on my best behavior." She rolled her eyes. "I ask you, would I embarrass you, my darling?" She turned to sweep an admiring glance over Jessica. "Doesn't Moira look beautiful?"

"*Jessica* does," Cyrus stressed, relieved beyond words Jessica wasn't wearing his father's golden pearls. She was wearing, instead, the very pretty peridots he had seen before. They were almost hidden in her cloud of hair.

"That's a seriously sexy dress, Jessica," he said, the note in his voice sending exquisite little shivers up and down Jessica's spine. "I'm extremely impressed." He made a little twirling gesture. "Turn around."

Jessica joyfully obliged. She wanted to remember *everything* about tonight. Her silk chiffon dress, strapless, in a lovely shade of mint-green, was draped closely around her body to the hips, from where the tapering hem floated from mid calf almost to her ankles. Her evening shoes— she had brought them with her on the off chance—were sexy gold heels, which gave her extra height. The plunging back of the gown showed an expanse of youthful skin as smooth as cream.

"Delightful. Delectable. Delicious." His mouth curled into a rakish grin.

"Sounds like an ice cream."

"Tell her you want her to have your children," Lavinia burst out, a tender smile on her face.

Long used to her outbursts, Cyrus didn't even blink. He replied gently, "Livvy, dear, if I come on too strong I'll frighten her off."

"No, no, no. She feels safe with you. This family made one dreadful mistake. We can't make another."

Jessica intervened quickly. Although she was pleased Lavinia was coming to the party, she was concerned about what Lavinia would say in company. It was becoming increasingly apparent Lavinia dwelled in the realm of fantasy. She had never *once* called her Jessica. Why should she start now? She touched Cyrus's arm, her heart in her eyes. "*You* look wonderful."

"Thanks." He gave a little bow. "Especially as it took me several hours to fix this blasted tie."

Lavinia gave him a tap on the hand. "It did not. When do you suppose we'll have the pleasure of seeing Robyn in her birthday finery? Pity she's got such a flat chest. Poor little Sharon was just the opposite. Top heavy. I must say Broderick looks very distinguished in black tie. Such a shame he's got a manner one wouldn't wish on a rottweiler." She smiled at them happily.

Cyrus shot her a near-despairing look. "Livvy, I hope this isn't a case of your starting out the way you mean to go on. It's very rude to criticize Dad. You've just promised me you'd behave."

"Ah, yes. I did say that. And so I shall. It's just that I'm too old to worry about a lot of things."

Jessica couldn't help wondering how long it was going to take before Lavinia's thunderbolts came down on the party.

ERIK MOORE'S HOUSE was very much one built to survive the elements. Darwin had suffered terribly in Cyclone Tracy of 1973, so the architectural firm that had designed the Moore house had made sure it could withstand the most severe cyclonic weather. The massive two-story concrete structure was elevated high on piers to protect it from floodwaters and topped by a broad, sheltering hip roof. The piers, surrounded by beds of agapanthus, gave the impression the house was floating. Jessica looked around her with great interest as they walked to the glass-enclosed stairway, which was the entry to the house. Its solidity and clean lines were complemented by a splendid garden full of lush and fragrant tropical plants, trees and shrubs, including four floodlit soaring date palms with the trunks bent at an interesting angle.

"Elizabeth was a great gardener," B.B. informed Jessica, sensing her interest. As usual, he didn't even bother to lower his voice. Indeed it bounced off the glass walls. There were guests both in front and behind them, rich, solid, substantial-looking people with a fair sprinkling of very beautiful Eurasian women, all spectacularly gowned. "She was responsible for all this."

"That's so unfair, Dad," Robyn protested, holding up the skirt of her sleek black, silver-trimmed creation. "Erik had considerable input."

"Without actually doing any of the work," B.B. replied with a thin smile. "Erik is a firm believer in not getting his hands dirty."

Jessica cringed in case anyone overheard him, but she realized by now Broderick Bannerman simply didn't care. Such was the fearful power of having a great deal of money.

The plant-filled central atrium was crowded with people who acted absolutely delighted by their arrival. There were lots of beaming hellos, calls of admiration and an outbreak of clapping for the guest of honor, Robyn. The general opinion may have been Robyn was a vain self-centered creature who could turn nasty when threatened, but what the hell! She was B.B.'s stepdaughter and his good will had to be preserved at all costs. It was the way societies all over the world played the game. No one was going to be completely honest. Honesty didn't pay.

Many smiles even came from people who had never forgiven Broderick Bannerman for doing awful things to them in business, but the instant Bannerman passed by, the smiles changed to expressions of bitter envy and in some cases open rage.

What *had* he done? Jessica wondered. Obviously not enough to come under investigation like a couple of multimillionaires currently in the news, but then, an investigation would take a lot of digging.

It was odd, therefore, to witness the way Cyrus worked the atrium. If he'd been running for the top position in the Territory, he surely would have been elected. The women loved him, and why not? The men gripped his hand, the smiles apparently genuine. On the one hand a Bannerman who was held in some awe and deep-running hostility, on the other a man who appeared to be universally liked and admired.

The living room was so vast there were still empty gaps between large groups of people. Erik immediately broke away from his circle, coming toward them, his expression so full of warmth it could have melted the polar cap.

"Now the party can begin!" he cried expansively. "Darling, you look sensational!" He kissed Robyn on both cheeks. Lavinia grandly extended her hand; Jessica was welcomed to his "humble abode" and the men shook hands. "I know this is going to be a wonderful night," Erik continued jovially, the picture of prosperity in a double-breasted, beautifully tailored black dinner jacket that hid his slight paunch.

"Ever the optimist," said Broderick Bannerman.

The truth was, Broderick couldn't control the anger that prowled around inside him like a wild beast. Anger seemed to be destroying him these days. Was that inevitable as one progressed into old age? He hated the thought of growing old. There was so much more he had to do. So many future possibilities! An opportunity to redo the past and get wider meaning to his life. He had come to think of it as his second chance.

But she hadn't worn his gift of the earrings.

That affected his self-esteem, his whole view of himself as a winner. He'd been absolutely sure she would. Ferociously ambitious all his life, as well as enormously successful, he couldn't grasp the possibility he couldn't buy anything he wanted. Now the fact that he felt thwarted, *worse,* scorned, did nothing to soothe his jangled nerves. So many forces were at play. He was aware Jessica and his son had reached some kind of an understanding. That manifested itself in ways that caused him anxiety. What was more natural than a young woman turning to a young man—only, no one was going to be allowed to get in his way. Cyrus, especially, who these days only served to remind him his best days were over. *Unless* he could form a new intimate relationship. The fact Jessica so closely resembled Moira would allow him to put the past to rest. Perhaps make amends to a stern God. Ever since he'd laid eyes on Jessica, the possibility had presented itself. He thought of it as his time of *transformation*. He could construct a new identity.

The experiences of his childhood had shattered him. Years had passed in a kind of terror, but he had survived. Not only survived, he had raised the family fortune to new heights. As a prime mover he was a superstar. If he had an eye for a woman, he didn't worry too much about getting her—his money pulled her in. His mirror told him he was still handsome, fit, virile. People called him a dynamo even if these days they didn't fully realize how much Cyrus propped up that image. He was *exactly* the sort of rich man who deserved a beautiful young wife. Fate had robbed him of Deborah. But by God, it wasn't going to rob him of his second chance.

Bannerman felt the hot beating urgency of his own plan. He wasn't in love with her. Nothing so sentimental. Love had little place in his life. But he *wanted* her as an avid collector wanted a centerpiece for his collection. Yet her refusal to accept his gift had left him with a dreadful aching emptiness. And goddammit, his head ached, as well. It ached a lot these days. He put it down to a high level of stress, even if he *had* lived with stress all his life. And he'd forgotten to take his blood-pressure medication.

It was Moira who had brought destruction on his whole family. So beautiful, so full of innocent allure. His father, the war hero, respected by all, had totally lost his head over her, though he had never doubted his father had put up a fight. Loving Deborah as he had, Broderick understood the power of passion. The two of them had simply been carried away. But they would never have run off together. His father had been master of Mokhani. His poor betrayed mother should have sent Moira away. Sometimes his son's resemblance to Steven, his father, turned him inside out. Then there was Hugh Balfour, so tortured and torn he had to escape life.

He had always thought Moira had deserved to die for what she'd done to all of them. But now?

Jessica Tennant was her *blood*. He'd known that instinctively the instant he'd seen her on TV. She might as well have admitted it with her own lips. And she was *real*, not a ghost. That he'd even seen the program was a miracle, and he came to recognize it as fate. He remembered the instant of recognition as an explosion in his head. Then gradually he had begun to see how he could rewrite history. It wasn't difficult for a man in his position to have had gathered for him every scrap of information on her and her family. Families always had secrets. Even from one another. He hadn't been too shocked to find out theirs. After that, everything had fallen into place.

Everyone was a slave to fate. In reaching out to Jessica, Moira's kinswoman, by making her his wife and showering her with all the gifts money could buy when Judgment Day came—he still believed in one, for he'd been through hell, so correspondingly there had to be a heaven—mightn't he be judged less harshly? For a time, after Deborah had been taken from him, he'd been seriously suicidal, but he hadn't been able to go through with it for fear of what lay on the other side. Deep down inside him was a very frightened man. As frightened as a child whose mother had to leave a night-light burning in his room.

JESSICA, SMILING BRIGHTLY as expected, was introduced to a lot of people as the clever young woman B.B. had chosen to decorate the new mansion. She could almost hear the speculation ticking in their heads. No matter how gifted she was as a designer, wasn't she too *young* to have won such a commission? Was it sheer chance she was good-looking, as well? Some reached out to her in a warm, friendly fashion; others, older, shrewd-eyed women probably one-time girl-friends of the great man, appeared cynical. The men looked at her rather too long. She might as well have arrived hanging off B.B.'s arm for all the interest she was creating. Tonight would start a lot of malicious rumors, she thought dismally, and in turn jeopardize the blossoming relationship between her and Cyrus. That *couldn't* be allowed to happen.

Robyn wouldn't like what was happening, either. Robyn in her ultrasophisticated, one-shouldered gown with a gleaming silver trim across the neckline and on the gathered hip, was wearing glittering two-carat diamond studs in her ears. She clung to Erik, who rested his hand for the most part on her taut rounded bottom. Jessica knew she would have asked him to remove it, but Robyn obviously didn't mind.

Hours on, with the party in full swing and many whispers of a possible engagement announcement, Jessica found herself worried Robyn could be in for a bitter disappointment.

She was standing briefly on her own, waiting for Cyrus to return with champagne when Robyn, smiling brilliantly, came up to her. "Oh, Jessica, this is a dear friend of Cy's and mine. Roz Newman. She's just arrived. She had to call in on a family party."

"Hi." A very pretty, dark-haired young woman wearing an absolute knockout of a red dress, made the more so by a push-up bra, held out her hand. "It's lovely to meet you, Jessica. Robyn has told me how clever you are."

"Lovely to meet *you,* Roz," Jessica responded, looking into doe eyes that were warm and friendly. "I'm glad to hear I've done something right. It's an important commission."

"Don't I *know!*" Roz made a moue of her luscious mouth. "Everyone thought Robyn would be handling it. She did such a great job renovating the homestead, but then, she has her businesses to look after. Love your dress. One of Robyn's?"

Jessica did what was clearly expected of her. "Yes." She smiled, holding out the lovely floating skirt.

"That's Robyn. She only caters to the young and lovely."

"Make that *rich,* young and lovely," Robyn said, looking around her. "Where's Cyrus?"

"He'll be back in a moment." Jessica realized that Robyn was moving her friend right into position.

"There he is!" Roz's eyes suddenly glowed like lamps, and her smooth cheeks flushed with pleasure. "I must talk to him. We haven't seen oneanother since Mum and I took off for New York, my favorite city in the whole world. Cyrus!" she caroled, as though Cyrus walking directly toward them holding two glasses of champagne was visually challenged.

"I'll leave you to it," Robyn said. "My beloved is jealous of every minute I'm away from him."

"Robyn must have rocks in her head to even consider him," Roz muttered sotto voce as Robyn moved off.

"Really?" Jessica's ears perked up.

"We all loved Liz," Roz said, becoming aware Jessica was vaguely shocked. "She had it pretty tough with a philanderer like Erik. But Erik will do anything to get onside with B.B. Ah, here's my darling Cy," she said eagerly as Cyrus joined them.

Roz stood on tiptoe and kissed him full on the mouth.

Where there's smoke, there's usually fire, Jessica thought.

"Oh, boy! That was just what I needed!" Roz enthused, tweaking his tanned cheek. "It's *sooooo* wonderful to see you! I missed you like you wouldn't believe. You haven't returned my calls." She cast him a wickedly flirtatious look.

"I fully intended to get around to it," he apologized. "But you know me, Roz. I'm always working."

"Too hard, if you ask me. Are those drinks for us?"

"Roz you look too young to be drinking," he teased, handing one glass to Jessica before giving the other to Roz.

"You know exactly how old I am," Roz said, taking a sip. "Oh, that's glorious!"

"And damned expensive," Cyrus said dryly.

"Erik wants to impress B.B.," Roz gurgled.

Jessica stared at them with a near-disembodied sensation. What did she know of his life, after all? "Look, you two have a lot to catch up on," she said brightly. "I'll see you later."

"You'll be sure to," Cyrus retorted as Jessica all but flew away.

It was the opportunity for Broderick Bannerman to move in. He reached out to grasp Jessica's arm. He was infuriated with his son. So jealous, the heat of it consumed him.

"You've met Roz," he said, powerfully proprietorial in his manner. "Scatty little thing, but she's always been wild about Cyrus. Her mother and father are here. You've probably met them. Max and Sonia Newman of Newman

Industries? Max and I sit on various boards together." He drew her toward the upper balcony, which looked out on the midnight-blue harbor scattered in the moonlight, with a billion sequined dots. "Your dress is beautiful, but the earrings you're wearing spoil the effect."

"I'm sorry. I thought they went well," Jessica said lightly. "I loved the earrings you picked out, Broderick. You have perfect taste, but no way am I deserving of such a valuable, *personal* gift."

"Don't be ridiculous," he said impatiently, fighting to keep his anger under wraps. "If I think you are, you *are!*"

With her instinct for people, Jessica was aware of the terrible tensions that were tearing him apart. He was very flushed in the face. "Do you feel okay?" she asked with concern, staring into his face.

"I'm fine when I'm talking to you." He dropped his hand to close it over hers, an action Jessica was certain was seized on. "This party and the people here are boring me stiff. I don't know what Robyn sees in Erik. He'll never make a tender, loving husband."

"Maybe she's desperate for love," Jessica suggested, withdrawing her hand under the pretext of checking a stray lock of hair. "She seems to be missing out on it."

He laughed roughly. "You amaze me, Jessica. No one else says things like that to my face."

"You were wondering, and I tried to supply a probable answer. Why *does* Robyn persist if she knows you don't approve? I don't think she's in love with him, either."

"Mostly because she's turned thirty," he said dryly. "She's no different from other women. She wants a man. She wants to be married. She's had plenty come courting. *I* didn't send them away, in case you're about to blame me. *She* did. She lost every one of them with her lack of charm. Now, would you care to dance?"

"That would be lovely."

What else could she say? She had to handle this situation as carefully as she'd handle a hive of hornets.

THINGS DIDN'T GET BETTER, they got worse. Roz Newman set about making up for lost time. Time and again, she attempted to chain Cyrus to her side, though to Jessica's immense relief she was far from successful.

"Ever tried saying no?" she suggested sweetly when Cyrus groaned. They were dancing.

His embrace tightened. He was a terrific dancer. "You might try doing the same with Dad."

Broderick Bannerman had continued to pay his strange court to Jessica. Already it had set tongues clacking like knitting needles. Was B.B. looking for a trophy wife? Would she be the one? As the night wore on, B.B. wasn't the only man who made a pass at her. Serious, solidly respectable types did, too. It was as Jessica had come to accept. Men behaved badly around blondes.

There was no engagement announcement before or after the sumptuous supper featuring the superb seafood of these tropical waters. Didn't Erik Moore see that's what Robyn had pinned her hopes on? Didn't he care? Did he think B.B.'s disapproval would in the end work against him? Who could tell? Robyn's rigid expression revealed that Erik had taken a massive swipe at her ego. Jessica sincerely hoped she would dump him and afterward seriously consider charm school.

It was Lavinia, who was having a fine old time catching up with all the gossip, who brought the evening to a spectacular end. She was seated on a comfortable sofa with a few older ladies, stately stalwarts of Darwin society, when she called to Jessica from halfway across the room.

"Moira, dear! Yoohoo!" There was little hope no one heard her even in a very large room. Lavinia's voice was her splendor. It had been big enough to project to the bleachers in her prime. To add to it, she held up her hand, setting several antique bracelets tolling like temple bells. "Come and meet my friends."

The whole area took a collective breath.

Moira?

The laughter, the animated conversation turned off like a tap. They might have all been waiting for a cataclysmic announcement.

"Funny old thing!" someone said, giving a nervous giggle.

"Moira, did you hear me, dear?" Lavinia raised the decibels as if she wanted to crack glass.

Another woman muttered an obscene word beneath her breath and her husband looked at her in astonishment. "Carole!"

"What the hell am I supposed to say?" Carole retaliated, although she wished she hadn't been shocked into a swear word. "That Lavinia frightens me to death."

"It's Alzheimer's," another woman said sorrowfully. "The family is in for a tough time."

Farther away Broderick Bannerman looked up from a discussion with a couple of his business cronies, the hectic flush on his face deepening further.

"That's just dandy," Cyrus muttered in Jessica's ear. "Frankly I don't know how we got through this much of the night."

"I better go to her," Jessica said, horrified to be the focus of hundreds of eyes. "She'll only persist."

"Yes. I guess they can hear her at city hall." Cyrus realized with a jolt that his father looked furious. But, hell, wouldn't it be fair to say it was on their own heads, bringing Lavinia? Without question, she was suffering some form of dementia, but why should she be condemned to stay at home? She was *family*, even if she was border-line nuts.

Cyrus and Jessica walked toward Lavinia as one. "Livvy, dear, perhaps we should consider making a move," he prompted gently, leaning over the sofa and clasping Lavinia's bony shoulder. "It's well after twelve. You must be tired."

"Just a teeny bit." Lavinia laughed, fighting to get up before someone helped her. "Josie, you remember Moira, don't you?" She addressed a very smart septuagenarian with beautifully coiffed platinum hair.

"Jessica Tennant," Jessica smiled at the woman.

"She's all grown-up," Lavinia said. "I've waited over fifty years."

Josie patted Lavinia's cheek. "You aren't supposed to talk about Moira anymore, dear," she chided affectionately, herself forcibly struck by Jessica's extraordinary resem-blance to the missing girl. "She's dead, darling."

"No, *no!*" Lavinia's voice took on a soaring wail. "She was just hiding. Weren't you, Moira?"

"Why don't you find Robyn and Erik? Tell them we're leaving," Cyrus suggested to Jessica in a low voice, quickly getting an arm around Lavinia.

"Robyn looks so damned unhappy," Lavinia moaned. "He might have been toying with the idea of marrying her, trying to work out if it was the right move, but he won't now. Broderick is against it. Probably the kindest stand Broderick's taken in his whole life."

"We'll say our good nights." Cyrus flashed the group the charming smile that worked miracles. He expected and got their understanding. It wasn't until the very last minute the woman called Josie caught Jessica's hand.

"Poor old Liv! No wonder she's confused. You're the very image of Moira, my dear. Is there any connection? I can't help wondering."

"I'm sorry, none." Jessica said. She could see that the woman didn't quite believe her.

B.B. GESTURED FOR THEM to meet him in the central atrium, which was diplomatically cleared in seconds, though the partygoers were dying to stay and watch. Everyone knew the Bannermans weren't like anybody else. And old Lavinia, bless her, was good for a laugh at any time. She was what Darwin society thought of as a real character, a welcome eccentric.

"You can't be trusted, Lavinia, can you?" B.B. bore down on her, his deep voice thin with anger.

"About what?" Lavinia demanded to know, turning fearlessly toward that hard face and glittering eyes.

"Please leave it, Dad." Cyrus had an authority all his own. "At least until we get out of here. I'll take her back to the hotel. I won't be coming back to the party. Robyn and Erik won't mind."

"You don't intend on leaving, as well, do you, Jessica?" Bannerman whipped around to ask, his tone oddly vulnerable.

A strange sense of sympathy flowed through her. She could hardly claim to like him—he didn't allow anyone to like him—but she was trying hard to understand him. "I'm only in the way, Broderick. People are talking. Robyn won't want me around."

"Don't worry about *her,* Moira," Lavinia advised, opening her evening bag and putting away her glasses.

"You always were a tender hearted little thing. It will all pass like a nine-day wonder."

Robyn rushed out from the living room in a fury. "God, I swear I'm going to scream! Lavinia isn't eccentric, she's barking *mad*. I told you, Dad, it was a mistake to let her come. She's made a show of us all."

"And you're about to make another one." Broderick shrugged a powerful shoulder as though he couldn't care less.

Cyrus, however, spoke to Robyn in an undertone. "Hey, the biggest mistake is your hooking up with Moore. Leave Livvy alone. She can't help what's happened to her mind. Jessica *is* the image of Moira, after all."

Jessica's heart skipped many beats. In her ear came a long, soft sigh. She wondered where it'd come from.

Broderick Bannerman stared at his son, his formerly flushed face now drained of color. "And how would *you* know?" he asked.

"By checking. Just like you, Dad." Cyrus locked eyes with his father. "What did you think you were doing, putting a portrait of Moira on the market? What did you hope to achieve?"

Bannerman's handsome features went slack for a few moments, then he laughed harshly. "I don't have to explain myself to you."

"Maybe you could explain it to *me*, then, Broderick," Jessica said, her sympathy evaporating. "It upsets me you didn't hire me for my professional skills. I could have been puttering away in my office earmarked for failure, for all you cared."

"That's not true." Broderick looked momentarily off balance. He searched Jessica's face for understanding. "I hired you because you've achieved recognition in your profession. Look, we can't argue here. You'd better go. Please remember, Jessica, that you signed a contract. You're obliged to finish the job. If you doubt it, you should have devoted yourself to reading the fine print."

Robyn stabbed a finger at Lavinia. "I could kill you," she cried emotionally. "You're a real witch."

Lavinia trilled aloud. "Takes one to know one," she retorted, quite unmoved.

A nerve twitched near Robyn's eye. She continued to accompany them down the stairs. "You have no business being allowed out, Lavinia."

"More of us out than in, Robyn," Lavinia told her sweetly.

"It was all destined," Broderick muttered.

"More like planned." Cyrus gave a short, angry laugh. "You've got a lot to answer for, Dad. You might have been only a kid, but you didn't escape it all. I think you know— or you learned—what happened to that poor girl."

"Yes, who did it?" Lavinia, showing her vocal range, toned her voice down to a whisper. "Did she die from a fall? Was it an accident?"

"Hello, you're *with* us, are you?" Broderick asked of his aunt, not without humor.

"Livvy, please stop." Cyrus spoke so firmly Lavinia responded by zipping her fingers across her mouth. "This conversation has to continue at another time."

"Trust me, it *won't!*" Broderick whipped out a snowy handkerchief and mopped his broad brow. "And don't take that tone with me, Cyrus." It was obvious he was barely keeping himself in check. "I *forbid* you to take Jessica."

"That's a pity, because take her is what I intend to do," Cyrus returned curtly. "It's what Jessica wants, after all. Let's finish this right now." He grasped both Jessica and Lavinia by the hand, then inclined his head toward the living room. "They must be just loving it inside. The feuding Bannermans. Have you heard what they're up to now?" He exhaled in disgust. "Let's face it, Dad. You don't inspire trust."

This charge suddenly reminded Robyn of her dearest role in life. She linked her arm through her stepfather's, chin up, eyes flashing, the picture of loyalty. "*I* know Dad better than *you* do, Cy!" she exploded. "I love him, unlike *you*. You don't deserve to be his heir. You're staying, aren't you, Dad?" She turned, imploring eyes on her stepfather, though he was standing stock-still, seemingly unaware of her. "Don't abandon me."

"Quit sucking up to him, Robyn," Lavinia advised. "It does no good at all."

That brought Broderick out of his semi-trance. "I'll stay for another hour," he said, his face impassive. "In my opinion, Erik humiliated you tonight, Robyn. But don't worry, he'll pay."

"That's right, make 'em pay, Brodie," Lavinia crowed as Cyrus and Jessica led her away. "You should get on with your own life, Robyn. The *D*-word comes around quicker than you think."

"What's the *D*-word?" Robyn frowned in perplexity.

It was possible there was great sadness in Broderick Bannerman's answering voice. *"Death,"* he said.

CHAPTER THIRTEEN

THEY WALKED TOGETHER along the waterfront with the trade winds blowing in off the Timor Sea. The great copper moon of the tropics hung over the vast expanse of the harbor cutting a bright orange path from the glittering water to the sky. It was a beautiful night with a lovely breeze that strengthened into intermittent gusts. It caught at Jessica's long hair and silk chiffon skirt, ruffling the surface of the water into peaks that broke in white ruffles on the shore.

Their minds, still frazzled by the events of the evening, they were just trying to relax. They had finally got Lavinia to bed—she'd been overexcited, difficult to calm—and now both Jessica and Cyrus recognized that either this thing mounting between them had to stop, or become a serious commitment. Nothing this desperate stood still.

"How did you know your father had sent Moira's portrait to auction?" Jessica asked, watching a pair of lovers blend into the night. "You didn't tell me."

"I *didn't* know," he said wretchedly "Dad just fell into the trap." Cyrus cursed himself for what he had to say. "You know you can't remain on Mokhani, Jessica, no matter what threats my father makes. I'll take care of all that. If you *don't* go, we're headed for an almighty showdown."

They were her own thoughts; nevertheless, she was

devastated to hear him put them into words. "Hang on a minute. I've scarcely arrived." The fact he was urging her to go, with good reasons or not, sliced into her like a knife. She had fallen crazily in love with him. She was ready to take her chances. Now he wanted to see her off.

Cyrus caught her into the half circle of his arm, so attuned to her he knew what was running through her head. "I know. It's one hell of a mess, but it's just too explosive. You *know* it is." There was a ragged edge to his voice. "I'm worried about you and I'm worried about my father. I've never seen him like this before. He's getting like Livvy. Mixing up the past with the present. Did you see how flushed he was tonight?"

She nodded, not trusting herself to speak, she was so agitated. "He lives under such pressure," she managed to say after a while. "It can't be good for him. Now there's this problem of *me*. Something *new* is driving him."

"You don't have to be Einstein to work it out." Cyrus's voice grated. "When Livvy looks at you, she sees Moira. It seems Dad does, too, in a way. Obviously, he's never been able to forget her. Maybe he's trying to bring Moira back. God, I don't know, but I don't like it."

Jessica shook her windblown hair from her face. "Do you suppose Moira could have been murdered all those years ago?"

Cyrus's groan was eloquent of unhappiness and confusion. "She disappeared, Jessica. This mystery will never go cold."

"Is that a yes?"

"It's a *no!*" He turned her to him almost desperately. "We're talking about *my* family, remember? *My* blood."

Tension was crackling like the flames of a bonfire. "I'm sorry."

They walked on, reaching a moon-washed clearing like a small park. Her stiletto heels dug into the grass as they moved off the pathway into the deep sapphire gloom. Colors of flowers came out of the darkness. Color and heady tropical scent. She could see timber benches.

"Jessica?"

She lifted her face to him with breathless urgency, her feelings for him invading every part of her, wiping out anger. "What?"

He stared down into her shimmering face "*You*. Just you." In his world gone mad, she seemed to be the only thing he could hold on to. He bent his head, kissing the side of her satin cheek, burying his face in her neck. "You smell like a field of flowers."

The way he said it was so seductive, so utterly thrilling it went a long way toward restoring her badly shaken confidence. She wanted to beg him to make love to her, furious with Broderick Bannerman for pursuing her and thus ruining everything....

"Hey." He lifted his head. "Are you getting shorter or what?"

She held on to him with a little shaky laugh. "My high heels are digging into the grass. I'm sinking. There's a bench around here someplace." She felt she had to sit down. *Lie* down. Her breathing had changed—short, faintly panting.

"So there is." Without warning, he lifted her high in his arms as if her weight were insubstantial. The bench was set on a concrete block. He lowered her gently onto it, keeping his arms around her. "You should wear that dress always. Though if I had you to myself, I'd peel it off you."

"When will that ever be?" she asked mournfully, aware the parameters of her world had shifted. She was so much in love with him she was ready to do things perhaps she shouldn't. Cyrus Bannerman was her one great leap into the unknown.

"Can't be soon enough," he said fervently. "I want *you* no matter how much baggage keeps getting in the way."

"Why should we let it?" That golden moon hovered over them, like a pathway to heaven. She lifted her arms, drew down his dark head.

Why indeed!

When he finally stopped kissing her, it was only to mutter, "I think we should finish this in your room—or *my* room?"

"What happens when your father comes looking for us?" she asked in a voice verging on edgy laughter. "God knows he's capable of it."

"We don't answer." Cyrus was almost afraid of what he might say and do if his father pushed him too far. The idea of his father wanting this young woman he had come to love drove him crazy. Clashes with his father were one thing, but this was so dreadfully inappropriate. "Kissing you is wonderful," he murmured. "You weave such a spell. Look at this hair!" He speared a hand through the pale moonlit tresses in wonderment. "I want to see your hair spread out on my pillow. You can wear your earrings—they're very pretty, after all, but nothing else." He twisted a long coil of her hair around her throat. "You'll make an exquisite bride."

Jessica's heart rocked in her breast. "Is that a proposal?"

"Why would someone like you want to marry into my family?" he asked with near despair. "Mokhani isn't a safe place for beautiful young women. Beauty seduces. Just as in the fairy tales, it can also carry a curse."

"Don't *say* that!" She put her fingers against his mouth.

He caught them and kissed them. "A world lost for love! I see nothing. I hear nothing. All there is, is *you* all around *me*."

"I might use the very same words," she whispered.

"I never want to let you go. I *won't* let you go." He stood up, pulling her to her feet. Their hunger for each other swept all before it. Tonight they were on the crest of a wave....

As THEY HEADED BACK to the hotel, cars whizzed back and forth, couples strolled arm in arm or came out of restaurants, laughing, ready to go on to nightclubs.

"So much we have to get to the bottom of," Cyrus said. "Dad knows a lot he's not telling."

"Why don't you try to speak to your aunt Barbara again?" Jessica hugged his arm, thinking for all that was happening she had never been aware of such happiness.

He sighed deeply. "My aunt finds the whole subject of Moira and her disappearance too painful. Not that she'd know anything. Whatever happened would have been kept from the children."

"Unless your father saw what happened with his own eyes," she found herself suggesting, albeit in a fuzzy way. Certainly she'd made no decision to say it.

"God, no!" A convulsive shudder went through Cyrus's lean body. "He *couldn't* have been there. Dad was only seven. He would have been able to ride, of course, but he'd have been forbidden to venture too far from the main compound. From all accounts, there was a bad thunderstorm that day, as well. I've gone over and over this, Jessica. Dad couldn't have been out there."

"Could he have gone with someone who was?" The compulsion to ask these questions was worsening. She couldn't contain them.

He flinched, his arm tightening around her. "My grandmother or my grandfather?" he asked bitterly.

"I know how upsetting this is for you," she said quickly. "It was only a suggestion."

"I want a life *free* of the past, Jessica. You've affected us all so much. But we now know your coming to Mokhani was planned by my father. The great irony is I have to thank him for that, otherwise our paths would never have crossed. Dad's getting you to Mokhani had little to do with decorating the mausoleum. I don't want to offend you, but he probably didn't care if you turned out to be the worst designer in the length and breadth of Australia. He hired you to rework his *life* in some way. It's almost as though he's trying to rewrite history. But nothing makes sense. I can't begin to understand his motives. I'm horrified Dad has become fixated on you. He doesn't want *me* to get in the way…. Oh, hell, what's the use of talking about it? I don't want to talk. I want to make love."

"You shouldn't have to be in conflict with your father over me. It's not *meant* to be that way," Jessica cried. "I love *you!*"

WHEN THEY ARRIVED BACK at the hotel, they found Broderick waiting for them in the lobby. The minute he saw them, he heaved himself to his feet.

Cyrus swore beneath his breath. Jessica felt she could swim an ocean to get away. The unthinkable was becoming a daily occurrence.

Broderick approached, his shoulders hunched. "All right, so you're back!" He glared at his son, so cruelly young and handsome. God, if he had his time over again! he thought. Aging was a whiplash across a man's back. Jessica appeared to float, a lovely fluid motion to her skirt, her eyes brimming with emotion.

But not for *him.*

She was Moira, only different. Stronger, far more confident, knowing her place in the world. The tears would never dry for Moira. Moira lying so secret, so hidden away from the world.

"Don't do this, Dad," Cyrus muttered, between clenched teeth. "How can you sit here waiting for us like we were children?"

"I'll remind you, Cyrus, Jessica is *my* responsibility," Broderick said aloud, in a hostile voice.

Jessica noticed several other hotel guests looking their way. She squirmed inside. "You must excuse me," she said in haste. "I'm tired. I'm going to my room." She didn't fancy getting her picture in the noon papers.

"We'll all go up," Cyrus said briskly.

Broderick didn't say another word until they were in the elevator. Just the three of them in a claustrophobic space. "It may seem an odd thing for me to do, Jessica," Broderick said, apparently in an effort to apologize to her. "But your well-being is important to me."

"It's highly unlikely I'd come to any harm with Cyrus, Broderick," she said. "Besides, I can take care of myself." She didn't want to say another word, sensing they were on the brink of a terrible argument. It couldn't be good for Broderick. His color wasn't good. In the space of a few hours, he'd aged ten years. All the virility had seeped out of him.

"You know Cyrus is involved with Roz Newman?" he announced abruptly. "Am I wrong, Cyrus?" he challenged. "I rather think she's expecting an engagement ring sometime soon."

"And she's as likely to get one as Robyn." Cyrus issued a humorless laugh. "What are you on about, Dad?"

"You know damn well!" Broderick snarled. "It's for Jessica's own good."

"I'm sorry. This is my floor." Jessica took quick steps forward. "It's best if I say good night."

She wasn't swift enough.

"Not yet!" Broderick grasped her bare arm, restraining her. The door closed while they all stood arrested. "I want you to come up to my suite."

"Oh, Dad!" Cyrus groaned, shaking his dark head. His formidable father, always cold reason, seemed to be disintegrating right before his very eyes. "What's going on with you?" He began to wonder if dementia was going to overtake the entire family.

"What do my actions possibly have to do with you?" Broderick said through gritted teeth.

"I'm your son, remember?"

"So maybe I want your support, not your opposition."

"To do *what?*" Cyrus appealed to him. "Can you let us know what's on your mind?"

"I don't trust you, Cyrus," his father snapped.

"Around Jessica, is that what you mean?" Cyrus watched the high color flare into his father's face. "I take it that's a yes," he said quietly.

They had arrived at the top floor where Broderick had his suite. Still clutching Jessica's arm, he stepped out into the empty hallway, Cyrus right behind. Broderick turned Jessica to face him. "I thought you liked me, Jessica." Incredibly he spoke like a suitor who having been led on, was left bitterly confused and disappointed.

"Of course I like you, Broderick," Jessica said, sick with pity and embarrassment. "But first and foremost you're my client."

Their voices were hushed, but the atmosphere couldn't have been more intense.

"That's the only reason I got you to Mokhani," he ex-

242   THE CATTLEMANTHE CATTLEMAN

plained, never taking his eyes off her. "So we could get to know one another."

Jessica dropped her head, quite unable to meet his gaze. He had placed her in a terrible position. "I can't talk about it anymore. I had no idea your thoughts were running on those lines. You actually got me to Mokhani under false pretenses, Broderick. I was so excited to get such a commission, too. I've done so much work already. All for nothing! Cyrus is right. I must go home."

"Go home?" Broderick's eyes flashed with shock and rage.

"You don't leave her with much alternative, Dad," said Cyrus. "There can't be any relationship between you and Jessica." He stretched out his hand to his father in sympathy.

But Broderick ignored the gesture. "You envy me, Cyrus. Envy fills your heart. Envy of one's father is a terrible thing."

"It's the other way around in our case," Cyrus said with weary sadness. "I don't envy you at all. You may have achieved a great deal in your life, but you're not a happy man. You've given everyone, including yourself, such a hard time. Let's end this discussion. Call it a night. You can't expect Jessica to want to stay on when you're starting to harass her."

"Harass her?" Broderick spat. "How dare you!" He shook his head like some sovereign of old, ready and able to put his own son's head on the block. "How dare you say such a thing! It's not *right!*" He twisted his body, shaking his head from side to side.

Tears were forming in Jessica's eyes. "Please stop, Broderick," she begged, laying a restraining hand on his arm. "You don't look at all well. You must see I can't stay."

Arrogance flooded Broderick Bannerman's expression. "My son is acting like he's trying to protect you. He really just wants you for himself."

"And you have a big problem with that, don't you, Dad?"

"You've always hated me, Cyrus."

Cyrus's handsome face contorted in distress. "God, Dad, we're *family*. The wonder is I *don't* hate you. You've always treated me like the enemy even when Mum was alive. You seemed to see me as a rival for her love and attention, isn't that right? You turned your back on me when I was just a kid. You didn't change even after she was dead."

Broderick's head shook as though he had palsy. "You can't know how desperately unhappy that made me."

"You could have turned to me, your son." Cyrus got a grip on his father's shoulder. "But that didn't cross your mind. You set out to bring me to my knees. I might have been another man's son. That really worried me when I was a kid, do you know that? I seriously considered I might have been a bastard. That would explain your behavior. But I look like you, don't I? I also look like my grandfather, Steven. I'm the Bannerman you rejected."

His father looked a bit mad. "With good reason. You're the—"

"Broderick, *stop.*" Jessica put herself between the two men. "Somewhere deep down, Broderick, I think you hate yourself."

It was a statement that seemed to strike Broderick Bannerman like a blow. He closed his eyes as though he were in terrible pain and slumped as if pierced through with a sword. "I do. You're right, I do," he muttered.

"Let's go, Jessica." Cyrus reached for her.

But like a man possessed, Broderick changed suddenly from passive to violent.

"Cyrus!" Jessica shouted the warning, but it was too late.

With a look of savage hatred in his eyes, his fist clenched, Broderick Bannerman launched himself at his son, screaming, "Do you understand what you've done to me? *Do you?* Treason—"

Almost without volition, Cyrus swung a defensive punch. It sent his father sprawling back against the wall, from there to the floor, where he slumped into a posture of defeat.

Immediately Cyrus felt an overwhelming disgust for himself. He stretched out his hand. "Get up, Dad. I shouldn't have done that. Neither should you."

His face marred by a look of terrible bitterness and defeat, Broderick allowed himself to be pulled to his feet. "Damn you to hell!" he swore.

"I'm sorry I hit you." The words were flat.

"We've got nothing to say to each other," his father snarled. "Take her if you want her. She's not who she says she is, anyway. She's Moira back from the other side."

It was meant to be a deadly parting shot, only Broderick staggered, clutching at his head with his two hands.

"Aaaaaaaah!"

"Dad!" Cyrus cried in alarm.

"Go to hell," Bannerman said, still clutching his head.

Cyrus turned to Jessica. "Call an ambulance," he said urgently, moving to his father to physically support him.

She needed no prompting.

CHAPTER FOURTEEN

OVER THE NEXT FEW DAYS, the family fielded innumerable questions from the media about Broderick Bannerman's condition. Finally Cyrus had to take the phone off the hook. Their stock answer had been the same as the spokesman's for the Royal Darwin Hospital. Mr. Bannerman was resting comfortably. He had not suffered a heart attack or a stroke. He would be in hospital a day or two, undergoing tests.

A media crew drove all the way from Darwin to the station, but got turned back by stockmen acting as security guards. A media helicopter flew over the main compound, taking aerial shots, but the pilot wasn't about to risk landing. This was the Territory and strangers didn't come onto a man's land without an invitation. B.B. especially had to be treated with respect.

What Broderick Bannerman was really suffering from was a tumor growing in the right posterior temporal region of his brain, dangerously close to the brain stem. This information was not released to the press. The tumor would most certainly paralyze him, cause deafness, blindness, in short, kill him if not removed or treated by chemotherapy, which he refused. Broderick Bannerman had elected to take his chances with an operation. His doctors gave him only a fifty percent chance of survival.

It seemed the family had found the explanation for the patriarch's frenzied behavior.

"So this is when we say goodbye to Broderick," Lavinia announced, crossing herself in a rare moment of religious fervor. "Who would ever have thought I might outlive him? I'm old, old, old. A nuisance to everyone, including myself. He was a beautiful little boy. Steven's heir. We all thought he was going to be fine. It's what happened to Moira that tore the family apart. Even now Barbara won't come to Mokhani, although she visited the hospital." Lavinia was seated in her favorite planter's chair on the front veranda. Jessica had taken a chair near her, holding the frail hand with its knotted fingers. The skin around the contours of Lavinia's eyes was a murky violet, but the eyes themselves were bright. Jessica had the idea Lavinia played a lot at being batty. "You should ask him before it's too late," Lavinia said.

"Ask him what, Miss Lavinia?" Jessica tried to smile into the old lady's face.

"What they did with you, of course."

That blew the notion of not being batty out of the water.

A little distance off in the trees, a bird sang one beautiful heart-piercing note.

Jessica stood up. "I think I hear the phone. It could be Cyrus." Cyrus was in Darwin meeting with the eminent neurosurgeon who was to head the team to perform the very difficult and risky operation on his father.

It wasn't Cyrus. It was Brett, saying he couldn't leave until the weekend, but he and Tim were coming up to join her and take her home.

"You need to be looked after, Jass," he told her, his voice filled with concern. "You sound unhappy."

"I seem to have been through a lot." A lot she hadn't told him.

"It's scarcely your fault, sweetheart." Brett tried to console her. "The tumor has probably been growing for years. Cyrus will probably want to continue the project at some point, but that will be the last thing on his mind with his father so ill. And right in the middle of it, you win the award. You have to show up for the ceremony, you know. Life goes on, no matter what. We have to celebrate it. I'm very proud of you."

ROBYN WAS TAKING her stepfather's illness very badly. In fact, she looked like she was coming apart, lost in silent, secret, desperation.

Jessica no longer doubted Robyn loved her stepfather. She was not prepared, however, for Robyn's anger. "He doesn't want to see me anymore!" she screamed at Jessica, having sent Lavinia rushing to her room as though she couldn't lock the door fast enough. "I'm nothing to him. *No one.* I never have been."

"He doesn't want to see Cyrus, either," Jessica tried to point out. Facing death, Broderick had turned in on himself. "He's not clear in his mind."

"No, he's not." Abruptly she changed topics. "So who are you really?" Robyn stared at Jessica with her deep-set dark eyes.

Jessica sighed. "Not a ghost, Robyn. It's all gone far enough, this Moira business. Your stepfather has an excuse. He's been diagnosed with a brain tumor. Lavinia's excuse is—"

"She's mad as a bloody hatter," Robyn interrupted bitterly. "God, why doesn't the old bat die? Oh no, she's got plans to stick around for Cyrus's wedding when it's just possible he won't get married for years he's so bloody choosy. Look, I've got to get out of the house. Why don't we go for a ride?"

"If you want to," Jessica agreed, not really wanting to, but realizing Robyn was suffering in her own way.

WHEN THE STABLE BOY led out Chloe, Robyn turned abruptly. "I don't like that horse. It's bad-tempered. Take her back."

"It's for Miss Jessica," the boy said. "She rides him."

Robyn stared at Jessica with something like outrage. "Since when?"

"Since Cyrus took me to the escarpment," Jessica said, having second thoughts about accompanying this volatile young woman. Robyn delighted in baiting Lavinia about her eccentricities. Was it possible Robyn was bipolar? She certainly had huge mood swings. "It was when you were in Hong Kong."

"Congratulations. So how did you manage to stay on?" Robyn gave a twisted smile, laced with challenge.

"She's better than you," the stable boy piped up, digging his hands into his jeans.

"Oh, shut up." Viciously Robyn flicked her whip at him but he moved out of range with natural agility. "Who's asking you?" she growled.

"Only tryin' to help." Unperturbed, the boy gave Jessica a big white grin.

"Don't worry, Robyn, I'll keep up," Jessica said. "I don't think we should go all that far. Cy is due home late afternoon."

"You're involved with him, aren't you?" Robyn swung her leg over her mount, a big gelding. Her tone was despairing, as though she could prevent nothing.

Jessica turned the question aside. "Cy's thoughts are only for his father."

AN HOUR AND MORE LATER, they were lost in the vastness that was Mokhani.

"Somewhere around here that blasted Moira's life came to an end." Robyn sat her horse, one hand on the reins, the other indicating the primal wilderness surrounding them. "I suppose if the truth be known, someone killed her. I can just see it happening. She was very pretty, from all accounts."

Jessica shuddered. "Do you really believe someone in your family was capable of murder?"

"Not *my* family!" Robyn gave a bitter laugh. "I have something to be grateful for, it seems. My poor mother was a saint. She put up with Dad, who treated her like dirt, just a possible brood mare Dad could never get his adored Deborah out of his memory. He even turned on Cy, his own son. I ask you, is that crazy or what? Anyway, there's been some haunting in this family. The legend of bloody Moira has survived the test of time."

"She ought not be *bloody* Moira, Robyn. She was a victim and so young!" Jessica stared out over the immense primeval landscape. Its extraordinary mystique was palpable. It wasn't just the wonder of nature, the vastness or the savage beauty. It was the *antiquity* of the Timeless Land, the oldest continent on earth.

They were taking shelter beneath the branches of the loveliest of all the Outback trees, the slender white ghost gums. A grove of six or more were growing luxuriantly out of the sand, highlighting the rust-red of the soil, the golden grasses that sprung out of it and the burnt siennas of the boulders strewn about like discarded devils' marbles. To the northeast, the purple escarpment stood out ruggedly against the brilliant cobalt sky. She marveled that she had actually been right to the summit. She'd walked the length of that magical canyon with its rainbow walls, caught the spray off the waterfall, pondered the mysteries of the deep dark green lagoon where the spirit of a beautiful *lubra* had made her home.

"It's easy to see how Moira could have disappeared." Jessica spoke her thoughts aloud. "Someone who didn't know the bush would be in a lot of danger out here."

Robyn's expression was chilling. "Easy to bury the body. We have cases of disappearance right now in the present. That English tourist—they'll never find him."

"What a great grief for his family." Jessica drew a deep sigh. "Moira's family must have been devastated. I don't think they could have faced the notion she might have been murdered. They had enough of a nightmare to contend with. I've never asked you about what happened to *your* mother, Robyn. You must have loved her dearly."

Robyn hunched forward in the saddle, frowning. "I did. She comes to me in my dreams. But when she was alive, she was little use to me. She was completely dominated by Dad."

"How did she die?" Jessica asked again, very gently.

Robyn's face, inexplicably, became distorted by anger. "Curious, are you?"

"I'm sorry." Jessica hastened to apologize. "I was actually trying to help. Sometimes it lightens the load if you can share it with someone. You haven't had an easy time, Robyn."

Robyn's eyes brimmed. "Don't feel sorry for me. Feel sorry for yourself. Cyrus is only using you. You're nothing in the scheme of things. Just a passing affair. He doesn't give a damn about you, really."

"I don't think you're in his confidence," Jessica said. She trusted Cyrus. She knew she was right to trust him. This was a clumsy attempt to undermine him.

"I know this much." Robyn looked at Jessica, hard-eyed. "He's going to marry Roz Newman. He doesn't need you. He needs Mokhani . He's there in Darwin pouring out filial love, but he's too late. Dad will see I get what I deserve."

"You can't be implying he'll make you his heir?"

Robyn gave a convulsive laugh that petered out. "Cyrus hitting on you was a disastrous move. It upset Dad greatly. From that moment, things started going well for me."

"I thought you wanted to marry Erik Moore." Jessica endeavored to follow Robyn's reasoning.

She shrugged. "Dad was right. He isn't worthy of me. Liz did try to warn me."

Jessica shook her head. "Don't you think it strange your stepfather doesn't want to see you now? Perhaps he was building up your hopes, Robyn, only to knock them down. A tumor affects the sufferer's behavior, sometimes in a disastrous way. I would say even before that, your stepfather liked to pull the rug out from under people."

"He's famous for it," Robyn confirmed. "People have warned me a thousand times but I was blind. Dad seemed like a god to me when I was a kid. My judgments were all wrong. I picked the wrong Bannerman to be my champion." Robyn sank in the saddle as though all the air had gone out of her body. "Cyrus tried to bond with me, God knows he got precious little love from his dad, but I shut him out. You know why? There's something dread-fully wrong with me. I'm even *happy* in a way that Dad's dying—put him out of his misery. He's said some rotten things to me. If there is a heaven, which I seriously doubt, Mum will be there. Dad, I'm thinking, is heading straight for hell."

THE SUN SANK IN A BLAZING BALL of fire toward a horizon brushed with great sweeps of pinks, golds, indigo and grape. The mauve dusk settled in quickly. They didn't seem to be getting anywhere. How was it possible for Robyn to get lost? She'd grown up on Mokhani. The horses were tired and sweating, especially the filly, Chloe.

Robyn ripped off her Akubra and smoothed her shiny black hair in agitation. "Listen, I have to go for help. You stay put. You'll just be holding me up."

"You don't expect me to stay here by myself, do you?" Jessica looked nervously around her, amazed that the Outback-bred Robyn seemed as disoriented as she was.

"You're not scared, are you?" Robyn taunted.

"I think anyone in their right mind would be. It's pitch black at night. There's no water. We haven't seen any dingoes, but I'm sure they're about. What about snakes? Are you sure you're not doing this deliberately? You want to punish me for some reason? You said yourself there's something wrong with you."

"Don't be so bloody stupid," Robyn snarled. "Cyrus will be home. He'll be expecting us back. All you have to do is stay put. That's the first rule in the bush. When someone knows the area you're in, you stay there. You don't move off. I'll ride back as fast as I can. I can cope a lot better without you and the filly tagging along. She's tired. She doesn't have the stamina of the gelding. Cyrus will be only too happy to come back for you. You might even rate a night under the stars. Make the most of it. It's all you're going to get."

ROBYN ARRIVED BACK at the homestead to a very hostile reception.

"Explain yourself, Robyn. And fast." Cyrus's voice

carried the strain of their wait. "You rode out together. Where's Jessica?" Cyrus generated such anger it was like a fire had been lit inside him.

"Yes, where is she?" Lavinia ran at Robyn raining blows on her. "Don't lie to us, you wicked girl. Where's Moira?"

Robyn ground her teeth with fury. "It's *Jessica,* you crazy old bat. You should have been locked up long ago. Jessica is where I left her. It's all her fault, wanting to wander around on her own, taking no notice of the time. She could easily have ridden back with me if she'd tried, but she's just a soft city girl. She's out by Wirra Creek. At least that's where I left her. I told her to stay put."

"You better not be lying to us, girl." Lavinia stared up at Robyn, wild-eyed.

It *was* a lie. Robyn had long felt she was under no obligation to tell the truth. All her efforts these long years, her bids for love and respect proved futile.

"Why the hell would I? You're nuts!"

Lavinia shook her head grimly. "You're not so sane, either."

Cyrus's voice cut them off like the crack of a whip. "Livvy, you'd better go up to your room. I'll come and see you the minute I get back with Jessica. Robyn, I'd advise you to leave Livvy well alone or you'll answer to me."

"I will, will I?" Robyn shouted, her face twisted with bitterness. "Let's have it. Dad's told you you're his heir?"

"He hasn't said a word." Cyrus regarded his stepsister with contempt. "And if I am, that's as it should be. You're not going to get anyone to disagree with that. But take heart, you won't be left out. I'll take the helicopter. You made Jessica understand the importance of staying where she was?"

"What do you think I am?" she asked with weary disgust. "Of course I told her. She mightn't have listened."

"You'd better be telling the truth." Cyrus was nearing the end of his tether.

"Yeah, yeah. Go to her," Robyn yelled. "It's pretty damned dark out there."

OVERHEAD, WATERFOWL, myriads of them, were flying in formation, squadrons of them at various heights, darkening the already fading sky. Jessica kept looking until they disappeared from sight. They were heading for water. Without water, all creatures died.

I can't sit around waiting for help, she thought. *I have to get myself settled in case I'm stuck here for the night.* In her saddlebag she had a canteen of water, a couple of teabags, two crisp Granny Smith apples, and a few little packets of dried fruit—sultanas and apricots. She had even found a box of matches right at the bottom of the saddlebag, though she hadn't put them there. Maybe one of the stable boys stealing a quick smoke while he was out exercising the filly.

Food and fire, at least. A cup of tea. No milk. No sugar. She didn't care. Her throat felt parched, a combination of heat and panic. Hot during the day the desert, she knew, could turn freezing at night. What could she use for warmth? She was wearing jeans and a cotton shirt, a bandanna around her throat. If the worst came to the worst, there was Chloe's saddle blanket. She didn't fancy that around her, but then it was still light and the temperature was only beginning to drop.

She found herself a stout stick just in case a couple of dingoes came calling. Beautiful-looking animals, she knew they could and did kill humans. She had to be ready for that sort of violence.

What a fool you are trusting Robyn.

Robyn had big problems, which she frequently demonstrated. Like today.

Jessica felt a bursting sensation in her chest. She had the dismal feeling she had walked right into a trap. But what had Robyn hoped to achieve? Had she simply wanted to give her a good fright? A miserable night spent alone in the wilderness, communing with the guardian spirits. With Moira perhaps? Poor little Moira, who had disappeared without trace. Jessica had no fear of Moira's shadowy ghost. Moira didn't threaten her. Moira was a friend.

You are, aren't you Moira?

She spoke exactly as if the young governess were standing near her. One needed a friend at such times, even if the friend existed in another dimension.

As she worked to collect enough firewood, Jessica cast her mind back over Broderick Bannerman's parting shot. *She's not who she says she is.*

Had he found out something about her family? Something no one else knew or about which no one had ever spoken? It had nothing to do with her beloved Alex, her nan. Virtually every minute of Nan's life had been well documented. Nan had been the only daughter of a prominent family.

Yet it was such a strange thing to say. If not Nan, who? Someone who had handed down the family face. Her great grandmother, Margo. Margo had gained quite a reputation for being "difficult." She had run off to Europe at one stage and her parents had had to go chasing after her. She'd been at that time engaged to an upstanding young

man who'd been devastated when she'd taken off without
a word of explanation. The miracle was he'd taken her
back and married her. Nan always told that story, an odd
expression in her eyes.

Jessica got the fire going without too much trouble. Fire
was beautiful and terrible. Tonight it was beautiful, wonderfully comforting. She made herself a cup of tea. Again,
absolutely delicious, and she wasn't a tea drinker; it
slicked the dry patches in her throat. She was hungry, so
she started on a packet of raisins. Good source of iron.

In no time at all, it was dark, except for the orange-gold
flames of her fire, which, as she piled on the kindling, rose
higher and higher. She couldn't let it go out. She'd collected a good amount of fallen branches, dried leaves and
grasses. Ordinarily, she wasn't frightened of the dark, but
then, she'd never spent a night in the vast desert where noc-
turnal animals were on the prowl. She had Chloe to protect
her. Or maybe she was supposed to protect Chloe, she
wasn't sure. Chloe wouldn't be hungry, at least. She'd had
her fill of the golden grasses, and Jessica had given her
some of her own water.

All they had to do was sit tight and wait for Cyrus.

Cyrus!

Just to say his name sent a thrill of warmth through her.
Images of her other loved ones kept coming.

*If you're up there, Nan, now's the time to make the
stars come out.*

They did.

As she watched with bated breath, the stars came out
in all their glory, spreading their brilliance across the sky.
There was Orion, the mighty hunter striding across the sky,
his faithful hunting dogs at his heels. The Southern Cross
beamed its magic down on her. Even the night wind sang

a song to her. Not mournful but shivery sweet. The rapidly cooling air was incredibly fragrant as the desert plants released their aromatic oils which blended subtly with the perfume of a little carpet of wild flowers, like a mauve mist that covered the sand nearby.

One by one, several kangaroos approached the fire. They remained there, standing upright on their powerful back legs, ears pricked, their large soulful eyes seeming to ask her what she was doing there and was she all right? It was clear they meant her no harm and expected no harm from her, but when Chloe wheezed, they bounded off into the night, their great sinewy tails pounding the earth. She was sad to see them go.

Time went slowly. The cold air acted like a drug on her tired body. It was almost possible to nod off....

At one point, she thought she heard a whirring sound. It grew louder. Had she really dozed off? She must have. Her eyelids were heavy and she was freezing! Her fingers encountered gooseflesh all over her arms.

She leaped up, staggering a little.

It was a helicopter.

"Cyrus!" she yelled like a madwoman, a loud melancholy wail. She began to leap around the fire like a dancer at an Aboriginal corroboree. Something skittered across her vision. She peered across the mounting flames where someone who looked very like her had joined in the dance. How was that possible? She had to be hallucinating. She fought to reassert logic. The cold had sapped her brain. "Is that you, Moira?" she cried confusedly. "Do you know this place?"

Moira disappeared with a little wave.

Jessica told herself everything would be okay. She

was being protected. She didn't know how she knew that. She just did.

And now, she could see the welcome lights of the helicopter beaming over the rough terrain, coming over.

HAD ROBYN LIED? Why? But then Robyn basked in lies, Cyrus told himself, even now scarcely crediting she had done such a seriously twisted thing as abandon Jessica in the desert. He could be heading miles in the wrong direction given that it was Robyn who'd told him where Jessica was. Nevertheless, he made a low pass over the area around dried-up Wirra Creek. It was as he was circling he spotted the glow of a fire several miles off.

Thank God.

His relief was enormous, sweeping from his head to his heart.

I'm coming for you, Jessica. Hang on.

All he wanted in this world was to gather her in his arms. To tell her how much he loved her and wanted her to be with him forever.

SO, IT WAS TIME TO FACE the music, was it?

Robyn heard the helicopter before she saw Cyrus put down on the home grounds. Him and his easy skills. Not a bloody thing he couldn't do. She stood at the French doors watching the rotors slow to a stop before he jumped out, disappearing around the other side of the chopper from where he emerged into the strong wash of exterior lights with a bundled-up Jessica tucked in his arms. He loved the bitch, Robyn realized now. She had seen the very real fear in his eyes when she had returned to the homestead alone.

He hadn't trusted her to tell the truth, of course. Never had. Very wise.

Her head ached. Her stomach cramped with nausea. She couldn't do a goddamned thing right. The bitch was back. Not that she'd really believed Cyrus wouldn't find her. Cyrus knew she'd been lying her head off since she was a kid, hell-bent on trying to get him into trouble. But what choice did she have, then or now? Nobody loved her. Well, her mother had, but her mother had passed through life without causing a single ripple. By rights, she should have hated B.B. if only because of the callous way he had treated her mother. Instead, in accordance with her perverse nature, she had singled him out as the one person in life from whom she wanted love and attention. That longing had taken on obsessive proportions. But then, she'd been an extraordinarily distressed and needy child. She had been drawn to Erik because he was something of a father figure.

"I'm a natural-born victim," she said aloud. "It's bleedingly, blindingly, bloody obvious!"

Her head spun. Why not? She was drunk. Her poor mother had turned into a real lush.

Robyn pulled back the opulent covers on her bed—fit for Cleopatra—then slipped beneath them. Turning groggily to look at her bedside clock, she was startled to see it was only seven-thirty. Little kids stayed up later than that!

But what the hell! She wasn't going to endure any tongue lashing from Cyrus, so madly in love with Jessica, who looked like bloody Moira…pardon me, *Moira*. There was always the chance Jessica and Moira were somehow related. If they were, B.B. would have found it out, B.B. the super sleuth. She'd locked her bedroom door. Cyrus could pound on it all he liked. Her entire existence could be summed up in one word.

Failure.

Robyn pulled her iridescent violet nightgown around herself. She'd shelled out a fortune for it. She'd intended to wear it on her honeymoon. Turn Erik on, though it would've been blood hard, damn pansy. Yawning helplessly, Robyn allowed her troubled spirit to sleep.

CHAPTER FIFTEEN

IT WAS A SILENT HOUSE they returned to, although enough lamps were blazing for a Christmas party.

"Robyn's not here, waiting for us," Cyrus commented, his tone grim. "I bet she locked herself in her room the minute she heard the chopper. Her pitiful little scheme—God knows what she hoped to achieve—foiled. It's about time Robyn was forced to stop and take a good long look at herself and what she's become. Dad was a terrible influence on her."

"Not tonight, Cyrus," Jessica begged. "I don't think she meant any real harm."

"How little you know her," Cyrus said. "How are you feeling now?" He looked down at her anxiously. She had stopped shivering. He had given her a brandy at the rescue scene which had quickly warmed her, then had wrapped her in the mohair rug. At the very least, he had expected and wouldn't have been surprised by a few tears. It was a pretty scary experience for anyone who wasn't used to the wilderness to be left alone in it. But she had been aglow with welcome, literally dancing into his open arms, wanting no fuss, even if she was chilled to the bone.

"What you need now is a hot bath," he told her. "I'll run it for you. Then I better tell Livvy you're safe and sound. I know she'll be worried."

"We'll both tell her," Jessica said, feeling utterly warmed by his embrace. "I can wait another few minutes. But I *am* hungry."

"I'll take care of that, as well." He dropped a kiss on her upturned mouth.

LAVINIA THREW OPEN HER DOOR at the sound of Cyrus's voice. She emerged in a crumpled pink nightie and a magnificent brocade full-length evening coat fit for Boris Godunov. "My darlings!" She threw her arms around Jessica and kissed her. "We couldn't lose you a second time. That bloody Robyn! She's a criminal. We ought to turn her in to the police."

"Have you had something to eat, Livvy?" Cyrus asked quickly, anxious to get Jessica settled.

"Molly brought me a tray. She's such a comfort. I hope Broderick has left her a tidy sum in his will."

"He's not dead yet, Livvy," Cyrus reminded her bleakly.

Lavinia sighed and touched his face. "It has to happen, my darling. What other ending can there be? Now, why don't you take Moira off and feed her? She must be hungry stuck out there in the bush, though I suppose she's accustomed to it by now. Good night then, my darlings." She made to shut the door. "You've got no chance of waking up Robyn. She's quickly falling a victim to the wicked booze like poor Sharon. At lease *she* had an excuse. Only, Sharon liked vodka, I think."

JESSICA TOOK A LONG TIME over her bath, letting the warm, scented water ease the tiredness and take the chill out of her bones. Afterward she didn't bother getting dressed again. She slipped on a nightdress, then covered it with the silk robe her mother had bought for her on her last trip to Hong Kong. It wasn't as magnificent as Lavinia's rich brocade coat, but it was very pretty. Pretty enough to wear out, considering some of her friends attended functions in what looked like their underwear.

She found Cyrus in the kitchen giving his attention to a meal.

"Omelets?" His blue gaze enveloped her.

"Sure you can make them?" She smiled. She went to him and slid her arms around his waist, resting her head against his broad back.

"Of course!" He stood perfectly still, in case feeding her didn't get off the ground at all. His heart was on fire. "You sure you're okay?"

"I'm fine. Don't fuss." Even now she was reliving the blissful moment when he had found her, swooping her into his arms, holding her so close their hearts had thudded as one.

That's what a man's arms were for, she thought. To hold a woman. To make her feel cherished. She had felt all that and more. She had felt a profound sense of homecoming.

"So come on," he said lightly, holding himself on a tight rein. "I'm going to feed you and *then* we're going to bed together."

. "Sounds like the most wonderful destination in the world," she murmured.

He lifted her hand and pressed it to his lips.

HE CARED NOT AT ALL if they ate but tried not to show it. "Two eggs or three?"

"Three please. You need three for a good omelet." She sat down at the table, watching Cy with a sense of wonder. There were oranges, lemons, grapefruit in a bowl. She picked up a lemon and put it to her nose savoring the smell.

"Where's Molly?" she asked belatedly. She had expected Molly to be around.

He picked up a handwritten note and passed it to her. "She's gone over to stay with Ruth for the night. Ruth is tremendously upset."

"I know. She loves your father." She read the note, put it aside.

"Some women love men who treat them badly. Probably some syndrome. She's worked for him for twenty years, but he's never noticed her as a woman. Poor Ruth, wasting her life like that! She should have gone off, met the right bloke and had a family."

"The right bloke isn't easy to find."

Their eyes met and clung. "Then isn't it nice you've found him?"

ARM IN ARM, HER HEAD RESTING lightly on Cy's shoulder, they went around the house turning off the overhead lights, leaving only a few wall brackets glowing.

"Thought about what room?" He kissed her light and fast, setting up all sorts of aching expectations.

"I'm too distracted."

"Then mine." He wrapped her closer. "I've dreamed about you in my bed."

"Have you?" She was fathoms deep in love with him and falling farther.

"Oh yes. I was drawn to you from that very first moment. Now I'm absolutely sure you're the woman I want to share my life with."

OUTSIDE THE OPEN FRENCH DOORS, millions of stars patterned the sky. He carried her to his bed, her hair spread over his shoulder, his head bent, his lips kissing and tasting her lovely soft skin.

Cy lay on the midnight-blue quilted silk, poised over

her, an arm to either side. She was so beautiful. The most beautiful thing in his loveless life. He could never let her go. He could never allow anyone to hurt her.

A combination of soap and body lotion wafted up to him, deliciously citrusy and fresh. There was a trifle of lace showing at the neck of her robe. Slowly, he pulled the silk sash and the robe parted.

"Jessica." He was trying to steady himself, not give in too soon to the tremendous weight of desire. "I'm going to undress you, okay?"

She looked up at him with tender, trusting eyes. "You'll have to. I don't think I could get my fingers to work."

"Allow me."

The robe came off first, falling from her shoulders. Ever so gently, he turned her, tugging a little so it slithered out from under her. His breath was coming shorter and deeper. Hunger for a woman could be an agony. He had to hold her up so he could pull her nightdress over her head like a child. A groan came from the back of his throat as he saw her for the first time naked.

Her skin seemed to radiate light, and blood shot to his head. He had to regain his composure just to go on. His hands caressed her shoulders, silky skin and delicate bone, moving slowly over her, deepening his sense of touch and heightening his pleasure. His hands moved back up to her breasts, so beautiful, so perfectly formed, dusky-pink-tipped. It was a kind of agony just to look at them, hold them, take their tender supple weight.

Jessica let herself go with it, excitement roaring through her bloodstream like the most potent drug. The more he caressed her, the more she needed. Sensation ran so high she had to press back against the pillows, her eyes closed against the galvanic surges, like sails caught in a high

wind. Didn't he know he tore the heart from her? His min-
istrations continued, unhurried but intense. She had to
clamp her lips shut so her little rasping breaths wouldn't
escape her and turn into moans.

Cyrus understood perfectly the feelings that racked her.
He was astonished at the depth of passion between them,
long imagined, now finally being delivered. He was en-
tranced by the slender perfection of her body, the curves,
the long lines, the creamy whiteness of her skin. He let his
mouth travel her body as though following a map that
utterly absorbed him. Her little moans were both agonized
and joyous, urging him on. Once, in a bout of intensity,
her whole body bucked, then fell back onto the softness
of the bed. She was reaching for him, inflamed into taking
action.

She tugged at his shirt. Tore it loose. Next the waist-
band of his jeans, thrusting her hand inside, giving him so
much pleasure he cried out.

"I want you right next to me," she commanded. "Your
skin touching mine."

He stood up, stripping off his clothes, a lean, powerful
living sculpture of a man, his skin in the glow of the lamps
a dense gold.

The sleekness and strength of him! Jessica sat up in the
bed reveling in his manhood. She thought she might catch
fire when he touched her. She threw out an imploring arm,
secure in the knowledge she had made it her business to start
on the pill for protection. "What's keeping you? I *want* you."

"How much?" He approached the bed, the planes of his
face taut with passion.

"Let me show you." She was maddened by even the
smallest distance between them. "I never knew it was
possible to feel like this."

He wanted to cover her right then and there. Bear down on her. Make her his. Instead, he rose above her bracing his weight on his arms. "Then we have to do something about it."

"Let *me* start." This time she did the seducing. Her hands took hold of his fully erect shaft, scorching him with pleasure. She stroked and stretched the velvet skin until he grew too weak to withstand her.

"What are you trying to do to me?" He grasped her head to kiss her beautiful mouth. She tasted of white-fleshed peaches. It was amazing!

"Don't talk," she ordered. "I want to make you *feel.* I want you to experience the same rapture I do."

She moved over him and he covered his eyes with his hand, drawing in the ecstasy.

The intimacy between them continued to gain pace and intensity, the tenderness changing to the faint violence of passion bent on release. Delirious tears streamed down her cheeks. She and Cyrus were coiled around one another like vines, one ascendant, then the other, anything permissible between them because of the love they felt for each other.

"It was meant to be like this from the beginning." He pressed his mouth to hers, rapidly approaching his climax but waiting for her to catch up.

"I love you. Cyrus, I love you." She knew such a thing only happened once in a lifetime.

"Then come with me." He was determined to hold back until her climax seized her.

She held on to him for dear life, pressing her mouth to his shoulder tasting salt. Her body was filled with such heat....

And then it began. Ripples gathered in the pit of her groin. They gained strength, spreading to all levels of her body like molten lava. Her eyes were tightly shut so she could lock in the incredible sensations. She reached down to where their bodies joined. He was moving against her, very slowly like a sleek, powerful big cat. Up and down. Deep. Deep. Her whole body seemed to be quaking, as though something inside her was about to gush open.

"Now!"

Did she shout it? She was beyond caring.

ROBYN DENIED EVERYTHING. Her head was pounding from a hangover. She looked so ill that Jessica, despite everything, felt very concerned. Jessica herself was looking as radiant as a bride on her day of all days, still trailing the glory of the previous night. She was ready to forgive anyone, anything. Even Robyn, who undoubtedly would never be her friend.

Cyrus wasn't feeling anywhere near so magnanimous. He was deeply perturbed by what his stepsister had done. Robyn needed help and he came straight out and said it.

"Are you talking about a shrink?" she gasped, looking panic stricken.

"I'm angry enough to tell everyone what you did unless you make an appointment to see one."

"But everyone knows me," she protested. "I'd be the talk of the town."

"Don't be ridiculous! You know all about doctor-patient confidentiality. I'm serious, Robyn. It's important you get professional help. It could be one of the smartest things you've ever done in your life. Obviously we can't discuss this any further today. You're hungover. You can count your lucky stars I didn't believe you, and Jessica found matches in her saddlebag and was able to start a fire, otherwise this could have ended rather differently."

"Whereas it ended just the way she wanted," Robyn responded bitterly, hell-bent on driving everyone away. She jumped up precipitously, winced as her head threatened to split. "I don't know why I'm sitting here. I should be in Darwin with Dad."

Cyrus sighed. "If you're determined to go, Robyn, why should I stand in your way? You'll be better there than sitting around the house plotting some fool mischief. You're welcome to go to the hospital. I happen to know Dad's given instructions—no visitors. That means us. Bad sign in a man, don't you think, when he doesn't want to see his family?"

Robyn gave a snort. "Maybe I can get him to change his mind."

"Good luck, then. You might as well stay in Darwin while you're at it. The operation is scheduled for 9:00 a.m. Friday."

That got Robyn's full attention. "Dad would have made sure his will is in order?"

Cyrus's voice was dry. "I'm sure you've been well looked after."

"Well, I *am* his adopted daughter. Can I get Bill Morris to take me in the chopper? I can't face the long drive."

"Sure." Cyrus nodded his permission. "I'm going out to have a word with the men so I'll tell him now. When do you want to leave?"

Robyn fixed her stepbrother, then Jessica, with a hard stare. "As soon as possible. I'm sure you two lovebirds don't want me around. Say, eleven o'clock? I have to do a few things first."

"Like sober up?" Cyrus grunted. "I'll tell him." He looked across at Jessica, who had sat silently through the exchange. "What about if I come back for you then, Jessica? We can spend the day together."

"I'd like that," she said quietly. Despite what was happening, joy that would not be denied welled up in her heart.

"Course you would!" Robyn's laugh cracked. "With Dad out of the way, we'll have to drop to our knees and worship at Cyrus's feet."

"Dad's not dead yet, Robyn," Cyrus reminded her. "Now, I'm out of here." He turned away, crisply business-like. "Be ready at eleven sharp, Robyn. I actually need Bill today, but I recognize you're in no state to drive into Darwin."

"Thanks a bunch." Robyn suddenly scooped up the delicate cup and saucer that held the rest of her morning coffee and flung them to the floor. They shattered into pretty pieces, the black coffee staining the rug.

BRODERICK BANNERMAN HAD BEEN on the operating table for four hours.

They all sat in the waiting room, Cyrus, Lavinia, Jessica and Robyn, their backs aching, their expressions betraying their strain. Robyn stared fixedly and, Jessica suspected, sightlessly, at the television, though Cyrus had insisted it be turned down. Robyn actually looked like she needed a hospital bed herself.

They all looked up as Barbara Nicholls, Broderick's twin, who had arrived from Sydney, came back into the room carrying a cup of coffee and a cell phone. "Nothing?"

"Nothing," Cyrus confirmed. "Babs, why don't you take Livvy back to the hotel? You're only ten minutes away. This could go on for hours yet. I'll call you the minute we have news."

Barbara Nicholls, with the same handsome features as her twin, but much less severe, stylishly confident, beautifully dressed, sank into a chair and sighed deeply. "I don't feel good about this."

"Better to die than finish up in a wheelchair or lying in a nursing home, Babs," Lavinia said. "That wouldn't suit Broderick at all."

Barbara shook her dark head. She had the same distinctive silver wings as her brother. "No," she agreed quietly. "Don't feel bitter, Cyrus dear, but he let me see him for a time." She laid a comforting hand on her nephew's. "Please don't hold it against me. Probably I'm the only person who can get inside Broderick's head. I'm his twin, after all. Broderick has always been his own worst enemy. Keeping you away from him, especially at this time, is part of his defense mechanism. You must understand that. You're so much like our father, Steven. For some reason that has always upset him. It takes him back in time. Then there was the damage left in Moira's wake. Of course, Broderick being Broderick found out I put that portrait of Moira on the market."

That hit Cyrus with stunning force. "*You* did? I didn't even know you had it. You've never said. I thought it was Dad."

They were all focused on Barbara now. Jessica reached out to take Cyrus's hand, seeing his agitation. Even Robyn dragged her eyes away from Oprah Winfrey for a moment, even though an extraordinarily slim Oprah was offering everyone in the studio a free car.

"I've had the painting in storage for years and years," Barbara said. "It was too beautiful to destroy and too upsetting to display. No, I was the one." Barbara looked at her nephew. "Your father never told you?"

Cyrus shook his head. "I accused him of it. He didn't deny it."

"That's Broderick all right," Barbara said heavily. "I did it on impulse. It was Hughie's anniversary. I always feel

badly around that time. I feel cleaner, freer, bringing his
portrait of Moira out of hiding. The tragedies of our childhood left terrible wounds. Wounds that were concealed,
but never healed. I knew Broderick would find out what
I'd done.There's nothing much that happens inside the
family—and out—he doesn't know about. He knew how
I felt about the portrait. He knew I had it. He knew I
unravel around Hugh's anniversary—he does, too. I
suppose he was waiting for me to let it see the light of day.
He's uncanny like that."

Cyrus's handsome face was baffled. "What else have
you and Dad been hiding all these years, Babs? We found
another portrait, Jessica and I."

"Where, in the storeroom?" Barbara made an informed
guess. "One could hide anything there. So much was concealed, you know. My mother couldn't bear to hear
Moira's name. It was all so very painful. Brutal as it
sounds, making all trace of Moira disappear was the only
way we survived as a family."

"Oh man!" Cyrus turned away, sighing deeply.

"Hugh was a wonderful painter," Barbara said. "He
could have made a name for himself, only his whole life
ran off the rails. What was this painting of?" she asked.

It was left to Jessica to reply. "A nude. A very beautiful rendition."

"*What?*" Barbara gasped. "No, no, that's impossible."

"Nothing's impossible, dear," said Lavinia, looking
worldly-wise.

Robyn sat as if struck dumb by all they were saying.

"A very erotic portrait," said Cyrus, searching his
aunt's face.

"Moira didn't pose for it." Barbara spoke with absolute
certainty. "Okay, I was only a child, but I *know.* A portrait

of Moira in her prettiest dress was one thing. My parents allowed that. Moira nude would never have happened."

"No, it wouldn't!" Lavinia shook her forefinger energetically.

"Hughie must have seen her like that in his *mind*. An erotic fantasy as it were. He was an artist, after all."

"Bloody odd, if you ask me," said Lavinia. "Wasn't he a pansy?"

Barbara was thoroughly rattled. "No, he was *not*, Livvy. Where did you get that idea? Look, I don't know how this happened, but there was nothing between Moira and Hugh."

"As far as you know," Lavinia piped up.

Barbara flushed. "Of course he could have fallen in love with her, but Moira certainly didn't love him. All Moira could see was—" She broke off abruptly, dropping her gaze.

"Steven," Cyrus supplied grimly, as if this were the piece that was missing.

Silence from Barbara, but a look of extreme gravity.

"We're all human," Lavinia pronounced. "Human beings fall in love." She reached out to pat Jessica's hand. "That's what Cecily was afraid of. He loved you."

"Livvy, will you stop that?" Barbara exclaimed in horror, rising to her feet. "This is *Jessica,* for heaven's sake. I have to admit, I got a great shock when I first saw her. The resemblance is uncanny, but sheer coincidence. We were talking about Hugh. I've always thought something terrible happened to Hugh. Something he would never talk about."

"Unrequited love?" Cyrus suggested, continuing to regard his aunt closely.

Lavinia frowned at him. "No, no, my darling, Hughie was in love with Steven. Not that Steven had a clue."

Barbara was visibly trying to keep control. "Livvy, sometimes you sound quite mad."

"And sometimes I don't," Lavinia returned darkly.

"If Hugh had been in love with anyone, it was Moira. I'm sure Hugh wasn't gay."

"Gay?" Robyn's voice came out so loudly it made everyone jump.

"He was, too." Lavinia stuck to her guns. "It explains everything."

Cyrus held his head in his hands. "If it does, I'm missing it."

"*Everything* has to do with what happened to Moira," Lavinia insisted. "I expect if Broderick doesn't die, the police will come and arrest him."

Robyn gave a contemptuous snort. "If anyone should be arrested, it's you, Lavinia. You're long overdue for the giggle house."

"And you should be coming with me," Lavinia told her tartly.

Barbara acted. "Darling Livvy, I think we should go back to the hotel for a while. You need to lie down."

"You'll stay with me?"

"Of course." There was great confusion in Barbara Nicholls's gray eyes and the glint of tears.

SHORTLY AFTER THEY'D LEFT, Erik Moore made an appearance.

On seeing him, Cyrus straightened, his gaze challenging. "What are you doing here, Erik?"

"Yes, tell us." Robyn actually switched off the TV. "After my lousy birthday party, I vowed never to speak to you again."

Erik searched her face, looking for understanding. "You've no idea how I've missed you, my darling."

"That's the reason you came, is it, Erik?" Cyrus stood

up, towering over the other man. "To tell Robyn you've missed her?"

"That and to find out about B.B." So confronted, Erik sank strategically into a chair. "It was B.B. who warned me off, Robyn. He let us get to the stage of talking marriage, then right out of the blue he told me to butt out of your life. That was the very night of your birthday party, when we should have been deliriously happy. I had the ring. I still have it."

"You didn't dump me?" Robyn stared at him, apparently poleaxed by the disclosure.

Cyrus exhaled in wonderment but never said another word. His conscience was clear. He'd tried all he could with Robyn. None of it had worked.

A look of dawning wonder put life into Robyn's pale face.

"Would I dump the love of my life?" Erik asked, apparently always at the ready no matter what life dished up.

Robyn's look of shock had been replaced by hope. "Dad did that to us?"

Erik nodded, letting his head drop as in deep regret.

Obviously he was smart enough to know when actions spoke louder than words, Jessica thought cynically, not taken in by what she saw as a performance.

"Why didn't you tell me?" Robyn went to him, half kneeling so she could get a closer look at his face.

"Why bother?" he said forlornly. "B.B. means everything to you. I knew you wouldn't go against him in the end."

"The *end?* Now that, I think, is highly relevant," Cyrus cut in. "Your goddamn brain is always ticking over isn't it, Erik? Dad mightn't pull through. I bet you've got your sources inside the hospital who gave you a complete rundown on his condition. Many people survive brain tumors, however."

"Of course they do!" Erik heartily agreed. "I'm hoping and praying that will be the case with B.B."

"So who told you it was a brain tumor? We never gave out that information. It could be stomach cancer, for all you know."

Robyn was thoroughly roused from her stupor, apparently dead set on standing by her man. "Erik is a highly regarded member of the community, Cyrus." She ran a loving hand down Erik's cheek. "It would be easy for a man like Erik to be given certain information. After all, everyone knows we're as good as engaged."

"Really? I thought it was all over Darwin you'd broken up," Cyrus said with weary sarcasm. "So if Dad doesn't survive, Robyn will never know if you're telling the truth, Erik?"

"Robyn knows her father." Erik shook his head ponderously.

"Her stepfather," Cyrus corrected curtly.

"Robbie, would you like to have a cup of coffee in that little place across the street?" Erik said quickly, rising to his feet. "The coffee here is deplorable."

"I'd love to!" Robyn all but sprang to the door.

"Is that okay with you, Cyrus?" Erik asked before joining her.

"Sure," Cyrus drawled. "Thanks for coming."

Erik totally missed the sarcasm. "No worries. We'll be back."

THEY SAT IN A STUNNED SILENCE for a few moments after Erik and Robyn had gone.

"Sweet Jesus, can you believe that guy?" Cyrus sighed.

"She fell for it, hook, line and sinker."

Cyrus nodded. "He got the inside story. He knows just how bad Dad is. Obviously with Dad out of the way, he's home free. He can control Robyn and her money. And I'd say we're talking a lot of it."

"Reparation for not treating Robyn very well?"

"Probably." Cyrus shrugged. "I don't mind. Dad did adopt her when she was only a child. She's entitled. Erik is prepared to take his chances. That's how he runs his businesses."

"He's in big trouble if your father pulls through."

"I don't think the world holds any more appeal for Dad," Cyrus said, an expression of resignation on his face.

BRODERICK BANNERMAN DID NOT pull through, however great the combined skills of his surgical team.

As the neurosurgeon, Dr. Jung, who headed the team came toward them, Cyrus and Jessica stood up, their hands clasped tightly together for mutual support.

Something in the surgeon's expression alerted them the news was far from good.

"I'm so very sorry," he said, looking first at Cyrus, then Jessica. "Mr. Bannerman has gone. We did all we could, but we lost him. Please, let's sit down a moment."

Dr. Jung sat with them, explaining the various reasons why everything had started to go haywire. "I think your father had already decided he didn't want to live," he told Cyrus gently. "He was such a strong personality, such a powerful and influential man, he found it extremely difficult to consider the possibility of a greatly changed life. We had discussed every possible outcome of the operation, of course. He went into it with his eyes wide open. If there was a chance, he was going to take it. I wish things had turned out differently. I understand how deeply distressed you are. We did all we could."

But it hadn't been enough.

"SO WHO *WAS* THE LAST PERSON in the family he saw?" Cyrus asked after the surgeon had gone. Despair and a deep hurt were in his voice. "Whose face did he light on last? Not me, that's for sure. Not poor unwanted Robyn. But Babs, his twin. Sons and adopted daughters don't count. You, the young woman he became so infatuated with. In the end he shunned you, as well."

"In his mind, I betrayed him," Jessica said. "He was living a fantasy. I was no *real* part of it, Cyrus. Barbara was his twin. She loves you and she knows much, much more about your family's history than she's ever let on. Except maybe to her brother."

"That's obvious," Cyrus said harshly, pulling out his cell phone to start making the necessary calls. "Well, it doesn't matter now. Dad's gone. The secrets he'll take to the grave are probably too shattering to know, anyway."

LATER, AS THEY WERE about to leave the ward, a tall distinguished-looking man in his late fifties came toward them. He was wearing a clerical collar.

"Mr. Bannerman, Cyrus Bannerman?" he asked, putting out his hand. His voice had a soft Irish lilt. "I'm Father Brennan. I was with your father last night. I've just been told he passed away. I'm so sorry. Please accept my deepest sympathies."

Though stunned by the revelation—his father had been anything but a religious man—Cyrus responded courteously, shaking the clergyman's hand. "Thank you, Father. This is my friend, Jessica Tennant."

"Miss Tennant." The priest's dark eyes wandered to her distressed face.

"You're a Catholic priest, Father?" Cyrus asked, trying to grasp what the man was saying. Clergymen had freaked his father out.

"Yes. I heard your father's last confession," the priest said in a perfectly calm voice.

"But we're not Catholic, Father." Cyrus forced himself to speak quietly when he was agitated and upset. Just when he'd been thinking there were no surprises left, up popped a Catholic priest.

Father Brennan smiled. "Your father and his twin sister, Barbara—is that right?—were baptized in the Catholic Church. I understand there was a tragedy in the family many long years ago and the faith lapsed, but your father called for me, as a matter of fact. He wanted to see a priest."

Cyrus shook his head as if to clear it. For the moment, he had to rely on the man's word, but he saw nothing but truth and dignity in the clergyman's eyes. "Father, I have to tell you I'm stunned."

"I can see that, Cyrus. May I call you Cyrus?"

"Of course." Cyrus stared into the quiet, focused face.

"If it gives you comfort, I can tell you your father was a peaceful man at the end. Strangely happy, accepting of his fate."

"You gave him absolution?" Did a man automatically get it? Cyrus wondered.

"Certainly," the priest confirmed gently. "You probably have some clergyman in mind for the funeral service. If you haven't, if I can be of help to you, you have only to let me know. I'm at St. Mary's. God bless you both." He lifted a hand in a gesture that was both a blessing and a salute.

CHAPTER SIXTEEN

BRODERICK BANNERMAN WAS LAID to rest according to his wishes in a closed ceremony with only his family and a handful of lifelong associates present. Because of his status in life, a memorial service was to be held in Darwin at a later date when it was expected a huge crowd would attend.

Like most great Outback stations, Mokhani had its own cemetery. The graves of five generations of Bannermans were arranged within a large enclosure bounded by a tall black wrought-iron fence and double gates, and shaded by massive banyan trees that spread their long weeping branches over the graves. In a far corner, removed from the intersecting concrete pathways, was a species of cassia in gorgeous display. It caught Jessica's artistic eye. It was the only bright spot in that quiet place; the spent golden blossom covered the built up mound beneath it.

How beautiful! The long perfumed sprays moved like floral arms, even though there was scarcely a breath of air. Cyrus had spoken to Father Brennan, who presided at the service in the calm dignified manner Jessica remembered. If Broderick Bannerman had called on a priest at an extreme moment the same priest ought to bury him, Cyrus had decided when the family had discussed it. He'd met with no opposition from anyone. From now on, everyone would defer to him as head of the family.

Broderick Bannerman's last will and testament had already been read. Overnight, Cyrus had inherited the bulk of the Bannerman fortune, making him one of the richest men in the country—and thus one of the most eligible, though no one, not even Robyn, made reference to it. Robyn might have been cut out of all Bannerman business operations, including the pastoral empire, but what she did get was splendid enough for her not to rock the boat and had Erik Moore talking wedding dates.

Barbara, already a rich woman, was made a whole lot richer, not that she cared, and that was that. For a notoriously tight-fisted man, B.B. had been extremely generous. His longtime secretary, Ruth, who had loved him from afar and was crazy with grief—she'd had to be sedated when she'd been told of his death—wouldn't have to work another day for the rest of her life. A godsend for most people, but looking at Ruth, anyone could see she would much rather have had Bannerman back. Handsome bequests were made to various longtime employees, including Molly, who had gone so far as to burst into tears and start planning to join her widowed sister in Tasmania. Charities had a bonanza. Hospitals, medical research centers, an educational institution to be set up in Darwin, also a park— B.B. had owned the land—bearing his name. A huge monetary gift was made to the city. The list went on and on. No mention whatever of Jessica, for which she was greatly relieved. She couldn't have handled even a tiny bequest. Nothing about her stay on Mokhani had been *normal.*

After the funeral, Jessica had made the decision to go home and give Cyrus breathing space. She had thought about it long and hard. Cyrus needed time to clear his mind and focus on his future. Whether in the light of momentous events she was going to be part of it, she still had to give him space. For all the bitterness Broderick Bannerman's behavior had engendered in his son and nigh on everyone around him, Cyrus *was* grieving.

Brett and Tim were due to arrive on Saturday, which was two days off. They would take a look around Darwin, make a quick courtesy visit to Mokhani to meet the new master and take a look at the great folly Broderick had caused to be erected in his honor. Indeed a mausoleum. It was up to Cyrus now to decide what would be done with it. Had it been a timber structure, Jessica thought Cyrus would have burned it down. Her own idea was it should be turned into a huge conference center with every facility. As Cyrus was to take over all of his late father's business concerns, which spread to Southeast Asia and New Zealand, such a center made sense.

They hadn't discussed it. Broderick Bannerman's death and the events leading up to it had cast Cyrus into an inevitable state of depression. He wasn't immune to grief, sadness for what might have been, and quite starkly, the knowledge that at the end he had been met with rejection. What extraordinary place he had held in his father's mind. His heir and, quite simply, his *rival.*

It was late afternoon before everyone left after a subdued reception at the homestead. Barbara couldn't avoid staying over at the homestead even if she wanted to. Her husband was at a conference in London, where he was a guest speaker, and had been greatly relieved he wasn't required to return home. Barbara had been staying at the same Darwin hotel the family favored. It was obvious Lavinia was very fond of her niece—after all, Barbara had had Lavinia stay for years on end—so to humor the old lady and offer some comfort to her nephew, Barbara had agreed to stay over at Mokhani, the Bannerman ancestral home where Barbara felt she no longer belonged. She didn't think she would ever get over the desolation of her childhood, she'd confided to Jessica. The *loneliness,* the internal struggles. Hitherto inseparable, overnight her twin had been shut off from her. Her mother had changed into someone else. Her wonderful father had never been the same. After Moira had disappeared, they hadn't worked as a *family.* For years, her mother had gotten all choked up if anyone so much as mentioned Moira's name. Her father had looked as though he had lost something irretrievable. Uncle Hughie, who was the nicest man in the world, had killed himself on the station. Something had caused him so much pain, he couldn't go on living.

Small wonder Barbara seldom visited her old family home.

Strangely, Barbara didn't appear to have those feelings now that her twin was gone. Was it because there was no more Broderick with his stinging tongue? Broderick, always trying to wrong-foot everyone. And his secrets? Broderick had been her mother's favorite. Their mother, Cecily, had loved him far more than she had her daughter. Broderick had been on the receiving end of all Cecily's attention. That had incensed and alientated Barbara right up until the time she had married and made a new life for herself.

Because everyone felt terribly sorry for Ruth, the woman was pressed into staying, instead of going back to her own comfortable bungalow.

"You don't need to be alone, Ruth," Cyrus told her kindly. "We all know how devoted you were to my father."

"Head over heels in love with him more like it," Lavinia the irrepressible piped up.

"What of it?" Ruth countered, distraught. "I'm not ashamed of it."

Barbara's voice was soft and sad. "You have no need to be, Ruth. Loving someone can never be wrong."

"What about Moira?" Lavinia asked, adjusting her monk's robe, which she had worn to the funeral, along with blue socks and sandals. "I mean, loving the wrong man must count as one of the worst things you can do in the world."

"Certainly one of the most painful." Barbara put a hand over Lavinia's in an effort to quiet her. "I told you, Livvy, dear, I didn't want to talk about Moira."

Lavinia did a double take. "But she's sitting right opposite you, love."

Robyn threw down her linen napkin. "The only bloody difference between Lavinia and Zelda, the mad old bag lady in Darwin no one seems to do a thing about, is occasionally the authorities have to lock Zelda up."

"How unjust," said Lavinia. "She does no harm, but she does go on a bit about *sin*. The reason you don't like me, Robyn, is that I see through you. I think Broderick's leaving you all that money was a dreadful mistake. Erik will only glom onto it, mark my words!"

Barbara's eyebrows shot up like birds' wings. "Livvy, it's scarcely the right time for all this."

"There are only two kinds of times," said Lavinia. "The good times and the bad. Let's drink to Broderick. He up and died on us and left my darling Cyrus with all his problems."

For the first time in days, Cyrus laughed. "Don't worry about me, Livvy. I can handle it."

"That's right, my darling!" she encouraged him. "Build a new life with Moira." Her bright eyes moved to Jessica.

"I don't know that there's any better color for a beautiful ash-blonde than black. No news, I suppose, but that's my expert opinion."

IT WASN'T UNTIL MUCH LATER in the evening that Ruth came out onto the veranda to speak to Cyrus. He and Jessica were sitting out there talking quietly.

"Sorry to interrupt!"

"No problem, Ruth. Can I help you?"

Ruth's eyes filled up again with tears. "You're so good to me, Cyrus. I must thank you." She shifted her gaze to Jessica. "Don't think I don't appreciate how nice you've been to me, Jessica, since you arrived." Although she was obviously sincere, Ruth spoke in a flat monotone. She was clutching a padded bag in her hand. "Your father asked me to give this to you, Cyrus, should anything happen to him," she said. "I've been so desperately upset, it all but slipped my mind, so I'll give it to you now."

"What is it?" Cyrus made no move to take it.

"A video." Ruth passed the package to Jessica, who was nearest, and Jessica in turn passed it to Cyrus. "Your father wanted to speak to you."

Cyrus stared down at the package. "He could have done that very easily, Ruth," he said, making no attempt to extract the video from the padded bag. "I waited for hours on end at the hospital."

Ruth shook her head. "You know your father was a very strange man, Cyrus, but in his own way he loved you. Remember, I knew him well. He suppressed so many of his true feelings."

"Wouldn't it have been easier for all of us if my father could have shown a shred of appreciation, let alone affection?"

Jessica could feel Cyrus's tension. The knuckles of his lean, tanned hands were white.

"I don't believe he knew how to, Cyrus. That was the cross he carried. You should thank God you're like your mother."

"I do, Ruth. I do." Cyrus slowly withdrew the video. "You have your job, Ruth, if you still want it. I'd never find anyone else as good as you. For that matter, you know more than I do."

Ruth looked amazed. "You're serious, Cyrus?" The flatness in her voice turned into an emotional quiver.

"Perfectly," he said. "My father found you indispensable and he was a hard taskmaster. Of course you'll need time to think it over. Time, too, for a holiday. Something to look forward to. Let me know."

Ruth pressed her hand to her agonized breast. "Where else would I go, Cyrus? I'd be honored if you'd give me a chance."

Cyrus leaned forward. "Get some confidence in yourself, Ruth," he said gently. "Somehow my father stole it. You're absolutely first class at what you do. I'll *need* you."

He couldn't have hit on a more powerful argument if he'd tried.

"Oh, thank you," Ruth said in a heartfelt voice and fled back into the house.

"So what am I going to do with this?" Cyrus asked Jessica, looking down at the package in his hands.

"What do you suppose it is?" Jessica felt a bit fearful.

He sighed. "You can bet your life it's not to tell me how much he loved me. The strange things he was doing—the intimate connection he was trying to make with you, Moira's double, calling in a priest, making his confession, I'd say it was an extension of all that. I don't think I want to know."

"I don't blame you. Still, it would be unthinkable to

throw it away. You've lived through bad times. You can handle it. Perhaps at the end he wanted to explain himself. He could even be asking forgiveness."

"So." Cyrus let out a sigh. "Where do we see it, in the study? Somewhere private anyway."

"Are you sure you want me?" Jessica asked, very sensitive to his grief. "These are probably your father's most private thoughts. I wouldn't blame you in the least, Cyrus, if you wanted to see it on your own."

Cyrus stood up drawing her to her feet. "You love me, don't you?"

Her voice broke a little at the expression on his face. "With all my heart."

"Then from this moment on we do everything together." He cupped her face in his hands, looking directly into her eyes. "I've been waiting for you my whole life, Jessica. I can't let you go. All right, you can leave with your uncle— I'm looking forward to meeting him—but that's only to go back and see your family. I'll need to meet them. They'll want to look me over. I love you, Jessica. I want to marry you. Not at some hazy time in the future. I want it to be right away, but that would be seen as too soon. Besides, I want our wedding day to be wonderful. I want to see you as a bride. I want the memory of that day to stay with us forever. Say you'll marry me?"

"You've got it all planned?" She smiled through her tears, believing herself to be truly blessed.

"Within seconds of meeting you," he confirmed.

"The miracle of love at first sight." Her eyes luminous with love, Jessica put up her arms and drew his dark head down to her in a long, loving kiss.

Cyrus was her life. Mokhani was her home.

Together they would bring it back to the light.

CHAPTER SEVENTEEN

BRODERICK BANNERMAN WAS SEATED somewhere that looked like a law office because of the legal tomes in the bookcase behind him. He was directly facing the camera. Just for a moment both Cyrus and Jessica forgot he was dead. He looked very much alive. He addressed himself to his son: "The best son a man could wish for!"

"Dear God!" said Cyrus. "I actually heard that, did I?"

Jessica, seated close beside the man she loved, held his hand, understanding Cyrus took great comfort from her presence. All that passion with tenderness and need, besides! Sublime sex wasn't all that connected them, but rather the *depth* of their connection, the perfect matching. They were truly meant for each other.

There were points along the way when Cyrus had to stop the video to get up and pace around the room. Jessica sat, head bent, appalled by Broderick's tale told in such a matter-of-fact tone. *Some people put more emotion into reading a grocery list,* she thought with some wonderment.

Bannerman's voice never faltered, not once, during the telling of his harrowing story.

Uncle Hughie and I followed Mom and Moira at a safe distance. They didn't keep to the usual trails like we thought they would. They ventured out into the wilderness, heading toward the escarpment. The weather was terrible, hot and thundery with the sky piled up with clouds. I knew Uncle Hughie was worried. He didn't have to say anything. I just knew. Once or twice, I'd overheard a couple of the stockmen sniggering about Dad and Moira. The father I worshipped and my *governess?* It didn't seem possible. Babs and I really liked Moira.

Mum was mistress of Mokhani. But Moira was a servant. There was a huge gulf between the two.

Uncle Hughie and I waited until Mum and Moira reached the top of the escarpment, then we followed using the scrub for cover. Mum began speaking angrily to Moira. My mother could be really scary when she got angry. Moira fell to her knees. Mum told her to get up. I remember every word like it was yesterday.

"Adultery is a sin, Moira. A terrible sin. No decent young woman in her right mind would allow herself to be seduced by a married man. Unless she's the sort who seduces men. And what about Hugh? You want him as well?"

I've never believed, like poor old Livvy, Hugh was homosexual. Maybe he did have a sexual encounter with Moira. Who would know? Lovely little Moira turned out to be a slut anyway. She had to be guilty because she did nothing to defend herself even when my mother began to hit her. Mum sounded like she was going out of her mind. That's when Uncle Hughie broke cover, yelling at Mum to stop. Maybe Hugh did love Moira, but it was my father Moira had set her sights on.

Mum was shocked when she knew we were there. The words she threw at Uncle Hughie were so ugly I had to cover my seven-year-old ears. I didn't even know Mum knew words like that.

"Sins have to be paid for, Hugh."

That's when Moira asked very quietly, even sorrowfully, "Is love a sin then?"

Mum whirled about and slapped her, struck her so hard Moira went reeling.

"Marriage is sacred, you wicked little bitch. Sacred, you hear? You'll never break up my family. Destroy my marriage."

That's when I knew what I had to do. A son fights for his mother's honor even if he's only seven years old. I was big and strong. We were all standing close to the edge. What could be easier than pushing Moira off the cliff? She deserved what was coming to her. No way was she going to be allowed to break up my family. So I ran, propelled by hate and the need for action, my mother's agonized cries ringing in my ears: "No, Broderick, no! Stop!"

It was impossible to stop. I evaded Uncle Hughie easily. Poor Hughie, he was sobbing like a woman. Moira just stood quietly with her face turned toward me as though accepting her fate. She only had time to get out a few words, but I've never forgotten them.

"I'll always be here, Brodie. You'll see me."

Sure enough I have.

Appalled and in thrall Cyrus and Jessica listened as the voice droned on with the same peculiar lack of emotion.

Afterward, wrapped so tightly in my hysterical mother's arms she could have broken bones, we

watched as Uncle Hughie went down into the
canyon. There wasn't the remotest chance Moira
could have survived. We all knew that. But surely no
one would blame me? A child of seven couldn't be
held responsible for the outcome of his actions. It
was a terrible accident. I hadn't meant to push her
so hard. Except I *had.* I knew precisely what I was
doing. I was the Bannerman heir. The family honor
was at stake. I had chosen to send Moira to her death.

Of course the whole business turned Uncle
Hughie's mind. That and the booze. He buried Moira
under cover of night. "Out of sight, but in a sacred
place," he told us, not that Mum and I ever wanted
to know. Poor man! It was my mother who locked
him and me into living a lie. She was the strong one.
She made up the story. We had to get it straight.
Moira had gone out riding alone. It had been
drummed into Moira not to venture too far from the
main compound. For some reason she had anyway.
The horse came home. Moira didn't. She was never
seen again.

My father turned into a madman instigating a
mighty search. My mother aged overnight, but she
never broke her silence. All that mattered was that I
be protected. No one thought to question me. Not my
father, not the policeman who traveled from Darwin
to the station. I was a child, heir to Mokhani. My
family was powerful, well respected. The mysterious disappearance of our governess joined Outback
lore. Another tragedy of the bush, people said.

Only as it turned out no one could protect me
from my memories or the apparitions. They ruined
my life, twisted my soul. The whole story should

have come out at the beginning. Perhaps the truth
might have saved me. They could have locked me
away in a home for the insane, and I wouldn't have
cared. But my mother insisted I could never do
anything so dangerous as to tell. My father would
never understand.

"He would hate us, Broderick. Could you stand
that? Your father would hate us. It was never your
fault. How many times do I have to tell you? It was
Moira's. She got what she deserved."

Did Moira really deserve such a terrible fate? These
days, of course, I'd say, no. She was so very young and
love is madness. Of late I've contemplated making my
confession to a priest. My mother had been born into
the Catholic faith. Babs and I had been baptized. What
I so desperately need is absolution. God knows I've
long repented yet, I often dream of the gates of Hell
opening for me, then shutting me inside.

There was more. Jessica knew there had to be more. She
placed a hand over her mouth as Bannerman explained the
rest of the secret he had unearthed. There had been no
stopping him once he'd laid eyes on Jessica's face in that
interview. It was Moira's face. They had to be related by
blood. Such a resemblance was too uncanny to be mere
coincidence, though such things happened.

Before her marriage, Broderick's image said, Jessica's
young and beautiful great-grandmother, Margo Townsend,
had had an ill-fated affair that resulted in the birth of a baby
girl. Her parents, knowing Margo was engaged to another,
had been shocked out of their minds. Such disgrace would
taint the whole family. Something had to be done and
done quickly. Word was deliberately put out that Margo

had gone off alone to Europe, and her parents were obliged to go after her. In fact though Margo spent her confinement on a remote farm in central Queensland. Her baby daughter was given up for adoption hours after the birth to two good people—he was a doctor—who hadn't been able to have children of their own. They named their baby Moira, never speaking to her of her adoption. Margo and her mother waited until Margo was fully recovered before they returned home. Margo's fiancé, genuinely puzzled by it all, still wanted her, and they were married a few months later. A year after that, their daughter, Alexandra, Jessica's grandmother, had arrived to a fanfare of joy.

JESSICA AND CYRUS were still sitting stunned in front of the television long after the tape had come to an end and this extremely tragic story had sunk some way in.

"So it turns out Moira was murdered, after all," Cyrus groaned, and passed a hand over his eyes.

"Could anyone hold a seven-year-old child responsible?" Jessica asked, as appalled as he was. "It must have been unbearable for a small boy watching his mother so furious, hitting out at Moira, screaming that she wasn't going to be allowed to break up the family. Her actions incited the child. Cecily would never have meant what happened to happen, but what your father did on that day tortured him for the rest of his life. It made it impossible for him to like himself. He was right. It all should have been brought out into the open. Brodie should have had counseling."

Cyrus shook his head. "My grandmother would never have allowed that, for Moira would have *won*. The marriage would have broken up. She took on the responsibility. Only, they all suffered, no one more than her own son. Even Hugh found a way out."

"I feel strongly that Hugh *did* love Moira," Jessica said.

"Those paintings surely lent credence to that." Cyrus's eyes leaped to the portrait of his grandfather. "God knows where Livvy got the 'pansy' bit from."

"She mistook the nature of Hugh's love for your grandfather. Probably Hugh had never found a girlfriend. But who knows what goes on in Lavinia's mind?"

"She was right about implying Moira's disappearance was not an accident," Cyrus pointed out bleakly. "How could my poor father show love when he believed himself a murderer? I won't accept that he was, no matter what he says. He couldn't have understood the full consequences of his actions."

"I think I know where Hugh laid Moira to rest." Jessica stared down at her clasped hands.

"A sacred place? That could be anywhere." Cyrus was in despair. He began thinking of all the Aboriginal sacred sites on the station. "That poor girl was hardly more than a child herself."

His words brought tears to Jessica's eyes. No wonder she had felt such a bond with Moira; the bond of blood was impossible to ignore. "Hugh buried her in the family cemetery," she said with an amazingly clear belief in what she had said.

Cyrus's face betrayed his shock. "Jessica, sweetheart, how could you say that? There's nowhere—"

"Yes, there is," Jessica said in a quiet sad voice. "Beneath that beautiful golden tree, the cassia, in the far corner. I was drawn by the way it captured all the light. I'm sure that's where Hugh buried her, then planted the tree. Sacred ground, not out in the wilderness—he loved her too much to do that. Cecily must have begged Hugh to keep quiet, probably appealed to him on bended knee. Hugh must have thought lying about what happened was a gift of mercy to his cousin and to his lifelong idol, your grandfather. They were protecting Broderick and the family. Only, Hugh couldn't live with the lie. The guilt and the grief were always there."

"Poor Hugh," said Cyrus, not wanting to think of the anguish that had led to his suicide. "So how do we lay Moira's ghost to rest? Start the whole sorry business up again?"

"Why don't we ask her?" Jessica said. "We'll go out there together and call to her."

"Jessica!" Cyrus stared at her, his love and need for her spilling out of his eyes. He stood and drew her into his arms. "Out of all this suffering, I have to bless my father for bringing you into my life."

Jessica lifted her head to kiss the sculpted line of his jaw. "I think all Moira wanted was for us—you and I—to know what really happened to her. She wasn't looking for vengeance, but recognition. I acknowledge her as my great-aunt. I am happy to do so. We can turn that area of the family plot into a garden of remembrance with a seat beneath the tree where one could say a prayer. I'd like that. Instead of living inside our heads, Moira can be set free."

Cyrus's somber expression brightened. "I'll say a simple amen to that, and goodbye to all the heartbreak." He bent his head and kissed her long and lovingly. "I'm almost afraid to be so happy with you, Jessica. I'm not used to such happiness."

She smiled up at him radiantly. "Well, you'd better get used to it, because we're going to have a lifetime of it ahead."

Cyrus enfolded her in his arms, speaking into her beautiful cloud of ash-blond hair. "Everyone I have, everything I am, is yours!"

EARLY THE FOLLOWING DAWN, they walked hand in hand to the family cemetery, paying their respects first to Broderick Bannerman, who finally lay at peace, before moving to the corner of the enclosure where the cassia bloomed in all its glory.

"It blooms for months," Cyrus murmured gently as the tree spilled blossom and soft perfume on them like wedding confetti. "Like a beacon."

"We'll think of it as Moira's tree," Jessica said.

It might easily have been a trick of the rising sun dappling the light green leaves and the pendulous branches of bright yellow, but looking up, Jessica fancied she glimpsed a smiling young face. A face very much like her own.

An illusion or Moira bidding farewell?

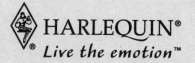

Detective Maggie Skerritt is on the case again!

Maggie Skerritt is investigating a string
of murders while trying to establish her
new business with fiancé Bill Malcolm.
Can she manage to solve the case
while moving on with her life?

Spring*Break*

by *USA TODAY* bestselling author

CHARLOTTE DOUGLAS

HARLEQUIN®

HN33

Available March 2006
TheNextNovel.com

If you enjoyed what you just read,
then we've got an offer you can't resist!

Take 2 bestselling
love stories FREE!
Plus get a FREE surprise gift!

HARLEQUIN®

Super Romance

OPEN SECRET
by Janice Kay Johnson
HSR #1332

Three siblings, separated after their parents'
death, grow up in very different homes,
lacking the sense of belonging that family
brings. The oldest, Suzanne, makes up her
mind to search for her brother and sister,
never guessing how dramatically her
decision will change their lives.

Also available:
LOST CAUSE (June 2006)

On sale March 2006

Available wherever Harlequin books are sold!

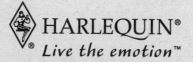

HARLEQUIN®
Live the emotion™